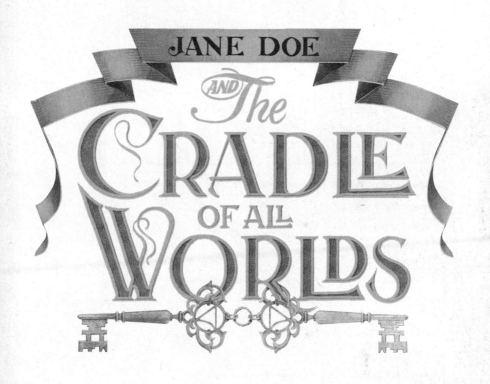

JANE DOE

AND The CRADLE OF ALL WORLDS

JEREMY LACHLAN

CAROLRHODA BOOKS
MINNEAPOLIS

First American edition published in 2019 by Carolrhoda Books

Text copyright © 2018 by Jeremy Lachlan
First published in 2018 by Hardie Grant Egmont

Carolrhoda Books
A division of Lerner Publishing Group, Inc.
241 First Avenue North
Minneapolis, MN 55401 USA

For reading levels and more information, look up this title at www.lernerbooks.com.

Cover illustration by Iacopo Bruno.
Photo of columns: AndresGarciaM/Getty Images.

Main body text set in Bembo Std regular 12.5/17.
Typeface provided by Monotype Typography.

Library of Congress Cataloging-in-Publication Data

Names: Lachlan, Jeremy, author.
Title: Jane Doe and the cradle of all worlds / Jeremy Lachlan.
Description: Minneapolis : Carolrhoda Books, [2019] | Originally published: Sydney, Australia : Hardie Grant Egmont, 2018. | Summary: "Jane Doe and her father, John, appeared on the steps of the Manor the night the earthquakes started and the gateway to the Otherworlds closed. Fourteen years later, Jane enters the Manor to save her missing father . . . and the world" —Provided by publisher.
Identifiers: LCCN 2018033080 (print) | LCCN 2018038644 (ebook) | ISBN 9781541541771 (eb pdf) | ISBN 9781541539211 (th : alk. paper)
Subjects: | CYAC: Missing persons—Fiction. | Adventure and adventurers—Fiction. | Fantasy.
Classification: LCC PZ7.1.L214 (ebook) | LCC PZ7.1.L214 Jan 2019 (print) | DDC [Fic]—dc23

LC record available at https://lccn.loc.gov/2018033080

Manufactured in the United States of America
1-45123-35938-9/24/2018

FOR
MUM
AND
DAD

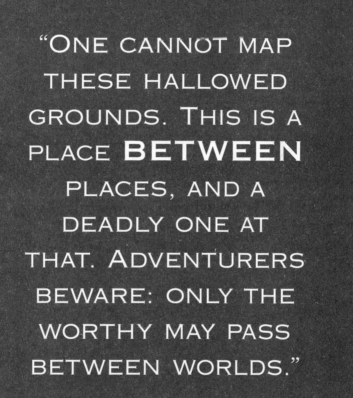

"ONE CANNOT MAP
THESE HALLOWED
GROUNDS. THIS IS A
PLACE **BETWEEN**
PLACES, AND A
DEADLY ONE AT
THAT. ADVENTURERS
BEWARE: ONLY THE
WORTHY MAY PASS
BETWEEN WORLDS."

—*Arundhati Riggs and the Colossal Door*

THIS IS NOT THE BEGINNING

THE HIDDEN SYMBOL

Her lantern chases shadows through the dark. Cobwebs tear at her fingertips; spiders flee. She runs a hand over the stone wall of the tunnel and breathes in deep, savoring the damp, the dirt, the unknown. She had missed this. People call her an old relic, but they are fools. Winifred Robin is one of the Great Adventurers. She may be old, but her story is far from complete. Tonight, something has changed. She intends to find out what, and why.

Winifred was conducting research down in the catacombs when the quake struck. The ground shook, the scrolls trembled. Candles toppled from the walls, snuffed out. A deep sound rumbled toward her—the echo of breaking stone—but it is not so much what she heard as what she felt moments later that intrigued her. A sinister breath. A breeze.

It blows toward her now, making the cobwebs dance. She is close.

There is a chasm around the next bend. A long, black void so thick with thousand-year dark even the lantern light shies away from it. Winifred does not consider turning back, not for a second. This is a woman who has defeated armies, cheated death, battled gods. There are only two things she fears in all the worlds. Height is not one of them.

Lantern hooked onto her belt, she climbs around the edge. A rock clatters into the chasm. The darkness takes it. She never hears it land. She swipes away the odd spider as she navigates the wall. Hairy, palm-sized things. The breeze swirls around her from the depths, but she makes it safely to the other side. Straightens her crimson cloak. Chances a smile.

She proceeds with caution now. The island of Bluehaven is riddled with abandoned mines and passages, but this one has sat here in secret for thousands of years, sealed off from the world. Now, on the second anniversary of the Night of All Catastrophes—two years since the quakes began—it has opened.

She does not believe in coincidence. She knows secrets are kept for a reason.

There is a small, rock-hewn chamber at the end of the tunnel. Winifred's lantern splashes golden light upon the walls when she steps inside. She frowns. There are no chasms in here, no spiders. In fact, there is nothing at all. The chamber is empty.

She turns on the spot, searching, hoping for a secret passage, another path. Could somebody have been here before her? Climbed up the chasm from a different tunnel?

The floor is bare. No footprints. No deathly triggers set into the stone. She paces around the chamber, runs a hand over the back wall, and that is when she finds it. A small, faded symbol: rust red, like dried blood. An ancient hiero-glyph. A triangle with one inward-curving side, like a ship's sail or a wave, encased within a circle. Incredible. Winifred knows the symbol—has been scouring the Great Library for two years trying to uncover its meaning, and here it is. It has been right under her feet all along, but how? Why?

The symbol calls to her. Whispers in a foreign, archaic tongue.

She touches it. The symbol flashes, white and blind-ing. A phantom gust of wind howls through the chamber, kicking up her cloak, swirling dust. Winifred tries to pull her hand away from the wall, but it is stuck, fixed to the symbol as if seared to a burning hot plate.

The pain is excruciating. Not in her hand, though.

In her head.

Winifred sees things. Flashes before her eyes. A story unravelling in her mind like a book read at speed. But not *just* a story. This is real—or at least, it will be.

This is a vision of things to come.

There is a chase. A cage. A sacrifice. There is a long journey, a trickster, and an ally. There are horrors from Winifred's own past, born from the sands of a distant world that fill her with a certain cold dread she hasn't felt in years. There is rock and ruin. Death and destruction. Just as Winifred thinks she can take no more, the phantom wind ceases, the stone in front of her splinters into a thou-sand cracks, and she is thrown back from the wall. The darkness takes her, too.

Winifred is not certain how long she is out. By the time she comes to, her lantern has almost burned dry. The dust has settled. The symbol has vanished. She feels strange. Drained of all energy, yet filled with something more. A grim sense of purpose. The vision was a gift, a warning, a set of instructions from the Makers themselves. Winifred has *seen*, but more than that, she understands. There are things she must do.

Terrible things.

This godly gift comes with a price.

Winifred stands. Holds a scarred, bony hand to the cracked wall. She now knows what lies beyond this stone. A wonder beyond wonders. Her hand trembles. She cannot remember the last time she cried, but she allows herself a moment now. She weeps for the things she has done, for the things she is about to do, and for the long road laid out before her. When she has finished, she clears her throat and straightens her crimson cloak once more.

Enough. She must leave this place—leave and never return—for the wonder beyond the wall is meant for someone else. This is not Winifred's story, after all.

It is Jane Doe's. The child with the amber eyes.

PART
ONE

TWELVE YEARS LATER

I'm in trouble again. Occupational hazard when you're known as the Cursed One, the Unwanted, the Bringer of Bad Juju, a Djinn. Bad weather, spoiled crops, missing pets—I always cop the blame. I don't have a clue what I've done this time. All I know is, Mrs. Hollow's performing another cleansing ritual at the top of the basement stairs, spitting on the landing, flapping a sprig of thyme. Muttering things like "repugnant abomination" and "catastrophic blemish of unfathomable proportions" under her breath.

Clearly, she's been looking up big words in the dictionary again. Never a good sign.

Normally, I'd settle in for the long haul. Sit in the shadows, chew my fingernails, hum a tune. Not today, though.

Today, I actually have somewhere to be. Today, I have a secret.

I step into the wedge of light cast by the open door. "Um. Mrs. Hollow?"

"Shh!" The woman's tall and lanky. Twitchy eyes ten sizes too big through her glasses. Basically a six-foot-tall praying mantis on the edge of a nervous breakdown.

She pulls half a lemon from the pocket of her apron and squeezes it along the doorframe. "Need to focus."

"Right. The spit-and-twirl. Sorry."

Mrs. Hollow ditches the lemon and thyme, spits on her hands—*ptooey, ptooey*—spins in a circle and shouts, "Be gone!" Then she freezes with her hands held high, fingers splayed.

Nothing happens, of course, but it sure looks impressive.

"Good one," I say. "Thing is, I'm kinda busting for the loo."

"Ugh. Damn it." Mrs. Hollow snaps out of her trance and wipes her hands on her apron, shakes her head. "It's gone. The vibe. You've ruined it. I'll have to start again."

"Maybe if you just told me what it is you think I've done."

"Not you. Well, not *just* you. Him too." She jabs a finger over at my dad, lying in his little alcove, still awake but calm at last. We live in the basement, see. Rats and all. "Keeping us up all night, shrieking like a banshee. We've had it! Learn to control him or he's out."

My face flushes red hot. "It wasn't his fault. The quake scared him, is all."

"The quake *you* caused, you freaky-eyed little—"

"*Beatrice!*" a voice screeches from upstairs. Her husband, Bertram, a little weasel of a man perched semi-permanently at the kitchen table. He hardly ever leaves the kitchen because a) that's where the food is, and b) he's terrified—of everything. Germs, animals, pollen, books, simple human contact, me. The man squealed at a coat hanger once, I swear. "*Give her The Speech.*"

Uh-oh. Anything but The Speech. Not now.

"Excellent idea, Honey Bucket!" Mrs. Hollow stares down at me, suddenly so earnest, so wounded. "This is how you repay us, is it? We take you in, purely out of the goodness of our hearts. We feed you. Employ you. Heck, I even bathed you when you were a baby, and all you can do to show your appreciation is keep us up all night? Well, let me tell you something . . ."

The woman drawls on, but I learned to ignore her a long time ago.

Sure, some of it's true. The Hollows really did take me and Dad in, but only because they drew the short straw. Nobody wanted us after we showed up on Bluehaven, so the town council threw the names of every couple on the island into a barrel and picked the lucky winners. Half an hour later, we were dumped on the Hollows' doorstep with two chickens and a cow to soften the blow. There's no "goodness" in their hearts. They have no friends, they pretend Violet—their own *daughter*—doesn't exist, and they've treated me like a slave for as long as I can remember. I clean the outhouse, do their laundry, collect eggs, milk the cow, shovel crap, and mop the floors, all while caring for Dad full-time.

Jane Doe, Jack-of-all-trades.

"Are you listening, girl? I said *that* is why you deserve a horrible, lonely death."

"Oh." My turn now. "I apologize, Mrs. Hollow. You're absolutely right. I'm a bad seed. Rotten to the core. I promise I'll try harder in the future. Ma'am."

Thankfully, the woman's never been good at catching sarcasm.

"Good. We'll be leaving for the festival in a few hours. You know what to do."

I nod. "Stay here. Stare at the wall. Pray for forgiveness. Same as always."

"Precisely. The Manor Lament is an important day for us all." She jabs a finger at me. "Don't ruin it! With any luck, the Makers will grant us mercy this year," she adds, meaning with any luck I'll be struck by lightning, attacked by rabid dogs, or stung to death by bees.

"We can only hope," I say, but I'm pushing it.

Mrs. Hollow frowns at me, then nods at Dad. "Keep. Him. Quiet." And with that, she steps back and slams the door.

"Finally," I mutter.

I skirt round my raggedy mattress on the floor and duck into Dad's alcove, squeeze alongside his bed. He barely slept at all last night, thanks to the quake. Tossed and screamed, sweated through his sheets. Just like the quakes, his outbursts have been getting worse lately. More intense. Almost violent. Now his big brown eyes are glazed again, fixed in that thousand-yard stare. Most people would see an empty shell of a man, but I know better. The slight crease in his brow. The tremble in his hands. I know he's in there somewhere, and he's scared.

He wants me to stay.

"Thought she'd never leave," I say, forcing a smile. "You doin' okay?"

He doesn't answer, of course. I've never actually heard him talk, not once.

Caring for Dad's the one chore I like. It's hard work. Beyond sad. I have no idea what kind of nightmare he's stuck in, and I gave up trying to guess a long time ago. Sure, he can stand and walk if I help him. A slow two-step shuffle. He can drink and chew and swallow, use the toilet in the corner, but that's pretty much it. He can't talk. Can't laugh. Can't hug me. I can't play games with him or take him outside. Worst of all, I can't make him better. All I can do is plump pillows, tuck blankets, spoon soup, tear bread, brush teeth, wash hair, trim fingernails, and ask myself the same old questions that have drifted into my head for years: What was he like before he got sick? What's his real name? When did his hair turn this premature, smoky gray? What were his favorite foods, colors, seasons, and songs? And the bigger questions: Where did we come from? What was Mom like? What's *her* name? Does *she* have eyes like mine? Is she out there somewhere, waiting for us on the Other Side? Why isn't she here with us now? In short, what really happened the night we came to Bluehaven?

I know Dad has all the answers—he must—but they're trapped inside him, like scuttling bugs in a jar. All I can do is imagine. Some days it drives me mad, but I love him, simple as that, which means I wouldn't have things any other way. Sure, I wish he'd snap out of it and steal me away from this place, but wishes are dangerous, distracting things. *This* is our life. Always has been, probably always will be. At least, that's what I used to believe.

Now I'm not so sure.

I woke at dawn to a quick *rat-a-tat*. Wiped the drool from my chin and the sleep from my eyes just in time to see a note slip through the crack in the tiny basement window. Not just any note, though. An old photograph. A picture of Dad, sleeping in a chair in a grand, sepia-toned study: still sick, I think, but slightly younger, his face less lined. I felt like I'd swallowed an anvil. I'd never seen a photo of him before. I dragged a crate under the window and stood on my tiptoes, desperate to see who left it, but they'd gone. I held up the photo to the milky light, and that's when I noticed the message on the other side.

My place. White Rock Cove, 10am. Come
alone if you want answers. —E. Atlas

Eric Atlas. It didn't make any sense. Still doesn't. Bluehaven's illustrious new mayor skulking around town at dawn, sneaking messages through windows? The guy was here in the house just a few weeks ago. I didn't see him, of course, but I could hear him through the basement door. The heavy boots. The gravelly voice. He said he was checking up on the Hollows. Sat in the kitchen for an hour while they listed their grievances. So why all the secrecy now? Why today? I paced and pondered, scratched my head. Debriefed, plotted, and planned with Violet when she sneaked down to say hi before her parents woke up.

"You have to go," she said. "It could be a trick, but you have to go."

And she's right. It probably is a trick. A ploy to lure me out into the open. Festival shenanigans or something, I dunno. But I have to go. I have to risk it, have to *know*.

This feeling doesn't come along every day, the feeling that everything could change.

I pluck the crumpled photo from under Dad's pillow. Best hiding place in the basement. Dad has a blanket tucked over his legs in the photo, and there's a desk beside him. A fireplace, too. Behind him, a cabinet stocked with books, weapons, and vases. It sure as hell wasn't taken in the Hollows' place, so where was it taken? And when?

Dad's breath quickens. I hold his hand, give it a squeeze.

"Don't sweat it, Johnny-boy. I'll be back before you know it."

I need to hurry. The old clock on the wall says it's almost nine-thirty, which means Violet's signal should come any moment. *Just a diversion*, I told her. *Nothing over-the-top. Don't blow anything up.* She promised, crossed her heart and all, but I saw the glint in her eyes.

I tie my hair back—long, dark, so knotted I swear it'd snap a comb—then shove the photo into my pocket and kiss Dad on the cheek.

"I'll fix you something to eat later on, okay?"

I turn away, don't look back. Leaving him alone is hard enough as it is.

There was a time when I could squeeze through the basement window, but those days are long gone, so I grab my cloak and creep up the basement stairs. The Hollows won't lock the door till they leave, so getting out's no problem. Even so, I sit tight a moment, breath held.

Then it happens.

There's a sharp *crack*. Somewhere out back, I think. Mrs. Hollow yells, "Not again! The bucket, Bertram, where's the bucket? Violet! You get back here now!"

I smile.

The girl's incorrigible. Eight years old and already a pyromaniac.

The back door screeches open, which means it's time to move. I step out into the hallway, ease the basement door shut, and sneak down to the front door as quickly and quietly as I can, doing my best, as always, to ignore the Three Laws hanging above it, framed and embroidered, covered in a fine film of dust. Standard in every house on Bluehaven.

> *We enter the Manor at will*
> *We enter the Manor unarmed*
> *We enter the Manor alone*

OUTSET SQUARE

Bluehaven's a hole. A crumbling mess of ramshackle houses and dead-end alleyways sandwiched together all the way around the rocky shore of the island. Wooden beams support bulging walls and sagging eaves. Potholes mar the narrow streets. The quakes have taken their toll. I doubt there's a single surface in town without a crack in it—one of the main reasons the townsfolk make me feel as welcome as a fart in a bathtub on the rare occasions I step outside. So even though the sun's shining, even though it's hot as hell and I haven't breathed fresh air in three days, I pull the hood of my cloak forward the moment I set off down the street. I can't take any chances. Gotta keep my head down, walk fast, look out for the usual suspects.

Old Mrs. Jones, who wails whenever she sees me pass by. Mr. Annan, who shutters every window and sobs in the dark. The old woman in red, Winifred—freakin'—Robin, who stalks me from the shadows nearly every time, walking when I walk, stopping when I stop, vanishing the few times I've doubled back to tell her off. Creepy, sure, but I'm used to it. All of it. Kids usually run the other way when they see me, like I'm carrying an infectious disease. Doors are slammed shut, locks click. Old folks whisper prayers.

This morning, though, it's a ghost town. There's no one in sight.

"Oi, wait up!" Violet darts round the corner behind me in her little red boots, beaming like a thousand suns. "Before you start, I didn't blow anything up. I just set fire to the trash." She falls into step beside me. "Something *inside* the trash exploded, but that isn't my fault."

"You do realize you could've just called your mom upstairs or something, right?"

Violet scrunches up her nose. "Where's the fun in that? Besides, I can't help you if I'm stuck at home, can I?" She claps her hands. "So, what's the plan?"

"I'm heading to White Rock. You're going home."

"Uh-uh. If you're caught breaking curfew, you'll be locked in the basement for a month. Or worse. They could banish you. Stab you. Oh! Oh! They could stab you and *then* banish you!"

"Wow. Try not to sound too upset about it, Violet."

"Obviously, I don't want any of that to *happen*. But let's face it, you're stuck in the basement with John every day, which means I'm your only friend; you're not allowed to go to school, which means you're not the smartest kid around; and now you're going for a walk on a day when people literally gather round to burn effigies of you in Outset Square."

17

The fact that kids on Bluehaven know effigy-burning is a *thing* can't be normal, can it? This place, I swear. "You're saying I need all the help I can get?"

"I'm saying you need *me*."

"Fine," I sigh. "You can walk with me to the edge of the cove, but then you have to go. The message said 'come alone.' If we spook Atlas, this could all be for nothing. And if anything happens before then, you run home. Don't stop. Don't look back. Deal?"

It doesn't seem to bother her, but Violet gets teased enough for living under the same roof as me. I don't even want to think about what would happen if people found out we're friends.

"Deal," she says.

I hang back at the corner of Sunview and Main. Violet ducks ahead to make sure the coast is clear. She tries to whistle but hasn't quite got the knack of it yet, so she coughs and clears her throat till I get the point and join her. A bunch of kids have just walked by. A woman's sweeping her stoop a few doors down. I sneak across the road, stealthy as a bandit, and lead Violet into an alleyway quick smart.

Bluehaven's like a giant maze, but I know every street, every shortcut. Sure, I only step outside to run the occasional errand for the Hollows nowadays—collecting wood, buying rice—but I used to sneak out all the time, mostly at night. I'd wander the streets by moonlight, raiding the neighbor's bins for any clothes or knick-knacks they might've thrown away, maybe even a midnight snack for me and Dad. Sometimes I'd head on up and raid the mango and coconut groves and bring back a feast. Didn't take long till I'd walked every path a thousand times.

"I've been thinking," Violet says now. She dives and rolls under a window to make sure nobody sees her. A pointless move, seeing as the window's boarded up, but at least she's enjoying herself. "If this really is an ambush—" she leaps up, dusts herself off "—I reckon you should just go with it. Have fun. Be the baddie. Run around and scream and tell 'em if they don't give you a crate of flint you'll sink the whole island or something."

"Why would I want a crate of flint?"

"Why *wouldn't* you?"

A busy intersection. A right onto Kepos Road. No choice but to blend in for a bit, go with the flow. Hide in plain sight and hope the passing townsfolk don't clock us. I pull my hood down even lower. Focus on my feet, let Violet lead the way. Keep expecting a hand to grab me and spin me around, the crowd to turn on me as one.

Violet stops. I bump into her back, and someone bumps into mine. I brace myself, get ready to run, but the guy actually says, "Excuse me," and keeps on walking. I almost laugh.

If only he knew.

"What's going on?" I whisper.

"Two carts up ahead," Violet whispers back. "They're stuck. Blocking the road. Idiots. We could try ducking under them, but—"

"No," I say. "Come on. It's risky, but we're gonna have to cut across Outset."

We duck into a side alley and start jogging. I can feel the seconds slipping away from us. We sidestep bins, jump over potholes, duck under a clothesline and scramble over a stack of crates and barrels, the hum and buzz of Outset Square growing louder all the while.

I check my pocket. The mysterious photo's still there, safe and sound. I hold it tight, fighting the urge to run back to the basement and make sure Dad's okay. Sometimes I swear there's an invisible thread connecting us that spools out, stretches, then tugs at my heart and guts whenever I stray too far. Whenever I'm gone too long.

It's pulling stronger than ever today.

Violet catches the look on my face. She knows it all too well.

"He'll be fine, Jane," she says, huffing and puffing beside me. "I mean, he's much safer than you're about to be. But don't you worry, the square'll be packed. Everyone'll be way too busy setting up for the festival to notice anything. You'll see."

And she's right. Outset Square is heaving. Everybody's busy building stalls and stages. Trundling carts of fruit and roasted spits of suckling pig. Hanging flags from the lampposts. Unfurling long banners between the columns of the surrounding buildings. The Dawes Memorial School. The Museum of Otherworldly Antiquities. The grand Town Hall. The flags and banners are white, symbols of peace and slates wiped clean. The Manor Lament marks the anniversary of the Night of All Catastrophes. It's the one day of the year the townsfolk come together to celebrate and remember the adventures of old. To praise their gods—Po, Aris, and Nabu-kai—otherwise known as the three Makers. To chant, pray, feast, dance and—yep—burn effigies of me and Dad. There they are right now. Towering wicker things on wheels.

Maybe the festival started out as a somber affair, but it's more like a party nowadays. And I'm most definitely not on the guest list.

I really, *really* shouldn't be here.

"I *love* festival time," Violet groans as a wheelbarrow full of fireworks rolls by.

"Calm down, little pyro." I drag her into the crowd. "I like the idea of these losers running from something other than me, but do you really want a repeat of last year?"

"Hey, if they didn't want kids around the Dragon Wheels they should've put up a sign or something. And I only let off half of them."

"They were still in storage. I could hear the explosion from the basement."

Violet sighs. "Yeah, you should've seen it." Then she goes all puppy-eyed on me. "I *wish* you'd come tonight, Jane. You've never been once. Why don't you just give it a go?"

"Do I really need to answer that?"

"We could dress you up. Like a tree or something. Get a few sticks, some leaves—"

"I'm not coming to the festival, Violet. Ever. Now can you drop it?"

"Fine. I'm dropping it. It's dropped. Do you reckon it'll happen this year, though?"

"Do I think you'll blow something up? Probably."

"No, stupid. The thing everyone's thinking. Do you reckon it'll finally wake up?"

I look around at the crowd. Between the trundling, building, sweeping, and cleaning, everyone keeps glancing up the Sacred Stairs on the far side of the square. Straight as a tack and crumbling at the edges, the colossal staircase stretches all the way up the steep hill in the center of the island, raised above the terraced farms by a series of towering arches. Up, up, up they climb, scaling the rugged, rocky slope of the hilltop—a dizzying height now, almost as steep as a ladder—until they're devoured by an enormous stone door. The gateway to Bluehaven's great lamented treasure.

The Manor.

With its towering columns and crummy stonework, the Manor looks more like an ancient ruin than anything. A gigantic gargoyle crowning the island, born of the cliffs themselves, as old as the sea and sky. Crumbling statues flank its windowless walls. Dying vines creep up its sides. For thousands of years, the people of Bluehaven worshiped it, praised it, journeyed through it to the Otherworlds, but it has stood like this—dormant, lifeless, closed to all—for well over a decade now. Fourteen years, to be precise.

Ever since Dad and I came to town.

They say there was a storm. They say Dad fell through the gateway and collapsed at the top of the Stairs. A man without a past. Without a name. John Doe, they called him. John Doe and his baby, Jane. Apparently, I was bundled up in his arms, crying.

They say the first quake struck at once.

"Jane? Ugh." Violet tugs at my cloak. "I said, do you think it'll wake up?"

"Don't know, don't care."

"All right, all right. Grumpy-pants. I don't reckon it was your fault, by the way."

"I know."

"I mean, *you* caused the Night of All Catastrophes?" Violet hocks a loogie and shines a cobblestone between her feet, a refined skill I taught her last year. "You're afraid of the dark, you slobber in your sleep, and you can't even *swim*, let alone curse an entire island. And yeah, your eyes are kinda creepy, but you're not an aboma—I mean, abomo—"

"Abomination."

"Yeah, that. Point is, nobody knows where you and John came from. Or what really happened inside the Manor that night. Miss Bolin reckons you cursed your home world. Ruined everything. She told the whole class yesterday that John must've been trying to dump you in a different world, 'cause he was so ashamed and all, so you cursed him, too, like some sort of evil baby mastermind, and that's why he's sick." She shakes her head. "Nonsense."

"It's actually a pretty popular theory, but still. Thanks for the vote of confidence."

Violet squints up at the Manor. "At least you can say you've been inside it. You're pretty lucky, if you think about it."

"You there! *Hey!*"

Damn it. Old Barnaby Twigg just spotted me through the crowd.

"Alaaaarm! Devil in our midst! Be gone, despoiler!"

"Get down." I pull Violet behind a crate of bananas.

Barnaby's obsession with the Manor is on a whole other level. Determined to witness the reawakening first-hand, the pot-bellied maniac sleeps, eats, sometimes even bathes beside the well in the center of the square, just so he can be first up the Stairs every morning and the last at night. He's dressed in his best safari suit today. Thankfully, everyone's so used to his rambling that they completely ignore him.

"Leave now or I'll destroy you," he bellows, clambering atop the well, "just like the demon soldiers of Yan! Killed 'em all, I did. With a slice, boom, cha, huzzah! True story."

"Yep," I mutter. "I'm the luckiest girl around."

Violet grabs my arm. "Jane," she whispers, and points at a pocket watch dangling from the hand of a stranger nearby. I lean in, can only just tell the time from here.

My gut twists.

It's already a minute past ten. "Oh crap . . ."

We leave Barnaby to his theatrics and scoot back into the crowd, heading for the road that leads down to White Rock Cove. Violet tries to convince me to let her come.

"No way," I say. "Skirt around and wait for me on the western side of the cove. If I'm not there in, I dunno, fifteen minutes, head home, check on Dad for me, and sit tight. Don't come looking for me. Got it?"

"But I can just hang back and—"

"No time to argue, Violet. You go. I'll be fine."

"Okay," she says. "Okay, okay, okay." She's pacing on the spot like she needs to pee but fixing me with a Super Serious Stare. "Good luck, Jane. I'll see you on the other side."

And she dashes off into the crowd.

CATCH OF THE DAY

The streets of Bluehaven might be fair game for me on the odd occasion, but I'm banned from entering all public buildings. Never really cared, either. The museum? The Town Hall? Boring-with-a-capital-Ugh. But as far as school goes, curiosity got the better of me years ago. Trying to resist this colorful place where kids gathered every day to learn, read, laugh, and play was like resisting the urge to pee. The longer I held it in, the more I had to go.

I used to sneak down a few days a week. I learned my times tables crouched beneath an open window. Learned the names of clouds hiding in an alleyway outside a science lab. When I was nine, I sneaked into an *actual* classroom and spent most of the day stowed away in a cupboard. Peering at the class through a crack in the doors, I learned how their ancestors came from across the seas, having fled the Dying Lands. I learned the difference between a labyrinth and a maze. I even learned that booby traps have nothing to do with actual boobies. Unfortunately, the cupboard I'd chosen was filled with art supplies, so when the time came for the students to paint their favorite Otherworld, the teacher found me and threw me out the window. Security was tightened, the school scrubbed clean, cleansed with incense and all.

I've had to borrow books from Violet ever since.

So I'm no genius. Math, science, history? Forget it. What I *do* have is a noggin-load of street smarts. Survival skills honed from a lifetime of living in a place I'm not wanted. I know when to run, when to hide, when to lie. I know I have to stick to the shadows whenever I step into White Rock Cove because, like Mayor Atlas, the fisherfolk got over their fear of me a long time ago. Hell, over the years I've been pelted with fish guts, threatened with hooks, and chased with knives up the road. I'm pretty sure it's an act. I doubt they'd do anything if they actually caught me—one guy nearly did but he backed off right away, all shifty-eyed and awkward, as if someone or some-*thing* was gonna jump out from behind me and tear his head off. I'd rather not test that particular theory.

I creep behind the lobster traps and trays of dried kelp, take in the scene. Luck's on my side today. A new catch has just come in, fresh for the festival. The fisherfolk are busy unloading their sailboats, hauling buckets down the jetties, gutting their catches on these big stone tables, and flinging the scraps to the army of cats prowling around their ankles. The cove's namesake sits out a ways in the water, beyond the boats, a pale rock poking from the swell. Atlas lives down the far side of the cove, but there's so much junk scattered around the place I can pretty much crawl, dart, and creep my way there; under a sheet of canvas, behind crates and piles of netting.

I'm knocking on Atlas's front door in no time. Late, but only just.

I pull back my hood. The mayor's residence is huge. Four stories, arched balconies, window boxes weeping jasmine. Old Mayor Obi carked it a month or two back. Nice enough guy, I guess, in that his preferred method of dealing with me and Dad was pretending we don't exist. Never gave us much trouble. The man's ashes had barely cooled before a snap election was called. Atlas won in a landslide and wasted no time moving into his new digs.

I knock again, but still nobody answers.

"What the hell are you doing here, Doe?"

Joy of all joys. Not Atlas, but his dropkick of a son, standing right behind me. The kid's a few years younger than me but already nearly as tall. A real meat-safe in the making.

"Eric Junior," I say. "Yeah. Um. I'm just . . . here to see your dad."

He doesn't raise the alarm or shout for help. What he does is look me up and down, like he's trying to work out if I'm really here and not just some horrid figment of his imagination.

"Why would my father want to see you?"

"Oh, you know." I shove my hand in my pocket, hold the photo tight. "Catch up on old times, play some backgammon. Discuss plans for a statue of me and Dad in Outset Square."

Eric Junior frowns at me. I clear my throat, tell him I was joking, and miraculously I get a smile. One of those practiced, winning smiles. The kind of smile that's supposed to make me swoon and drool, quiver at the knees. And who knows? If I was into guys, maybe it would, but I don't think I am. Into guys, I mean.

"That's pretty funny, Doe," Eric Junior says. "But I'm sorry, he's not here." He cocks an eyebrow at me. "Let me just ask his mates, though. Surely someone knows where he is."

"No, don't—"

"Hey everybody," Eric Junior shouts. "Jane Doe's looking for my father. Anyone know where he's gone? Anyone want to help her out?"

The fisherfolk freeze. Even the cats abandon their fish heads and stare.

"Huh, guess not," Eric Junior says. "Actually, how stupid of me. I just remembered he's at the Town Hall, working on his speech. It's a good 'un this year." The little prick slaps me on the shoulder and stands aside, ready to enjoy the show. "Pity you're not invited."

A seagull squawks. A cat meows. A lonely buoy-bell clangs in the distance.

"W-well," I say in the general direction of the fisher-folk, "I'm running late, so I'll leave you all to—"

"*GET HER!*"

They charge. Naturally, I run for my damn life. Duck and dodge. Jump over a barrel, slide under one of the gutting tables, and leap to my feet again. For a second I figure

29

I'm gonna make it, too—there's a break in the crowd, an alleyway beyond—but then some jerk swings an anchor at me—an actual freakin' anchor—and I have to change course. I'm surrounded in no time. Everything's a blur. Everyone's shouting and screaming, closing in, so I head for the only clear space I can see. Before I know it, I'm running along a rickety old jetty stretching out into the sea. The fisherfolk weren't just closing in. They were herding me.

I'm trapped. Over water. Maybe not so street smart, after all.

A cheer from the fisherfolk now. Even Eric Junior joins in, whooping and howling.

I feel sick. I can hear the water lapping far beneath my feet. See my shadow drowning between the rotting planks of wood. A few sailboats are anchored nearby, but for a girl who can't swim they may as well be floating on the horizon. I turn around, slowly. The fisherfolk are already stalking down the jetty toward me, led by Eric Junior and a gap-toothed giant with a wooden leg. Peg, they call him. Yeah, they're really great with nicknames round here.

"We told you not to show yer face here again, little Doe," he growls.

The jetty groans under our combined weight. It sways a little.

"We *really* need to get off this thing," I say. "Please, I-I'll go home. Right now."

"You don't have a home," Eric Junior says. "You're a parasite, Doe. A leech sucking this island dry. You and your demented dad."

I barely get the chance to think *Nobody calls my dad demented, you overgrown turd* before he breaks away from the others and sprints right at me. The jetty cracks and buckles.

"Wait," I shout, "nobody move," but it's too late.

The jetty lurches to one side. The fisherfolk topple like dominoes. Eric Junior slams into me and we fall and fall and hit the water hard, shoot right under. My cloak's too heavy, dragging me down already, as if the pockets are filled with stones. I cling to Eric Junior. He kicks, thrashes, tries to break free, but I can't let go. I plead with him, scream bubble-shaped cries for help, my lungs heaving and burning. It's like I'm trapped in one of my nightmares.

And then he's gone.

Eric Junior disappears and an eerie quiet settles around me. I can hear my own heart beating, every spasm in my throat, but all I can think about is Dad, lying in the basement at the mercy of the praying mantis and the weasel. Alone. Hungry. Waiting. Worrying.

The invisible thread between us tugs and wrenches.

But now there's a different feeling. Some tentacled thing wrapping around me, squeezing, stealing me away. No, not away. Up. I'm rising, faster and faster, caught in a fishing net. I burst from the water in a flash of brilliant sunlight and glorious air fills my lungs. I'm not just breathing it, either, I'm flying through it. The net swings around, dumps me on the deck of a sailboat and I collapse in a tangled, panting mess. Even manage a smile, till I realize someone's watching me. An old woman in a red cloak, standing by the rope pulleys.

Winifred Robin, up close and personal. Her skin's wrinkled and scarred. Face like a chopping board. Hands like talons. As she strides across the deck toward me she pulls a shotgun from her cloak. Clearly my situation hasn't improved.

"I am sorry, Jane," she says. "You are going to wake up with quite a headache."

And she knocks me out cold with the butt of her gun.

VOICES IN THE DARK

My sleep's usually riddled with nightmares. Flashes of babies crying, strangers running from monsters, never-ending stone corridors, and a blinding white light. Most of the time it's just me, drowning in a faraway sea. No wonder Violet thinks I'm scared of the dark. I always wake up screaming, twisted in my sweaty sheets. This, though—actually being knocked unconscious—ain't too shabby at all, like being wrapped in a thick, warm blanket. A floating cocoon where no bad dream can touch you. A safe place, deeper than normal sleep.

Only problem is you have to wake up.

"I was surprised to get your message." A deep voice tugs at my ears. "Capturing her after all these years. Throwing her inside this thing. Quite the change of character, Robin."

"Perhaps." An old and scratchy voice. *Her* voice. "But I have my reasons."

"So you keep saying. You have not, however, told me what those reasons are. Nothing is ever this simple with you. You haven't set foot on a boat in years. How did you know she was going to end up in the water? You cannot tell me it was mere coincidence."

"Of course it was no coincidence. There is no such thing."

"Then how—"

"You have waited fourteen years for this moment, Eric. I am surprised you are asking any questions at all. I have handed over the girl. She is no longer under my protection."

A moment of silence.

"You know what this means, Robin. What you're giving me permission to do. You may have struck a deal with my predecessor, but I won't stand for it. Breaking curfew, wandering the streets, knocking on my door, bold as brass. Attacking an innocent group of people—attacking my own *son*. And another quake—today of all days—hours before the Lament? They're getting worse. We all know it. We cannot live like this. We won't."

"Like I said, I can protect her no more."

"And what of the other?"

"His time will come soon enough. Leave him be. Now, if you please, Ms. Doe is about to wake up. I would like a quick word with her alone."

"You think you can tell *me*—"

"I *know* I can tell you, Eric. Out. Don't even think about listening at the door. After I am through with Jane you may do what you wish, but until then I want absolute privacy."

I don't like the sound of this, but she's right about one thing. My cocoon's unravelling, slowly spinning me through the dark. A door slams shut. My eyes blink open. Shapes blur, senses sharpen. It's time to face the waking world again, whether I like it or not.

THE CAGE AND THE CURATOR

The worst thing about being known as the Cursed One is that when you're just minding your own business, following instructions from a secret message, you can somehow end up being chased, drowned, trapped in a fishing net, and smacked in the head with a shotgun. My head hurts, my mouth tastes like a rotten sock full of seaweed, and I'm pretty sure there's a dead fish trapped in my undies. I feel for the little guy, but at least its troubles are over.

Mine, it seems, have only just begun.

"Welcome back to the world of the living, Jane."

I'm sprawled on the floor of a cage. A cage lashed to the back of a wagon parked in a poky old boatshed. My cloak's long gone, my tunic's still damp, my wrists and feet are tied, and there's a rag stuffed in my mouth. A little rowboat's leaning against the wall to my right, surrounded by a clutter of crates and anchors. To my left—

Oh crap.

Winifred Robin's staring down at me.

"Don't worry," she says. "I am not going to hurt you. I trust you already know my name." I nod, just the once, my eyes fixed on hers. She doesn't shy away, doesn't blink. "Good. I am the curator of the Museum of Otherworldly Antiquities. Sorry about the cage and bindings, but I had no choice. I will remove your gag, but you must understand, crying out for help would be rather pointless." I flinch as she reaches through the bars. "Easy now. Easy."

I lean toward her, transfixed by the jagged scars crisscrossing her face, neck and hands. Are they claw marks? Battle wounds? Really, really bad paper cuts?

"Lovely," the woman mutters, throwing the spit-drenched gag to the floor. "There was another quake while you were in the water. Just a tremble, really, but I am afraid your little escapade has set everybody on edge. They feared you might summon another upon waking."

I try to spit the dirty taste from my mouth. It doesn't work. "Listen, lady—"

"Winifred."

"Right. Winifred, whatever. Look, you've got the wrong idea here. It wasn't my fault the jetty broke. If those idiots hadn't chased me out there in the first place—"

"I do not care about the jetty."

"Then tell everyone I was only following the mayor's orders. Where's my cloak? Check the pockets. There's a photo inside with a message on the back, and—"

"I know of the message." Winifred plucks a silver hipflask from her cloak, throws it through the bars onto my lap. "Drink. It is tea infused with a sprig of feverfew. An herb to soothe your head."

"Sure it is." I nudge the flask aside. "Thanks."

"For goodness' sake, girl, I am not trying to poison you. If I wanted you dead I would have let you drown. I understand it may be difficult for you to believe, but I am on your side."

"*My* side? I'm sorry, but did I wake up on a different island or did you accidentally whack yourself in the head as well? You do know who I am, right?"

"Of course."

"But you don't hate me."

"No."

"You're not scared of me? Not even a little bit?"

Winifred sighs, cocks an eyebrow.

"Okay," I say. "If you're my pal, why throw me in a cage?"

"That is . . . complicated." Winifred wanders over to one of the grimy windows set into the boatshed's double doors. "What would you say if I told you every man, woman, and child on Bluehaven was in grave danger and you were the only person who could help them?"

"I'd say you've clearly been sampling too many of your special herbs." I pick up the flask with my bound hands, give it a cautious sniff. "Why?"

Winifred turns around. "Because every man, woman, and child on Bluehaven *is* in grave danger and you *are* the only person who can help them."

Silence fills the shed but not for long. A bubble of laughter swells in my gut and bursts from my mouth. I can't help it. It's a real shame too. Unable to stand the taste in my mouth any longer, I'd just decided it was safe to take a swig of tea. It was hot and sweet, and it really did make my head feel better. Now it's gone up my nose and down my chin.

Winifred isn't impressed. "This is no laughing matter, Jane."

"But—but this is a joke, right? Some sort of prank for the festival?"

"Unfortunately for us all, it is not." Winifred circles my cage like a shark. "The tension that has existed between you and the rest of the townsfolk is about to reach boiling point. Mayor Obi and I came to an agreement long ago—gods bless his soul—but Eric Atlas is not as understanding or as forgiving. I was talking to him before you woke up. He is furious about what transpired earlier. Convinced you tried to drown his son."

"That's a load of crap! I told you, check my cloak. Atlas *told* me to meet him—"

"No," Winifred says, "he didn't."

I can't believe what I'm hearing. It was her. It had to be her. I can tell by the way she's looking at me, the sparkle in her damned eyes. "It was you. You gave me the photo. Why?"

"Because sometimes fate needs a little nudge in the right direction."

"What fate? What the hell are you talking about?"

Winifred stops pacing, grips the cage bars. "Everything is about to change, Jane. Something terrible is about to happen to this island—terrible yet absolutely *necessary*. Atlas will come for you soon. Do not fight him. Play along. You must trust me."

"Trust you? Lady, I don't even know you."

"But I know *you*, Jane Doe." Winifred swivels her wrist and plucks another photograph from her sleeve. "Better than you can possibly imagine." She places the photo on the cage floor, strides over to the big wooden doors.

"Hey!" I shout. "You can't leave me here. If you're on my side, help me."

"I am helping you," Winifred says. "I wish I could tell you everything now, but dusk is steadily approaching. Answers will come." She nods at the photo. "Trust me."

I lose it when she leaves. Kick at the cage, try to untie my feet with my hands and my wrists with my teeth, but the knots are all too tight. I even hurl myself into the wooden bars and try to tip the wagon over. The thing doesn't budge. With nothing left to do, I swear under my breath and shuffle over to the photo.

I freeze.

"No way . . ."

It's similar to Dad's photo: crinkled, soft at the edges, could've lived in Winifred's pocket for years. But this one is of me—baby me, I'm sure of it. Even though the photo's sepia-toned, my amber eyes shine a little too brightly. I'm sitting in some sort of library, smiling up at the camera, wearing one of the books as a hat.

I flip the photo and frown. There's some kind of symbol drawn on the back. An almost-triangle, like a shark fin or a thorn, surrounded by a circle.

And, beneath the symbol, another message.

Everything happens for a reason.

WORST-CASE SCENARIOS

My tunic gets clammy in the stifling heat. The sun creeps toward the horizon, beaming dusty shafts of light through the gaps in the boatshed walls. A mishmash of tribal drums drifts down from Outset Square, mingled with the faraway sounds of laughter.

The Manor Lament has begun. Hours must've passed since Winifred left.

Worst-case scenarios claw at my mind. The mayor and his goon squad crashing through the doors, pitchforks raised and ready to skewer. Mr. and Mrs. Hollow wandering in with a tub of popcorn, ready to enjoy the show. Peg throwing me back into the water. The fact that none of them have happened yet can only mean Atlas is planning something bad. Really bad. The man knows my weak spot, after all. He knows what would hurt me most.

He could go after Dad.

I haven't left him alone this long in years. Atlas could burst into the basement, drag him from his bed and throw him out onto the street, and I wouldn't be there to stop him. Peg could throw *him* into the water. Dad would sink faster than I did. Wouldn't stand a chance.

The thought alone makes my hands tremble.

I just want to get back to the basement and make sure he's okay. Rustle up some grub, settle him in for the night, maybe even tell him a story or sing him a song. Dad loves my songs. I can tell. I'm not one to blow my own horn, but I'm pretty sure I'm a great singer.

I should sing a bit now to pass the time, but I'm not in the mood. Instead, I fumble through my undies and throw the fish corpse across the room. No easy task with two bound hands. I tap my feet. I sweat. I try the ropes again, and sweat some more. Stare at the photo till my eyes ache and blur, then try to find a hidden clue in Winifred's message, a secret meaning behind the symbol. Strange, but I can't help feeling I've seen it somewhere before.

Also, I kinda need to pee. I'm seriously considering taking a squat in the corner when there's a flurry of tapping somewhere behind me. I drop the photo. Violet's waving down at me through a window high on the back wall, face painted in stripes of black, orange, and white. She's supposed to be a tiger, but she couldn't look less fearsome if she tried. She's wielding a toffee-apple half the size of her head. I've never been happier to see her in my life.

"Go round the front," I shout. "I don't think the door's locked, so you don't need to break the—" Violet shatters the pane of glass with her toffee-apple. "Never mind."

"Jane whatever-your-middle-name-is Doe." Violet

ditches her treat and clambers in, dropping down onto a stack of crates. "I leave you for one second and—*whoa*. That sucker on your forehead's the size of a chestnut! Does it hurt? It looks gross. Like, really, really—"

"I'm hideous. I get it. How did you know I was here, Violet?"

"Eric Junior. Heard him bragging to Meredith Platt at the festival. She was getting her face painted same time as me. Got a *butterfly* on her cheek. Can you believe that?"

"Focus, Violet. What did he say, exactly?"

"Eric Junior? He said you tried to drown all the fisherfolk and Winifred Robin caught you. And he said it's a secret. I don't think many people know yet. Cool cage, by the way."

"Yeah, I love it. Almost want to stay here forever."

"Yeah." She cocks her head. "Wait, really?"

"Of course not. Thanks for coming, kid. Look through that junk down there for something to cut this damn rope. We've gotta get out of here, pronto."

Violet leaps down from the crates and searches through the junk scattered around the shed. "By the way, I waited, like, half an hour for you. Even after the little quake happened. Then I went home, just like you said, and I waited and waited—"

"Did you check on my dad? Is he okay?"

"He's fine. I told you he'd be fine. I sat with him for a while, but then I got really, *really* bored, and thought maybe Atlas might've taken you to check out the festival, so I headed back to Outset and—well, then I got distracted."

She rummages through a tackle box. "You should've told me you were gonna wreck half the cove."

"It was an accident, Violet. And it wasn't half the cove, it was one jetty."

"Still. Would've been cool to see." She pulls a small fishing knife from the tackle box and skips toward the cage. "I could've helped you teach 'em a lesson."

Bless her little boots. She hacks away at the rope around my hands, chewing on her tongue. She always chews on her tongue when she concentrates. Her parents hate it. Actually, they seem to hate everything about her. Maybe they love her deep down, but they never show it. Truth is, they've resented her ever since she became friends with the girl in the basement.

They tried to stop it happening. For the first two years of Violet's life, Mr. and Mrs. Hollow made sure we were never in the same room together. Before I was let upstairs to clean the house, she'd be locked in her room. Before she was brought down to the kitchen, I'd be locked in mine. I'd hear her crying and giggling, blowing raspberries upstairs, but I never saw her. After a while, I heard her little baby footsteps. I'd hold my ear to the basement door and listen to the tales Mrs. Hollow would tell her over breakfast. Scary stories of bad things lurking under houses and demons posing as amber-eyed girls. But the Hollows didn't know who they were dealing with. Even as a toddler, Violet was enthralled. I began to hear her shuffling around outside the door. One day I looked through the keyhole and saw her eyeball staring right back. Mrs. Hollow dragged her away and told her she could burst into flames just by looking at me, which only made the little pyro want to see me even more. She sneaked outside a few hours later and made her way round to the basement window. I'll never forget that moment. Me, standing at the base of Dad's bed, looking up. Violet fogging up the glass with her breath, smiling down.

The rest, as they say, is history.

"So," Violet says now, "what was she like?"

"What was who like?"

"Winifred Robin." Violet tuts at me. "Come on, you could act a *little* more excited. She's only the most amazing adventurer Bluehaven's ever seen. She's been into the Manor more times than anyone. I've read all her books. Kids at school say she went batty after the Manor shut up shop, like most of the old folks round here, I s'pose. She lives under the museum. Never talks to anyone. She's pretty much a hermit, but, like, a cool one. And you *actually* got to meet her."

"Lucky me." Violet cuts through the last few strands of rope and it unravels to the cage floor. I rub the red-raw marks around my wrists and take the knife. "Thanks."

I saw away at the rope around my feet.

"Why didn't you just untie that with your hands?" Violet asks.

"I tried, but the woman ties knots like a pirate. As for what she was like?" Actually, I have no idea how to describe Winifred. On one hand, yeah, she smacked me in the head with a shotgun and stuffed me in a cage. On the other, she saved my life. Even offered me a refreshing, poison-free beverage. I cut through the rope and kick it away, stand, and stretch. "*She* was the one who slipped the photo through my window this morning, not Atlas. She wrote the message. She's messing with me, but"—I hand Violet my baby photo—"look."

Violet gasps, "Is that you? Aw, you're so little!"

"All those books. It's the Great Library, right? Under the museum?"

"Yep," Violet says. "And we thought you'd never been inside it, huh?" She shakes her head in wonder, flips the photo. "Everything happens for a reason? Weird. What does the drawing mean?"

"I dunno." I check the padlock and chain wrapped around the little cage door. Useless. Pace around the cage and give each wooden bar a shake instead, rub the shotgun lump on my forehead. "She said Atlas is gonna do something. She said something bad's gonna happen, but it's *necessary*, and I'm the only person who can help everyone. Maybe at dusk."

"*You're* the only person who can help everyone? We're in big trouble, then."

"Look, this knife isn't gonna do jack on these bars. We'll have to break through them. Have a look around for a hammer or something."

"Sure thing." Violet hands back the photo and hurries over to the pile of junk, has a dig around. She holds up a rusty screwdriver. "How about this?"

"Bigger."

"That?" She points to an enormous anchor.

"Smaller."

"This?" She twirls a crowbar through the air.

"Perfect."

She runs back to the cage, grinning. "So what do we do once you're free?"

"Sneak out of here"—I stuff the photo in my pocket, wedge the crowbar between two bars and pull—"head back to the house, make sure my dad's okay, track down Winifred again . . . and get . . . some . . . answers." One of the bars cracks. I smile and re-position the crowbar. "Atlas is gonna go mental when he finds an empty cage. Did Eric Junior mention what he was gonna—"

A hot breath of wind blows through the gaps in the boatshed walls, carrying with it the sound of the drums again. The drums and a distant chuckle. We freeze.

A voice. The slow clippity-clop of a horse. Footsteps getting louder.

"Go," I whisper, tossing the crowbar from the cage. "Out the window."

"No way, Jane. If they're taking you somewhere, I'm going too."

"Look, I appreciate that but we don't have time to— *what are you doing?*" She's crawling under the wagon, that's what. "No, Violet. Get out of here."

But it's too late. The horse's clippities have stopped clopping. The door rattles.

"Run first chance you get, kid," I mutter. "If they catch you—"

"I'll kick 'em in the nuts," Violet whispers. "Suckers won't even see it coming."

The doors burst open. Golden light fills the shed with a swirl of dust. Four silhouettes stand in the doorway. Atlas, Peg, Eric Junior, and a horse.

My worst-case scenario is about to begin.

THE MANUVIAN KNIFE

Dapper three-piece suit. Slicked-back hair. Chiseled jaw. Mayor Atlas is a pompous, barrel-chested statue come to life. Grade-A jerk and then some. "Who were you talking to, Doe?"

"Nobody."

"We 'eard voices," Peg says, hobbling around, checking behind the piles of junk. He's changed his clothes since our dip in the ocean. So has Eric Junior. "Don't deny it."

"No. I mean, yeah. I *was* talking to myself. I do it a lot. On account of the whole no-friends thing and all." Violet giggles under the wagon. I stomp my foot to cover the noise. "Sorry. Nervous tic." I stomp again for good measure. Eric Junior frowns at me, hanging back with the horse. I want to punch him. "By the way, I wasn't trying to drown you, *Junior*."

"Tha's a lie," Peg says. "I saw it all." He glances under the wagon. Thankfully, Violet's off the ground, stretched out between the axles, face-up. I can just make her out between the planks beneath me. They'd have to crawl right under to see her. "Nobody 'ere."

Atlas stands right in front of me, hands in his pockets. "You were bound and gagged when I left, Doe. Robin helped you out, did she? Made things more comfortable for you?"

"Maybe."

Peg reaches into the cage, gives the flask a pig-like sniff. "What'd you talk about?"

"The weather." I can't help covering for Winifred. My baby photo sealed the deal. An unspoken pact, for now. "Oh, and swimming lessons. Probably a good idea, really."

Peg punches the cage. "Cut the cheek, you little freak! What'd she say?"

"Save your breath, Gareth," Atlas says, and all I can think is, *Gareth? Peg's real name is Gareth?* "She isn't going to tell us what Robin said and she doesn't need to. After tonight, I am going to be heralded as a hero, and that old meddler will have no choice but to retreat to her precious little museum forever." He gives Eric Junior a curt nod. "It is time."

Eric Junior leads the horse into the shed and tethers it to the wagon. Violet shifts a little underneath. Peg gathers the severed rope and knife from the cage floor.

"Want me to tie 'er up again?"

"Leave her. The crowd will find it more dramatic if there's a hint of danger involved."

My face falls at the c-word. "What are you gonna do?"

The mayor's lips flicker with a smile. "Tell me, Doe, have you ever heard of Manuvia? No? Pity. Beautiful place. Turquoise sky. Endless jungle, all of it teeming with life. I journeyed there on my first adventure through the Manor."

"Eric Atlas and the Red Temple Siege," Eric Junior says, buckling the last strap on the horse's harness. "It's an awesome story."

"The best," Peg says, which surprises me. He doesn't exactly seem like the reading type.

"If you weren't forbidden to lay your eyes upon the Bluehaven Chronicles, I would highly recommend it," Atlas continues. "Not that I like to brag. Anyway, I passed through the Manor with ease. A couple of booby traps—nothing too serious. But trouble was brewing in Manuvia. Upon my arrival, I discovered that an evil tribe of cannibals known as the Gothgans had stolen something from the Great Kingdom of Manu. A relic. It's just a knife, really, but to the tribes of Manuvia it was considered a mysterious and most powerful weapon. According to legend, the knife had the power to harness the energy of those it slayed or injured, and transfer that energy to whoever wielded it. So, my calling was simple: retrieve the knife, save the world.

"The journey to the Gothgan caves was long and fraught with danger—I won't burden you with the details, for they were many and quite extraordinary. I got the knife. Naturally, the Gothgans were not pleased. Even after I'd made my triumphant return to Manu they laid siege to the Red Temple, the resting place of the knife, for ninety days and nights. I battled and bled alongside the Manuvians for three whole months and the Gothgans were defeated. The Great Kingdom of Manu, nay, Manuvia itself, was saved."

I don't like where this is going.

"After we had claimed victory, Kucho, the tribal elder, called everybody to the base of the temple stairs." Atlas starts pacing. "You see, the Manuvians believe—and I say *believe* because, although I have never returned, I am sure they are still alive and prospering—that everything has a spirit. Air, stone, water, flame, and bone. Everything. They also believe these spirits can be tainted. Broken. The spirit of the Red Temple, having weathered such a lengthy and vicious battle, was in the greatest danger of all. It had to be saved. Revived. *Sated.*"

I glance down between the planks, see Violet's wide tiger eyes staring up at me.

"They'd captured thirty-seven Gothgans in the battle," Eric Junior says. "Out of those thirty-seven, nine were women, six were elders, and . . . four were children, right, Dad?"

"Correct, Junior. They were taken to the stairs, their lives spilled upon the stone one by one, fed to the temple not in the name of battle, but in the name of ceremony. Of sacrifice. It had been done many times before. That was how the temple had received its name."

"Red Temple," Peg says. "'Cause of all the blood, see?"

"Thanks," I tell him. "I got it."

"And they cut them with this." Atlas pulls a knife from his vest. A sharp, curved blade with an ivory handle carved into the shape of a hundred writhing, intertwined bodies. He steps up to the cage, twirls it through his fingers. "The Manuvian knife itself."

I swallow hard. "They . . . gave it to you?"

"After a fashion. I deserved it after everything I'd done for them. A mighty gift for a mighty warrior. Lifted it just before I made the journey home. It holds absolutely no magical or mythical properties, of that I'm certain, but it is remarkably sharp." The mayor traces the blade across his neck. "One cut per sacrifice. That was all it took. People have done it for thousands of years in the Otherworlds. Cleansing rituals on temple stairs. Offerings to gods and monsters." He shrugs his blocky shoulders. "I don't see why we should be any different."

"Don't see no reason at all," Peg sneers.

"You have terrorized this island for the last time, Jane Doe," Atlas says, and smiles. "We are taking you to the festival. We are going to sacrifice you to the Manor at dusk."

THE MANOR LAMENT

There was a time when I was obsessed with the Otherworlds. I used to sneak into the storeroom of the Golden Horn and hide behind the barrels of ale, listening keenly as the old folks at the bar told their tales. Back in the basement, I'd reenact them for Dad, dwelling on the fine details of these different places, these worlds without curses and curfews. Better worlds where smiling wasn't a punishable offense, and maybe—just maybe—Dad could walk and talk and play. Maybe even a world where Mom was waiting for us both with open arms, ready to take us home—to our *real* home.

It was a prospect too exciting to ignore.

I even used to love the Manor Lament. Locked in the basement, I'd listen through the open window, trying to guess which stories were being celebrated, savoring the scent of barbecued sausages and sugar-roasted nuts. Come nightfall, I'd cheer on the unseen fireworks, every *crack* and *bang*. Marveling at each flash of light that burst over the neighboring stone wall like a shattered rainbow. I pictured stars exploding over the island and wondered if you could catch the pieces as they fell. But all of that was way back when. Before I understood what the meaning of the word *outcast* truly was. Before I realized the festival was damning me and Dad.

The Manor Lament quickly slipped into the long list of things I couldn't care less about. The sounds, the smells, the stories, the very idea of the Otherworlds themselves. That mythical home-sweet-home. I bottled up the desire to embark on a quest to find my mom, buried it deep. I knew I had to make a choice. Spend my life wishing for something that would never be or focus on what I had. What was *there*, right in front of me. What was real. Caring for Dad. Protecting him.

Now I'm about to become the festival's star attraction.

And Dad's gonna be all alone.

My prison-on-wheels rattles and clanks up the road to Outset Square, drawn by the horse. I can only just hear Violet's voice over the racket, which is good, seeing as she chose the worst hiding place in the history of stupid hiding places. She asks how I'm holding up.

"Peachy," I mutter through frozen lips.

"Hang in there, kid," she says. "At least you finally get to see the festival, right?"

Nobody notices us when we emerge from the alley. Atlas, Peg, and Eric Junior stop the horse beside a cluster of barrels and wait, soaking up the scene. The ecstatic crowd. The busy food stalls. The flags, banners, and confetti tinted pink in the light of the setting sun. The jugglers and fire-breathers. Barnaby Twigg striding around the well, twirling a sword.

I spot Mr. Hollow in the crowd, desperately trying to avoid touching anyone, a handkerchief clasped to his mouth. Mrs. Hollow's laughing and clapping beside him. The effigies of me and Dad haven't been lit yet, but they've been used as target practice for eggs and arrows. A group at the base of the Sacred Stairs chant and shake their hands in some sort of ritualistic dance. Kids watch, enthralled, as red-faced old-timers act out their Otherworldly adventures on every stage, complete with homemade props. Battles with beasts. Epic wars. Narrow escapes from ancient, booby-trapped temples. The whole square is a heaving mass of people, color, and noise.

The Manor looms above it all, silhouetted against the sunset sky, its features lost in shadow. I can't help but feel it's staring down at me, a hungry toad watching a fly.

I can't hold its gaze for long.

That's when I realize Mr. Hollow's looking right at me. He flaps his handkerchief at me. Grabs Mrs. Hollow's arm. She sees me too and turns a dirty shade of green.

They scream together, long and loud. An ear-piercing, blood-curdling shriek.

One by one, the performers stop performing, the jugglers stop juggling, the fire-breathers let their flames die to curling wisps of smoke. Barnaby keeps on marching and singing until a rogue sausage flies from the crowd and hits him in the chest. Then he too stops and stares along with the rest of the crowd.

A grim, heavy silence settles on the square.

"What's happening?" Violet whispers. "Why's it so quiet?"

I feel naked, exposed, like a hooked worm dangling over a school of fish.

"Um . . . hi," I say to everyone.

Mr. Hollow clutches his chest. Someone lets out a stifled cry. Old Mrs. Jones faints into the arms of some idiot dressed in a bedsheet toga, but Atlas doesn't miss a beat.

"Fear not, good citizens of Bluehaven. The Cursed One is our prisoner at last!"

A collective gasp ripples through the square. I signal Violet to run with a jerk of my head. She stares defiantly back. The crowd doesn't know what to do, what to feel. Relief? Happiness? Terror? They aren't sure whether to celebrate and cheer or dash home and hide. But Atlas stirs them up, milks them for all they're worth. He assures them of their safety, my treachery, his undying love for them all, and sure enough the good sheep of Bluehaven start a freakin' slow clap. A slow clap that quickly turns into outright applause. The idiot in the toga drops Mrs. Jones and kisses some guy standing next to him. The Hollows even hug for three whole seconds.

"The Cursed One attacked a group of perfectly innocent fisherfolk five hours ago in White Rock Cove!" Atlas cries. "Ran at them with a machete! Threatened to kidnap their firstborn children! When they tried to flee, she herded them onto a jetty and tried to drown them all. Tried to sink the whole island with another quake!" Cries of outrage from the crowd now. "But my son leapt onto a nearby boat, trapped the beast in a fishing net, and brought her ashore to face her crimes!"

Eric Junior flashes a cheesy smile and punches the sky. Everyone *hoorahs* and *huzzahs* and sends gleeful praises to the Makers. It's amazing, to be honest.

Insane, but amazing.

Atlas raises his hands, silencing the rabble. "The sentencing, Gareth, if you please."

Peg unfurls a scroll from his vest and clears his throat. "By the powers newly entrusted to 'im as Mayor of Blue'aven, the Honerababble Eric Nathaniel Atlas, son of 'ighly esteemeded adventurer Nathaniel Constantine Atlas, does 'ereby sentence Jane Doe, daughter of what's-'is-face Doe, to—'ang on, can't read me own writin'. What's that last word there?"

"Death," I say, adding in a much quieter voice, "idiot."

"Oh yeah—DEATH!"

Surprise, surprise, the crowd goes wild. Right on cue, a bunch of fisherfolk haul large wicker baskets through the crowd, handing out rotten eggs, fish, fruit, and vegetables.

"Fourteen years ago, this filth and her father intruded upon our world," Atlas cries above the uproar. "Cursed our home!" He pulls the Manuvian knife from his vest. "Now her death shall set us free! Gone are the days of injustice! Gone are the days of fear and sorrow! Tonight we end our long years of suffering! Tonight we take destiny into our own hands!"

DUSK

By the time the cage reaches the Sacred Stairs I feel like a compost heap and smell even worse. Violet's no better off, drenched in the sludge dripping through the planks between us. At least she was shielded from the harder projectiles. Rocks, boots, stage props, torn-off pieces of the stages themselves. All I had were the cage bars fending off the occasional attack and half a watermelon shell to wear as a helmet. I'm resourceful like that.

"What do you think of the festival now, huh?" I ask Violet, but I don't think she can hear me. What else am I supposed to say? Look away? Close your eyes? Run home and don't look back? Please, please, please take care of my dad? Don't let them hurt him?

The invisible thread tugs at my heart and guts. I feel like throwing up.

This can't be happening. This can't be it. None of this feels real.

I try to fight Peg off when he snatches me from the cage. Wave my arms, kick my legs, say the things I expect people always say when they're about to have their throats slit. Pointless things like "let me go" and "get your stinkin' hands off me." He doesn't listen, of course, just drags me to the Stairs and pins me down with his wooden leg as the drums bump-ba-dum and the crowd claps to the beat. Eric Junior grabs my ponytail, pulls my head right back. Atlas holds the Manuvian knife high, and every idiot in the square cries out for my blood.

"I don't suppose there's any point asking you to— ouch—forget all this, is there?"

"You can beg all you want, witch," Atlas growls. "Won't make a difference. We should've done this years ago." Then the drums *thud, bam, boom* and Atlas cries, "In the name of the Makers! Po, Aris, Nabu-kai!"

I clench my eyes shut. Try putting myself in a happy place. Any place but here.

But then a voice says, "Wait!" and silence reigns again. I open one eye, then the other. The knife's hovering above me, dangerously close. Atlas is glaring down at me, veins pulsing on his forehead. Eyes bloodshot, twitching.

Peg removes his leg from my chest, turns to the crowd. "Who dares in'errupt?"

"I dare," is the only response he gets.

Atlas pulls me to my feet then, twisting my arm behind my back. He knows as well as I do who it is. "Ladies and gentlemen," he shouts, "we are joined by a living legend."

The red cloak. The scars. Her presence here is clearly as rare as mine. Those closest to her in the crowd step back in awe. Only one person stays by her side. A stooped figure with a hooded cloak of his own. Someone from the museum, maybe? An apprentice?

"Winifred Robin," Atlas says. "Such an honor. What brings you here this evening?" And in a lower, aggressive yet undeniably pleading tone, "We had an agreement."

"The agreement stands." I swear Winifred's eyes flick to the wagon where Violet's still hiding, huddled behind one of the wheels. "Everything is as it should be."

"*What?*" I shout. "How can you say that? You said you were on my—"

Atlas covers my mouth with his hand.

"I merely wanted to congratulate you, Eric," Winifred says. "You are putting on quite a show. And I must say I am dreadfully sorry for the interruption."

"No problem." Atlas clears his throat. "And—and thank you."

Whispers ripple through the crowd. Everybody looks from Winifred to Atlas and back again, expecting something else, something more. But the old woman just stares at him, doesn't even blink. It's enough to make his palms sweat. I should know. I can taste it.

"Is there anything else?" he finally asks. "Ma'am?"

"Yes. Actually, there is."

"Oh?" Atlas mutters. I can't help but feel relieved. Winifred has just been toying with him. She's about to tell him it was all a game. Demand he let me go or—

"Could you conduct the sacrifice a little higher up the Stairs?"

Wait. No. What?

"My friend here is not quite as tall as me, you see. I'd hate for him to miss out."

"Oh," Atlas says again. "And, ah, who is your friend?"

Winifred places an arm around the mystery man's shoulders. That's when I notice his swaying stance. The tendrils of gray hair weeping from his hood.

"To you, Eric, he is nothing. To Jane, on the other hand, he is everything."

She pulls back the hood, and the invisible thread tugs again, pulling at my insides so hard I almost pass out. I can't move, can't think how it's possible, but there he is, staring at the ground as if nothing's going on at all, as if he hasn't even left the basement.

Winifred Robin has brought my dad to the party.

"How dare you bring *him* here," Atlas growls. "Gareth! Take him into custody!"

Peg and his men charge into the crowd, weapons raised. Panic flushes through my body and everything seems to slow down. Winifred vanishes into the crowd, leaving Dad unprotected, alone, adrift in an angry sea. Now they're calling for his blood as well as mine. I scream and try to break away from Atlas, anger swelling inside me, a furious tide. The stone trembles beneath my feet. The sky's no longer caught in a tug-o-war between day and night. The bloodred clouds are bruising.

Dusk has come.

The crowd scatters. Atlas tells me to stop, but I keep screaming, fighting, reaching out to Dad. I'm thrown onto the shaking Stairs. Eric Junior holds me down, but nobody sees Violet coming, not even me. She slams into Eric Junior, who falls into Atlas, who staggers back but recovers all too quickly, swinging his knife again.

I pull Violet close, shield her with my body and swipe at Atlas as I turn away, but the blade gets me, slicing my left palm open, cutting to the bone. My hand hits the Sacred Stairs. Something snaps inside me, breaks free, and the furious tide overflows. I can feel the cracks in the stone snaking their way up and down the Stairs, tearing across the square. I can feel the whole island shaking to its very core.

ROCK AND RUIN

What just happened? I'm holding my palm against my chest, stemming the flow of blood with my tunic, covered in a cold sweat and shaking. Violet's yelling in my ear, but I can't focus. My hand's killing me. My vision's gone fuzzy. The air's thick with noise.

"Come on, Jane, we have to go!" Violet slaps me, hauls me to my feet. "Now!"

Bluehaven's being torn apart. It's chaos. The horse gallops around the square, still tethered to the wagon. Peg is out for the count or worse. Some of the crowd flood into the alleyways, heading for their homes or the ocean. Others stick to the open spaces, but no where's safe. The ground cracks at their feet. Windows shatter, walls crumble. I can't see Dad anywhere.

"We have to get out of here."

"Oh, really?" Violet says. "Where'd you get that idea, genius?"

She grabs my uninjured hand and pulls me down the Stairs. I'm too slow and clumsy. Don't even see Atlas coming till he's nearly on top of me. He has that damn knife out again, but one swift kick from Violet and he's on his knees, clutching his groin and grimacing.

"Told you I'd get him," she says.

Through the screaming crowd now. A lamppost falls. A stage collapses. We change course again and again, ducking and stumbling across the square. I feel lightheaded. The blood from my hand's running freely down my chest, but I can't stop. I have to find Dad.

The thought fuels me.

A woman screams and points behind us. Enormous chunks of the Sacred Stairs are breaking free, crashing down the hill. Bouncing through the terraced farms, flattening trees and farmers' huts, tumbling into the square and obliterating both effigies in a shower of sticks. The cracks at our feet open wide, some half a meter or more. Me and Violet jump one, hand in hand, take a hard left when the horse and wagon thunders past. We're running alongside the Town Hall now, weaving between the stone columns.

Definitely not the safest place to be.

The column ahead crumbles. I pick Violet up, leap over a fallen boulder, and dive into the Town Hall foyer just as the great doors slam shut behind us, blocked by the falling rubble.

"Inside?" Violet cries. "You brought us *inside*? What if the roof collapses?"

"Working on it." The checkered floor's covered in dust and debris. The high-domed ceiling's falling apart, and the statue in the center of the foyer has already lost its head. There are other survivors in here too, none of them happy to see me. The Hollows. Eric Junior. Old Mrs. Jones. Meredith Platt. Basically, everyone dumb enough to head *in*doors during a quake. They arm themselves with any weapon they can find—rocks, paperweights, shards of glass from the broken windows high on the wall, a chair. "Oh, give me a break . . ."

Mrs. Hollow snatches Violet from my arms with a high-pitched "Hands off my daughter!" Violet tries to get free, but Mr. Hollow grabs her too. Not, I suspect, to protect her, but to use her as a human shield. Nobody else moves. They're not as brave as Atlas. Even Eric Junior hangs back now.

Everyone's terrified. Well, everyone but Winifred Robin.

She's in here too, walking calmly toward me. "Hold out your hand."

"Where's my dad? What did you do with him?"

"Your hand, Jane," she says. The domed ceiling cracks again. More chunks of rock rain down. People scatter and shout but Winifred doesn't blink an eye. "Hold it out. Now."

"Dad," I cry, even though I know he can't hear me.

I trip and fall backwards. My tunic's drenched in blood, my head's spinning. But then Winifred grabs my left arm, tucks something small into my bloodied hand, and everything changes. The ground gives a final, almighty shudder, as if the island itself has shrugged, sat down, and sighed. The quake has stopped.

Everything's gone quiet. If it weren't for the settling dust I'd think time itself had frozen.

I sit up, blinking. Winifred smiles at me. But before either of us can say a word, somebody screams outside. Several people, actually. Cries of outrage, of fear. Eric Junior tries the doors, but they won't budge. People crane their heads up to the broken windows high on the wall instead, gathering beneath them like little light-starved flowers.

"What's going on out there?" Mr. Hollow asks.

"It has happened," Winifred says, and she closes her eyes, as if listening to a beautiful song. A favorite tune she hasn't heard in years. "The Manor has woken from its slumber."

THE DEPARTURE

At first, everyone in the foyer's too stunned to move, but it isn't long before they're all bustling around the doors, trying to get them open. I'm still on the floor, staring at an old, tarnished brass key resting alongside the gash in my palm. I let it slip between my fingers. It lands on the floor with a dull thud. Winifred bends down and quickly ties off a bandage around my hand. I can feel her watching me, hear Violet calling my name, but I can't stop looking at the bloodied key lying there in the dust. There's a symbol on its handle. The one Winifred drew on the back of my photo. The almost-triangle in a circle.

"Jane, you better come look."

Violet's standing on her mom's shoulders, looking through one of the broken windows. Strange. It's probably the most intimate moment I've ever seen them share.

"Don't talk to her, Violet," Mrs. Hollow grunts. "You know you're not allowed. Why should *she* look anyway? The last thing we want to do is let her curse us all over ag—"

"It's your *dad*, Jane," Violet says. "He's outside and he's . . . he's . . ."

I'm up in a flash, heading toward a small upturned desk in the corner of the foyer. I pick it up, turn it over, and slam it against the wall beneath another broken window, shooting daggers at Winifred Robin all the while. "I swear if anything happens to him—"

"You cannot stop him, Jane."

"Stop him from *what*?"

Onto the desk now. I leap for the tall, narrow window, pull myself up, and look through the shattered glass. It's a war zone outside. The square's a mess. Pillars of smoke rise from the town beyond. The horse and cage have disappeared. People are stepping out of the shadows. Stumbling. Crying. Staring and pointing up at the Sacred Stairs.

"Violet, where—"

And then I see him, my dad, scrambling up the Stairs, already halfway to the top.

"He is about to enter the Manor, Jane," Winifred says. "He has been chosen."

"*WHAT?*"

It isn't even me who says this. It's the Hollows. Eric Junior. Pretty much every idiot in the room. Everyone's glaring at Winifred.

"Now listen here, you homewrecker!" Mrs. Hollow shoves Violet back into Mr. Hollow's arms. "First you break into my house and free that—that *man*. Then you interrupt the festival just when it's getting interesting, and now you have the nerve to suggest—"

"I have the nerve to do a great many things, Beatrice. Do not forget who you are talking to. I have let you get away with many horrible deeds in the past, but those days have come to an end. A new age in Bluehaven has begun, and John Doe is leading the way. Now, are you going to keep arguing with me or are you going to stop Jane from joining him?"

I really hate this woman. Nobody had noticed me hop down from the desk and start toward the back of the foyer. Now they're all looking at me like a bunch of ravenous wolves, which are these big ferocious dogs that howl and hunt in packs. I read about them in a book once.

"Run, Jane," Violet shouts.

So I run. Past a grand staircase, down a long corridor. I kick my way into some sort of office and push through the upturned furniture to a window. Mrs. Hollow shouts after me, "Get back here, Doe! You are a scar upon this island! A catastrophic blemish." But I'm already out the window, already sprinting for the Stairs. I trip more than once— over a rock, a plank of wood, Peg. Whenever I stumble or hit the ground, I pull myself up and keep on moving. Dad's just an ant-sized speck now, three-quarters of the way to the top. I wish I could reach out, grab the invisible thread, and reel him back to safety before it's too late.

Because I'm not the only person trying to stop him.

Atlas has found a pistol. Someone must've dropped it in the square. He's running for the Stairs too, but he hasn't seen me coming. He fires at Dad. Misses by a long shot. Raises the pistol to fire again. I jump over a boulder, and that's when we collide. We hit the ground hard and roll. The pistol goes flying. I manage to slip out from under

Atlas, but he grabs my ankle, pulls me back, and before I know it he's on top of me, hands wrapped around my neck. He squeezes. Leans in.

"No more games, *girl*," he snarls.

I'm choking. Can't breathe. I reach out with my uninjured hand, feel around for something, anything, to help me. The pistol, a piece of wood, a club.

"Your little friend's not here to save you now and neither is Winifred Robin."

A rock. I grab it, hold it tight, smack Atlas in the head as hard as I can. A dull thud and he collapses beside me.

"Lucky I can take care of myself, then," I wheeze.

I stagger to my feet, coughing and spluttering, rubbing my neck. Only manage three steps before my legs buckle and someone catches me from behind.

Winifred's here, holding me up, holding me back.

Dad's at the top of the Stairs now. A tiny red dot of a man dwarfed by the sheer size of the Manor and its great stone door. It strikes me that we've never been this far apart before.

Why is he leaving me? How can this be happening?

He doesn't stop. Doesn't look back. He scrambles right up to the Manor, and we can't even see him anymore for the angle of the Stairs. But we can see the great stone gateway opening wide, ready to swallow him whole. Nothing can stop him now.

"A door opens," Winifred whispers. "An adventure begins . . ."

I'm not a big crier—hell, I reckon I could count the number of times I've cried in my life on one hand. But as the Manor gateway shuts again and I feel the invisible thread stretch and tug and snap with a sickening jolt, I can't stop the tears from coming. I struggle in Winifred's arms. I want to follow Dad, run up to the Manor, and smash my way inside, but I'm too weak. Exhausted. Broken.

He's gone.

I can't go up the Stairs now anyway. A flock of people have beaten me to it. Dozens of townsfolk stream around us, shouting, pushing, desperate to try their luck on the gateway. Barnaby Twigg's in the thick of it, warning everyone to back off.

"It's my turn," he bellows. "My destiny! My time!"

"We must leave," Winifred says. "That door will not open again for a very long time. Atlas will come for you again when he wakes. We must get you somewhere safe."

Dad's gone. I've lost him. I've lost him and I don't know how I'm gonna get him back.

"I have to . . . have to go after him."

"You will," Winifred says. "But not that way. There is another."

That's when I notice my bloodied handprint on the Stairs. Every crack in the stone spiderwebs out from its center. Up and down the Stairs. Across the square.

My left hand throbs again. The bandage is already spotted with blood.

"Did . . . did I do this?"

"Come, Jane," Winifred says. "We need to talk."

THE MUSEUM OF
OTHERWORLDLY ANTIQUITIES

The foyer's deserted. Winifred bolts the door the moment we step inside. The place is a mess. Tapestries hang askew on the cracked walls. The domed ceiling looks perilously close to collapsing. Some of the enormous stained-glass windows have shattered.

"This way," she says.

Our footsteps echo through the cavernous space. My hands are shaking. I feel numb. I'm covered in blood, sweat, and vegetable gunk, and the invisible thread's trailing behind me through the dust, untethered now, disconnected from Dad.

He's gone. He's gone. He's gone.

Why am I even following this woman? Isn't this all her fault?

Maybe I'm in shock. I'm definitely in shock. Hell, I'm not even supposed to be in here. I'm not allowed. I swear the larger-than-life-sized statues lining the walls are glaring down at me. Sayuri Hara. Atticus Khan. K.B. Gray. Finn Pigeon. They look like ancient guards. Sentinels bearing weapons, compasses, globes, and books. These are the Great Adventurers. The people whose exploits through the Manor have become the stuff of legend.

The statue in the center of the foyer's the largest of all. That Dawes guy everyone loses their mind over around here. There are all sorts of impressive words people use to describe him. Imposing. Fierce. Ferocious. All I see is a ponytailed fool in a loincloth. The plaque at the base of the statue says he entered the Manor over two thousand years ago.

Apparently, he was the first to step inside. And he never returned.

Dad's gone. He's in danger. Go get him.

"We are going down," Winifred says, heading toward a spiral staircase in the far corner. "Like you, I have grown accustomed to underground living."

So down we go, twisting deeper and deeper under the museum. Getting further and further away from Dad, step by step.

At the bottom of the stairs, Winifred opens a hefty wooden door. "Welcome to the Great Library. Or perhaps I should say, welcome back . . ."

The library's enormous, lit by hundreds of oil lamps hanging from the walls, lined with rows of stone columns and seemingly never-ending shelves. The same shelves from my baby photo. It looks like an underground city, and smells of dust and old parchment.

"This way, if you please . . ."

Winifred plucks a lamp from its bracket, sets off down one of the aisles. I catch a few titles on the shelves as we go. *Isobel Harper and the Tomb of the Serpent King. Hugh-lance Boone and the Glacial Blade. Jack Lee and the Darkling Light.* There are thousands more in this aisle alone. The Bluehaven Chronicles. Some look well preserved. Others have cracked leather bindings and faded, flaky lettering. It's impressive. All of it. Even I can't deny it.

"There are so many."

Winifred nods. "One book for every adventure undertaken through the Manor, written by the heroes themselves upon their return."

We head through an archway, down a staircase, along a stone-walled corridor and into a warm, cozy study—the same study from Dad's photo. There's the crackling fireplace, the desk littered with parchment, the massive cabinet packed with antique swords, rifles, globes, and vases. An enormous painting hangs on the wall next to the cabinet. A canyon riddled with caves. One of the supposed infinite realms connected to the Manor, I suppose.

"Your hand," Winifred says. "Are you in any pain?"

"Of course I'm in pain." I'm feeling bolder now. Angrier, too. The shock's starting to wane. "Why did you bring me down here? Where's my dad gone?"

"Your father is merely following the path that was laid out before him." Winifred strides over to her desk and pulls a small decanter and two crystal glasses from one of the drawers. She pours a dash of golden liquid into each. "Just as I am following mine."

"We should've stopped him."

"You cannot stop what is meant to be, Jane, any more than you can stop the moon from rising." Winifred downs her glass in one gulp, places the other in front of an empty chair across the desk. "Drink. It will help ease the pain in your hand. And your head."

"It smells disgusting. More special herbs?"

"Whiskey."

"Oh." Who gives *whiskey* to a fourteen-year-old? "Thanks, but I'm . . . trying to cut back."

Winifred shrugs. "Very well, then. Let us talk about your path."

"*My* path?"

"Of course. You are the hero of this adventure, whether you like it or not."

"Look, I just want to get my dad ba—"

"And therein lies the adventure." Winifred pulls a crummy green rucksack from behind her desk and flings it at my feet. "There is a towel in there. I was unable to find any clean underwear or socks among your belongings while I collected your father, but I did salvage a clean tunic and a pair of pants. It may not be the best attire for the quest you are about to—"

"Quest? No, no, there won't be any *quest*, okay? Listen, thanks for rummaging through my underwear drawer and"—I pull a chunk of bread from the rucksack, spot a few dates in there too—"thanks for the snacks. But as soon as things calm down outside, I'm going up the Stairs, getting my dad, and taking him back to the basement."

"It is not going to be that simple, and you know it.

Every moment of your life has been building to this, Jane. You will enter the Manor, yes, but not via the Sacred Stairs." She places the key on her desk—must've picked it up before following me out of the Town Hall. "You must take this. Keep it safe. I have returned it to you, and with you it must stay."

"*Returned* it to me? Meaning what, exactly?"

"Meaning I took it from you when we first met, and now I have given it back." Winifred sits down, leans back in her chair. "I was there, Jane. The night of the first quake. The night you and John came to Bluehaven. I was the one who found you on the Stairs." She nods at the empty chair. "Sit for a moment. Please. There are things you need to know."

THE NIGHT OF ALL
CATASTROPHES

"There was a storm that night. I was crossing Outset Square when the ground started shaking. I looked up at the Manor just as a bolt of lightning struck. I saw the gateway open, your father collapsing at the top of the Stairs. I ran to help him." Winifred pours herself another splash of whiskey, swirls her glass. "He was in so much pain, but I couldn't discern any visible wounds. He seemed to be fighting something within, as if poisoned. You were crying in his arms." She nods at the key on the desk. "That was fastened to a strip of cloth around your neck, like a talisman. When I reached out to touch it, your father grabbed my wrist. *Hide it*, he said. *Keep it secret. Tell no one.* I asked what had happened, where he came from, but something had broken inside him. He passed out. I took you into my arms and hid the key in my pocket. I have never mentioned it to anybody since."

I scratch at a glob of egg on my neck to keep my hands from trembling. "Where'd it come from? What does it open?"

"John is the only person who can answer that. I do not know what happened to him in the Manor, but he had clearly been through a very long and horrible ordeal."

"And his illness? Do you think it's true I could've—"

"Cursed him? No. Unlike most of the fools on this island, I have seen several curses, even been cursed once myself. It is not pleasant, let me assure you." Winifred pauses, deep in thought. "Your father's illness is something altogether different. But what, I cannot say."

"So . . . what happened next? After you found us on the Stairs?"

"I knew I had to get you and your father to safety as soon as possible. The ground was still trembling. The quake wasn't as violent as this evening's, but it was alarming all the same. Bluehaven had never been struck by one before, at least not in my time. A town council meeting was in session that night. Spooked by the quake, they fled into the square. Eric Atlas, Idris—that's Mayor Obi—and a few others saw us. They helped carry your father down.

"The island was in chaos. People flooded into the streets, fearing the wrath of the Makers, converging in Outset Square. A large crowd had gathered by the time we reached the bottom of the Stairs. I wrapped you a little tighter in my cloak and then—well—the strangest thing happened. You stopped crying. The quake ceased. Nobody moved. We stood there in the easing rain, all of us, waiting—for what, we didn't know. Then you opened your eyes. They glowed like embers."

"The eyes of a monster."

"*Different* eyes," Winifred says. "Hardly monstrous. Rather striking, if you ask me."

"But people freaked out, right?"

"Simple minds fear what is different, Jane. Everyone was terrified, desperate for answers, and there you were. Some suggested we break the First Law and try to dump you back inside the Manor. Others suggested banishing you and John instead, casting you off to the Dying Lands. Idris and I protested, but we were drowned out by three simple words."

"She is cursed."

"Precisely. I am sorry, Jane. It all happened so quickly. Your future had obviously been set in stone long before you fell through the Manor doors. It was as if you were *destined* to be held accountable for the Night of All Catastrophes."

I grab my glass and try downing the whiskey in one go just like Winifred, but it burns like fire so I end up spluttering most of it back into the glass. I hate the very idea of fate and destiny. The thought that some*one*, some*thing*, some*where* is controlling my every move makes me feel like a puppet, and I've been kinda scared of puppets ever since the Hollows staged a cautionary play in the kitchen called *The Little Girl Who Defied Her Guardians*. It was a two-hour epic tragedy.

"Are you all right, Jane?"

"Yes." I'm pacing around the study now. "No. Maybe."

"Well"—Winifred nods at the rucksack—"now that you're up, you might as well change. Time is against us, and I refuse to let you enter the Manor looking like a rotten salad."

"Can't you just tell me where the second entrance is now? I sat. I listened. My dad's alone up there—*in* there—and he's probably lost and scared. I'm all he's got."

"Precisely, which is why you need to be fully prepared when you leave." I open my mouth to object, but Winifred simply nods at the rucksack again and says, "Chop chop."

Breathe, I tell myself. *He's not dead. He's okay. You'll find him.*

"Fine." My injured hand throbs as I reach into the bag. This isn't gonna be fun. My clothes are clinging to me like a damp second skin, and the thought of stripping in front of an old lady doesn't exactly float my boat, either. I start small, lose my boots and socks. "But hurry."

"Certainly." Winifred swivels her chair to the side to give me a tiny bit of privacy. "Oh, and do remember to clean behind your ears. Now, where were we?"

"The townsfolk." I take a deep breath and yank my tunic over my head, smearing veggie crap all over my face. "Being jerks," I add with a cough. I grab the towel and scrub at a papaya smudge on my ankle. Shake the watermelon pips from my hair.

"Ah, yes. Well, as frightened as the townsfolk were, I made it clear we would not be banishing anybody. Idris helped me. He was a dear friend. A good man. We took you and John down to Vintage Road, where I lived at the time. I assumed John would recover, soon wake from his trance. I believed answers would come. How wrong I was . . .

"Weeks passed. The quakes continued. People climbed the Sacred Stairs daily to no avail. The Manor had been the lifeblood of Bluehaven for thousands of years, but it seemed to have bled dry. It opened for nobody. Desperation turned to anger. Crowds gathered outside my house daily. A boat was readied for you both, but there was no way I was going to turn you over. Eric led the charge, of course. Turned the townsfolk against me. Called me a troublemaker. A traitor. My reputation stayed the gossip for a while, but fear is a powerful thing. Everyone but Idris and the council elders chose to believe you had infected my mind, driven me mad, just like John. But I weathered the storm, and Eric soon realized it would take much more than rumor and hearsay to break me.

"After a particularly frightful quake—and against the will of the council—he led a mob down Vintage Road. Fifty-odd men and women. There was the usual nonsense, of course. Chanting, pitchforks and so on. Suffice to say, the witch hunt had reached its climax. I was presented with an ultimatum: surrender you and John immediately or suffer the consequences. Thankfully, I'd had enough foresight to board up the doors and windows earlier that day, when news of the gathering had reached my ears. To cut a long story short, the siege began at midnight and ended an hour later, when Eric and that oaf with the wooden leg forced their torches through the downstairs windows."

I whip my pants off and wipe down the rest of my legs. "They tried to *burn us alive?*"

"Their plan was to flush us outside, and it worked, much to their horror."

"What does that mean?"

"It means I decided the time had come to remind everybody just how dangerous Winifred Robin can be. I stormed the street and subdued everyone who stood in my way."

I pull on the pants from the rucksack. "But you said there were fifty of them."

"Fifty-three, to be precise. I made certain there were no serious injuries. A few joint-lock and pressure-point attacks, the odd butterfly kick, nothing too flashy. The fire consumed the house, but Idris had already ducked inside and brought you and John to safety."

I don't know what to say. Winifred could probably spring across the desk right now and kick me into next Tuesday if she wanted. "That all sounds . . . wow."

"I do not wish to sound arrogant, young lady, but 'wow' does not quite do it justice." Winifred downs the last of her whiskey. "There was nothing I could say or do to stop the townsfolk from blaming you for the Night of All Catastrophes, but I told them that if any harm came to you I would unleash a fury upon Bluehaven to rival the old Gods of Chaos. As the house collapsed and embers filled the night sky, I told Eric he would be the first to pay the price. Idris and the other elders expelled him from the council at once."

"And everyone let us go?"

"Let?" Winifred says. "My dear girl, I'd given them no choice."

"So what went wrong?" I shake out the clean tunic and slip it on. It's the one I nabbed from our neighbors' bin last year. "Why'd we end up being raffled off to the Hollows?"

"There was no raffle, Jane. That was a lie created by the Hollows to keep you from knowing the truth about your past. To stop you from tracking me down in search of answers." Winifred swivels back to face me again, clears her throat. She looks uncomfortable. "The truth is, you spent your first two years on Bluehaven living under my care, here in the museum."

"The second photo." I fish the old happy snap from the pocket of my worthless tunic. The photo's soiled now, reeks of rotten pumpkin. "You took this while I was living here?"

She nods. "About a year after your arrival."

I stare at the photo, at my smile. "I look happy."

"You were," Winifred says.

"Not for long, though, right?" The words roll off my tongue before I even know they're there. Before I can taste how bitter they sound. "Why didn't we stay here with you?"

"I did not abandon you, Jane. Please understand this. If I'd had it my way, you and John would have stayed with me indefinitely, but there are other forces at work here. Yes, you've had a difficult time with the Hollows, but—"

"Difficult?" I throw the photo onto the desk. "They've treated us like dogs for years."

Winifred sighs. "Jane, Beatrice has been in my debt, grudgingly, for a great many years. I will not go into detail now, for it is another story entirely, but I once saved her life. Long before you came to Bluehaven. When I delivered you and John to her doorstep, she had no choice but to honor this debt and take you in. Besides, they have not always been so—"

"Horrible? Nasty? Evil?"

"*Complex.* Yes, they have always been dimmer than the average lantern, but Bertram and Beatrice are not evil. They didn't even participate in Eric's campaign against you following the Night of All Catastrophes. They had been living in their own scared little world for years, but that world came crashing down the moment I knocked on their door.

"Word of the move travelled quickly. Idris and the council elders had passed a law forbidding anyone from harming you and John—like me, they believed the Makers had sent you to us for a reason, for protection—but others saw the move as an invitation. A sign that I had finally given up. Still fuming from his expulsion from the council, Eric organized several assaults on you and John, some endangering the lives of the Hollows as well. I stopped them all, protecting you from afar. That is why Eric changed tactics, started manipulating the Hollows. He showered them with gifts, whispered things, suggested ways to make your life intolerable. You used to live upstairs, you know. It was he who suggested the basement."

"Gosh, he really is a piece of—"

"Work, yes."

"Actually, I was gonna say—"

"I know what you were going to say, but I don't tolerate foul language." Winifred pauses for a second. "Well, not in here, anyway. So you see, Bertram and Beatrice have always been in a difficult position: desperate to please Eric but terrified of betraying me."

"I'm supposed to feel *sorry* for them now?"

"Not at all. But remember, Jane." She flips the photo, taps the tiny scrawl beneath the symbol. "Everything happens for a reason. You have had a hard life growing up in that household, harder than any child should have to endure. You have suffered, oh yes, but this suffering has made you strong—far stronger than you realize. It has also forged a fierce bond between you and John." Winifred pushes back her chair and stands. "Most importantly, you are *alive*, Ms. Doe, and seeing as though the future of Blue-haven now rests upon your shoulders, that is a very fine thing indeed."

HIDDEN THINGS AND
PUPPET STRINGS

"Come," Winifred says, striding across the room to the cabinet. "It is time to leave."

"Oh, *now* it's time? Right after you tell me I have the future of a freakin' island resting on my shoulders? An island filled with people who hate my guts?"

"In a word? Yes."

I plunge my bare feet back into my squelchy boots. "Okay. But you better tell me the rest of the story before we get back to the square. You say the Hollows took us in because they owed you—fine—but that doesn't explain *why* you handed us over."

"We're not going back to the square." Winifred opens a small cupboard set into the base of the cabinet. Pulls out a brick-sized bundle of black cloth and stuffs it into her cloak. "Eric came to several minutes ago. At this very moment, he is breaking into the museum with seven armed and very dangerous men."

"How can you possibly know that? And what was that thing? What'd you just put in your—" I'm cut off by a distant crack, a gunshot, far away but close enough to fill my stomach with butterflies. No, bees. Wasps. Horned wasps with dirty great stingers. "Uh-oh."

"Never mind," Winifred says. "Everything is proceeding as planned."

She heads for the study door. Closes it. Locks us inside.

"Wait, I thought you said we were leaving."

"We are." Back to the cabinet now. Winifred leans a ceramic vase to the side and—*click*—the massive painting of the cave-riddled canyon swings open. There's a set of spiral stairs behind it. A secret passage. "Now, put the key in your pocket and don't forget the snacks. You must be famished." She picks up a lantern. "You may leave the dirty clothes."

I take the key from the desk and tuck it into one of my pockets, then stuff the dates and chunk of bread from the rucksack into another. "What about weapons?"

"Excuse me?"

"You've got one, right? That black bundle you pulled from the cupboard? I should get one too. I could take that sword there. Or the crossbow."

"You know the laws," Winifred says. "You enter the Manor at will. You enter the Manor unarmed. You enter the Manor alone."

"I don't even get a knife?"

I don't even get an answer. She just holds open the painting and nods at the stairwell beyond.

"Where does it lead anyway?" I ask, ducking inside.

"Down to the catacombs. Trust me, Jane. Move quickly, move quietly."

Winifred carefully pulls the painting shut behind us. Her lantern fills the cramped stairwell with a golden glow. The steps are old, the stone worn smooth. We move single file, Winifred taking the lead, twisting down, down, down.

"So," I almost-whisper, "the future of Bluehaven's resting on my shoulders, huh? That was just an expression, right? Like 'the world is your clam' or whatever."

"The world is your *oyster*, Jane, and no, it was not an expression. I told you earlier today that every person on this island was in danger. That danger has not yet passed."

"Of course it hasn't," I mumble. The wasps swarm and sting.

"Two years after you and John came to Bluehaven— two years to the day—I discovered a chamber hidden beneath the catacombs. In this chamber I found an ancient hieroglyph painted onto the wall. The symbol from the key."

I take the key from my pocket, turn it over in my hand.

"I couldn't believe it," Winifred continues. "After all my years of fruitless research there it was, right beneath my feet. It had been down there, lying in wait, in secret, since the Beginning, long before my ancestors came to the island."

"But what does it mean?"

"Again, the only person who can answer that is your father. But I was drawn to the symbol on the wall, Jane. I touched it and was granted a vision. Images flashed before my eyes. I saw every event leading to this day, this very moment. Me, delivering you and John to the Hollows' the next morning. The attempts made on your lives thereafter. The fisherfolk chasing you around White Rock Cove this morning. The cage. Eric raising that infernal knife on the Sacred Stairs. Violet coming to your rescue. Your father dashing up the Stairs, cloaked in red. You, setting off for the hidden gateway, a second entrance to the Manor. It is down there, Jane, in the chamber, waiting for you. The quake tonight has cleared the way."

"Wait a second. You're saying you handed us over to the Hollows because a creepy symbol on the wall *told* you to? You sound ridiculous. You know that, right?"

"I've been called worse."

"I mean, a *vision?* How is that even possible?"

"The Makers," Winifred says, a hush of reverence in her voice.

I should've known she'd say that. Po, Aris, Nabu-kai. The Gatekeeper, the Builder, and the Scribe. The three gods who supposedly built the Manor. "I still don't get how—"

"Nabu-kai. The Scribe. Seer of All Things. The symbol was painted in his blood."

"Oh, okay," I say. "Seer's blood. Well, that makes perfect sense."

"How else could I have known to lay the fishing net in that precise spot along White Rock today? That Eric would try to sacrifice you? That witnessing your father in such mortal danger would make you cause the greatest quake Bluehaven has ever seen?"

I freeze. "Whoa, whoa, whoa."

Winifred stops a few steps down, turns around. Her scars and wrinkles look garish in the shifting lantern light.

"When *I* caused the quake? You said I wasn't cursed."

"I don't think you are. But you clearly share a connection with the quakes."

My bloody handprint on the Sacred Stairs. The stone like shattered glass.

"The first quake struck when you fell through the gateway, Jane. It stopped when you stopped crying. This afternoon, there was a tremor when you fell into the water. It subsided when you drew your first breath. The quake that occurred during the festival—"

"Started when I saw Dad in trouble."

"And turned positively chaotic the moment your blood hit the Sacred Stairs. It only stopped when I reunited you with the key."

"But why? What's the key got to do with it?"

"I don't *know*, Jane. The point is, I believe the quakes occur whenever you are frightened. Whenever you truly fear for your life or the lives of those you love."

"But most of the quakes happen at night."

"And how do you sleep, Jane? Peacefully? You rarely did as a baby."

The wasps drop dead. "Okay, so I—I have nightmares. A lot of them. But that's normal, right? Everyone gets them. And anyway, I've been in danger plenty of times and nothing's happened. Today wasn't exactly my first run-in with the fisherfolk."

"Because fear has become second nature to you, Jane.

With all the torment you have endured on this island, fearing for your life has become commonplace. You feel fear, yes, but I believe quakes do not occur in these moments because you have learned to manage it. It is only when you lose control, when you are at your most vulnerable, that something snaps."

A second gunshot rumbles through the stairwell like rolling thunder, closer than before. The study door's been blasted open. I can hear Atlas shouting orders. A flurry of footsteps and other, muffled voices. Winifred just raises her eyebrows. *Told you so.*

"Okay," I whisper. "Let's say your creepy visions were real and I really do have wild quake powers. Why would you want to *trigger* them? If everything you're saying is true then you still had a choice, right? You could've ignored the visions. You could've let us stay here with you twelve years ago. You could've not slipped the photo through my window this morning."

"And leave you to the half-life you have been stuck in all these years?"

"If it means my dad stayed safe, then *yes.* None of this would have happened. I wouldn't have been paraded through the festival, Bluehaven wouldn't be, like, broken, and Dad—"

My throat tightens. Dad would still be here.

"I had no choice," Winifred says, placing a steady hand on my shoulder. "Terrible but necessary, remember? I haven't been shown every piece of the puzzle—far from it—but I have seen enough. The symbol was a message from the Makers, Jane. A warning from the gods themselves. Something happened to you and John inside the Manor—what, I do not know—but the key, the quakes, the Manor's reawakening, these things are all connected."

"How? Why?"

"That is precisely what you must find out." Winifred's grip tightens on my shoulder. "This is your story. Your adventure. You must enter the Manor and find your father. Only then will the mysteries unravel. Only then will your destiny become clear."

I wish I could say Winifred's words are bouncing right off me, but I can already feel that invisible thread—still severed from Dad—beginning to change. It's fraying, multiplying, morphing into something else. A tangle of puppet strings knotting around my ankles and wrists, tying a noose around my neck. If what she says is true, though, maybe the puppet strings have been there all along. Maybe everything really has been building to this.

THE CATACOMBS

It's cramped and musty in the catacombs. The ceiling's so low Winifred almost has to duck when we step out from behind a heavy tapestry hiding a secret passage door. To our left, a wall lined with flickering torches. To our right, dozens of shadowy archways. Tombs filled with stone-carved coffins and statues of strange winged creatures. I shudder.

"Do not fear death, Jane," Winifred says. "The dead have their secrets, but they are at peace."

"Uh-huh," I mutter. "Sure."

Every step I take feels harder than the last, like I'm wading through invisible water. It rises to my belly button, my chest, my shoulders, pressing in from all sides, making it hard to breathe. Because I'm surrounded by dead people. Because I have no idea what I'm doing. Because Dad's gone, and all my unanswered questions are still playing tag in my head.

What happened to us inside the Manor? What happened to my mom? Where did we come from? What about the key? What's the deal with the quakes?

"This way." Winifred leads me past the main, public stairwell. Angry voices and footsteps echo down toward us. "Quickly now." She turns down a skinny passageway. Tiny alcoves dot the walls, housing hundreds of ancient scrolls and half-melted candles. "The Scrolls of the Dead," Winifred says. "A record of every soul laid to rest both here and in the graveyard."

"Awesome," I say. "Um. Why is the second gateway all the way down here?"

"Because I was meant to find it," she says. "Just as you are meant to walk through it."

We take a left and a right and then we come to a dead end. Or at least it would be if there wasn't a dirty great hole in the ground. "This is it? I'm going down there?"

A pickaxe wedged into the stone. A knotted bundle of rope. Winifred picks up the tail end and ties it around my waist. I can smell the whiskey on her breath.

"I shall lower you down as gently as I can. There is a chasm a hundred meters or so down the tunnel. You will have no trouble climbing around it. Oh, but do mind the spiders. The chamber is on the other side. All you need to do is touch the gateway, and it will open."

"And once I'm inside? What if Dad's already gone to a different world? How do I find him?"

"That is something you must figure out," Winifred says. "The gateway could take you anywhere within the Manor. Nobody has even come close to exploring it all— to do so would be impossible, for it simply has no end— but I have seen more than most." Winifred gazes down at the hole, gets all nostalgic on me. "You will see, Jane. An infinite number of corridors and chambers intertwined. The walls themselves buzzing, so vibrant, as if the stone itself were alive. In each new room, a mystery. A surprise around every corner. So many secrets waiting to be uncovered. So many new worlds to find." She zeroes in on me now. "But you must take care. Believe me when I say it is not to be ventured into lightly. The Manor is a place full of wonder, oh yes, but danger also. And a great deal of it at that."

I remember some of the stories I used to hear in the Golden Horn. "You mean booby traps and stuff? Pits, spikes, swinging blades?"

"Ancient devices with one purpose only."

"To kill people."

"To ensure that only the worthy pass between worlds."

Winifred hooks the lantern to my pants and rattles off a few rappelling tips, but I just can't pay attention. A stale breeze brushes my cheeks, as if the hole's breathing. I can't see anything down there. It's pitch black. I bet Violet would jump in without thinking twice, but—

"Wait. Violet. Do you reckon she's okay?"

"She is fine," Winifred says.

"I should've said goodbye. I mean . . . how long do you reckon I'll be gone?"

"Time is a fickle thing, Jane. The Manor is a bridge to the Otherworlds. Each world operates on its own time-line, so one day on Bluehaven could equal one week, one year, maybe even one lifetime somewhere else. As for the

Manor itself, time can do strange things in there. Strange things indeed." She nods at the hole. "No more questions. Forward is the only way."

My throat catches. The invisible water rises to my neck, my chin, threatening to drown me on dry land. I step right up to the hole. "Okay, but you're *sure* Violet's okay?"

Winifred nods. I suppose I just have to trust her.

"Good. Can you tell her . . . tell her I said thanks. For saving me on the Stairs and all." My head's buzzing, my hands clammier than a couple of dishrags. "And tell her— tell her—"

"I shall think of something appropriate," Winifred says.

I turn to her now, unsure what to say. Yeah, she kind of ditched me and Dad because a possessed scribble on a wall told her to, but she saved our lives, more than once. Sacrificed her reputation, her whole life here on Blue-haven. All those times she followed me around the island, she was protecting me, watching over me, warding off threats. I should thank her. Hell, I should get real cheesy and give her a hug too, but I'm simply not used to thank-ing grownups.

I'm chewing on the words, but I can't spit them out.

"I know, Jane," Winifred says, placing a hand on my shoulder. Before things get too corny, though, Atlas's voice echoes down the passageway, screaming bloody murder, shouting my name, and Winifred sighs. "However, I would not thank me just yet if I were you."

And she pushes me.

FIRST INTERLUDE

THE WORK OF
WINIFRED ROBIN

Atlas and his men storm past the Scrolls of the Dead, weapons raised.

"Drop the rope, Robin," he says. "It's over. You can't hide the girl down there forever. Let's put an end to this madness once and for all."

The rope stops spooling. Jane has made it. A quick descent, but safe.

Winifred smiles.

Facing the men now, she tells them the truth. They are too late. Their lives now rest in the hands of Jane Doe. They do not believe her. They scoff, shake their heads. Atlas points the Manuvian knife at her chest, and she decides she will claim that too before the end.

Ancient relics deserve more respect.

"You're lying, old woman. Now step aside."

Winifred gives the men a chance to walk away, return to the surface, help their families. She tells them the hunt is over and pulls the bomb wrapped in black cloth from her cloak to prove it.

Five sticks of dynamite. More than enough to seal the tunnel below.

She quickly lights the fuse on a nearby candle. The bomb sparks and hisses.

Every man but Atlas takes a step back.

"Easy now," he says. "Stand your ground, men. She's bluffing. She wouldn't dare."

But Winifred can sense his doubt, his fear. She can feel it, smell it, see it in his eyes.

Forward is the only way, she told Jane, and that is the way Jane is going right now. Winifred is sure of it. She knows Jane is running through the tunnel as quickly as she can—swiping away spiders, tripping over rocks, grazing her hands and knees—because Winifred left a warning down there this morning. One simple, well-chosen word traced into the dust on the floor so that Jane will know exactly what is about to happen.

May Po, Aris, and Nabu-kai protect her.

"Put it out, Robin," Atlas says. "It's over."

The fuse is getting low. Winifred must time the drop perfectly. The men will fire their weapons the moment she lets it go, but she has dodged bullets before. It will only take her ten seconds to subdue them. The bomb will explode and Atlas will surrender at once. She will give him no other choice. And when all is said and done, when Jane is safe from pursuit, Winifred will go and find young Violet outside. She will tell the girl she will not see Jane for a very long time, but her role in this tale is far from over. Her training shall begin at once.

But first, the bomb.

She raises her hand, holds the sputtering dynamite over the hole. The fuse has almost burned through. Seconds remain. Once more, Atlas tells her to cut it out and step aside. She says she heard him the first time, but in her mind she is thinking *three, two, one* . . .

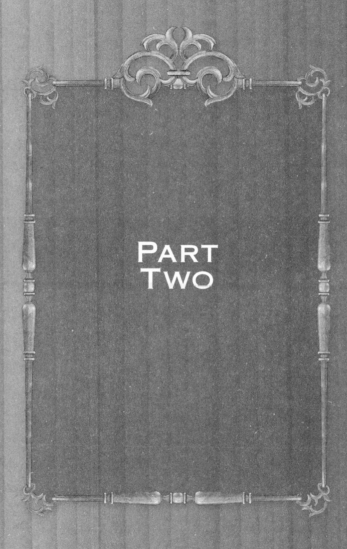

PART
TWO

THE WONDER BEYOND
THE WALL

"Jane, I'm gonna blow up the tunnel after I push you down it."

That's all Winifred had to say. It isn't exactly a tongue-twister. But no, that would've made things too easy. All I got was one measly, four-letter warning scrawled in the dirt.

Bang.

No exclamation point, no underline, no apology. I wondered for a second what the hell it meant, but then I remembered the black bundle she pulled from the cabinet, figured it had to be a bomb. All I could do was scramble, sprint, and climb. I dived into this crummy old chamber just in time. The bomb triggered a cave-in, of course. That was the whole damn point.

The tunnel is sealed. Atlas and his goons can't stop me now.

I'm lucky I didn't lose the lantern. Had to hook it to my pants again while I climbed around the chasm. Now it's back in my hand, lighting up the second gateway, which kinda looks like a giant tooth set into the wall. The stone of the gateway's pale and smooth, but there's a pile of darker stone heaped around its base. Remnants of the rock wall that's been blocking it all these years, I suppose. There's no sign of Winifred's creepy symbol.

This is the fifth time I've tried to work up enough courage to touch the stone. I keep telling myself it's just a door, nothing more, but it isn't just a door, it's a door that's been waiting for me. A gateway to a place I've never been.

I've paced around the chamber. I've peed in the corner. I've eaten the dates and bread. I've scraped smushed spiders from my boots. I've flipped the key through my fingers and wondered what Violet will do when she finds out I left the island without saying goodbye.

Now I'm wondering if it's even possible to find one man in the Manor. One man in all the worlds. It's a needle-in-a-haystack situation, no mistake. Only the haystack never ends.

I don't want to think about the future of Bluehaven. Can't think about the Makers or the quakes. I need to focus on one thing and one thing only: getting Dad back. I picture his face. His brown eyes. The way he almost-smiles sometimes when I tell him a joke.

I touch the gateway.

The chamber rumbles, and I pretty much crap my pants because the gateway grinds open at once—not outward like the main gateway, but up into the ceiling—and I'm blasted by cold air.

I've gotta do it. Jump. Right now.

I take a deep breath and leap over the rock pile into the darkness beyond. My feet land in something cold. A few black-bracketed candles flicker to life of their own accord on the walls either side of me. I'm standing in a short, empty hallway, ankle-deep in snow.

The gateway slams shut behind me at once.

Welcome to the Manor, Jane. Welcome to a whole new kind of weird.

THE SKELETON KEY

So it turns out snow is really, really cold. I shouldn't be surprised, snow being frozen water and all, but still. It's softer than I'd imagined. Drier, too. Tinted an eerie shade of orange under the candlelight. When I scoop some up and sift it through my fingers it drifts away, light as dust. When I put some onto my tongue it melts. I'm no Manor expert, but I'm pretty sure it shouldn't be here. Snow is an outside thing, an Otherworldly thing. Violet sure never mentioned snow-filled corridors whenever she banged on about the Bluehaven Chronicles.

Something's wrong. I can feel it.

Far as I can tell, there are no booby traps here. I scan the frosted walls either side of me, run a hand over the stone. It's nothing like Winifred said it would be. It isn't buzzing. It isn't vibrant. It sure as hell doesn't feel alive. It's just rock, cold and dead.

I take one step forward and quickly jump back. There's no *boom*, no *bang*, no *bam* or *twang*. It's just me and the snow and a silence so loud I can feel it.

There's a wooden door at the other end of the hallway.

Cracked and bulging, bleeding snow and ice. I'll probably have to dig my way into the next room.

Forward is the only way.

I take a few cautious steps, feet crunching softly through the snow, mouth puffing like a chimney. My hands are already shaking. When I reach the door I hold my breath and listen, but something presses down on me, an invisible weight. The quiet's too thick, too heavy. "Just a door, nothing more," I say to break the silence. A locked door, it seems. I wonder.

Could it really be this simple?

I take the key from my pocket, slip it into the lock, and *click*, bingo.

One mystery down, a billion more to go.

Dad found a key to the Manor, but how? Where? Manor keys must be rare if Winifred never made the connection. I can't recall any popping up in the stories I've heard. I do remember Violet saying people had to move on if they ever came to a locked door, try their luck on another, and trust that the Manor was guiding them the right way.

A key changes everything.

Hide it, Dad told Winifred. *Keep it secret.*

There must be more to it. Maybe the key opens more than this one door. Maybe it opens *all* of them. If it does, it'd be priceless.

But I can't linger on that now. Gotta keep moving before I freeze.

I tuck the key back into my pocket and clear away the

ice at the base of the door. When I wrench the damn thing open, it sounds like bones breaking.

There's a wall of snow behind it. Time to dig.

I start at the top, scraping and scooping, shaking now. When I slip, the snow sneaks down my neck, up my pants, into my boots, but it isn't long before I'm punching air, hauling my lantern up into the next—I want to say "room," but the word doesn't do it justice. It's even bigger than the museum foyer, soaring at least twenty stories high, and it's filled with arches, columns and balconies, all carved from the same ancient stone. Those creepy self-lighting candles have already flared to life, along with some larger torches too, many in places no human hand could possibly reach. There are no windows, only hundreds of wooden doors lurking between every pillar, under every arch. Most of the doors on this ground floor are three-quarters buried under the snow. The ones I can see on the floors above look frosted-over but otherwise clear. Icicles hang from every edge, a gallery of shiny daggers.

It's beautiful. Scary, but beautiful.

I want to call out to Dad, but that suffocating stillness holds me back. A feeling I've intruded on a scene undisturbed since the beginning of all things.

"*Dad*," I whisper-shout instead. "*You there?*"

No movement. No sound save the thudding of my heart.

There are too many doors. Too many pathways to choose. I really don't fancy another round of digging, so I head for the yawning, black archway at the far end of the hall, plodding through the knee-deep snow, cupping my free hand near the lantern to keep it warm. Stone-carved faces adorn the pillars. Women. Men. Beasts snarling down at me. Doesn't exactly make for a relaxing stroll. I turn around and watch my back, check for any sign of danger. I feel smaller and stranger than I've ever felt before.

I still can't believe I'm here. I still can't believe Dad left me.

Stepping up to the archway now, teeth typewriter-chattering, legs numb. The snow's banked up much higher in the next room, the ceiling so low I could almost touch it. The candles and torches in the grand hall snuff out behind me as soon as I step through, but at that same moment a black metal chandelier flares to life right in front of me— and a second, third and fourth beyond that—a whole line of them lighting up as far as I can see. It's a corridor. A long one, too.

I'm about to turn back when something makes the candles dance. A draft. It only lasts a few seconds, but a draft can only mean an opening, a way out.

Maybe a gateway Dad opened, but a gateway to where?

I set off down the corridor, trudging around the chandeliers, passing other archways, other halls, other rooms, balconies, and more buried doors. I come to crossroads and T-junctions, take a left, a right. See the odd statue poking out of the snow. The top of a helmet, a pair of horns, a spear. Sometimes I have to retrace my steps from a dead end. The place is a bigger maze than Bluehaven, and I lose the draft in no time.

It's hopeless.

Panic rising, I stumble up a slippery staircase. The snow isn't as deep up here. The chandeliers are high above my head, back where they should be. The air's just as icy, though, and the doors are still frosted over, sparkling in the candlelight. I fumble the key from my pocket. "Please, please, please . . ."

I slip it into another lock and turn it. *Click.* Bingo again.

I was right. It really is a skeleton key. One key for every door. Somehow it feels heavier now. More precious than ever. This is the kind of treasure people would kill for.

A fat lot of good it'll do me if I freeze.

I get a system going. Devise a set of rules for exploring the Manor.

1. *Open as many doors as you can before choosing a room to enter.*
2. *Pick the plain rooms. The ones without slits in the walls or holes in the ceiling.*
3. *Stay wily. This includes, but is not limited to: keeping your eyes peeled, listening out for Dad (or any creeps who might be lurking around the corners), and leaving every door open (because a quick escape is a good escape).*

Hours pass. At least I think they do. Time's getting harder and harder to judge in here. The Manor just keeps going, like a map that won't stop unfolding. Square rooms, circular rooms, the-kinds-of-shapes-I-can't-remember-the-names-of rooms. I jog to keep warm till my legs and lungs can't handle it anymore, the panic now a cold lump in my throat. When I see a wall covered in claw marks and stains that look like dried blood, I back away slowly and pick a different room. I think of nice things like warm blankets, hot baths, chicken soup, hot baths *in* chicken soup, but the nice things are never enough. My lungs burn from the cold. Frozen snot tickles my nose. I shout Dad's name over and over, suffocating silence be damned.

I get so cold and tired and grumpy that I forget to check for traps. All it takes is a close shave with a giant, swinging axe to snap me back, and I add another rule to my list:

4. *Take precautionary measures. Throw something into each room before you waltz on in and get yourself sliced, speared, torched, and/or decapitated.*

Later, when a candle I've nicked from the walls is chopped in half by a hidden blade before it even hits the snow, I decide to avoid the smaller rooms altogether.

Two eeny-meeny-miny-moes and a few icy stairwells later, I find the draft again, except it isn't a draft anymore; it's a howling gale. A damn indoor snowstorm. The candles on the walls whip around like tiny orange tongues flicking in the wind. Further on, they keep snuffing out and re-lighting. The doors tremble. I call out to Dad again, my voice a fleeting puff of steam. My vision blurs. I'm exhausted. Drained. I get the bright idea to hug my lantern and steal some of its warmth, but I must've dropped it way back when, because it isn't in my hand anymore. The key still is, though, snuggled tight in my white-knuckled fist.

And then I see it, through the blizzard and the blinking light. Another archway. A blueish haze. I stumble onto a balcony overlooking another grand, frozen hall. This one's dominated by an enormous stone gateway as wide as a street and fifteen stories high. It's covered in tiny holes, as if stone-munching termites have been feasting on it for centuries. The dull, blue light shines through the holes. The growling wind *blows* through them, driving the snow and ice. There's a frozen world beyond that door. An Otherworld.

If I were any other kid on Bluehaven I'd probably get all gooey eyed and giddy right now—standing here, seeing this—but all I'm thinking is there's no way Dad opened that door. The snow's piled too high at its base. There are no footprints. I've just wasted hours chasing a phantom lead. I know I'm new to this adventure stuff, but I'm pretty sure things weren't meant to turn out this way. If I wasn't feeling so weak, so cold, I'd scream. All I manage is a mumbled "sorry" as I huddle down against the wall. What if I've lost him forever?

But what's this?

A raggedy pair of boots. A man standing over me with an empty black bag in his gloved hands. I can't see his face, just a scarf and pair of goggles. I can't cry out, can't run, can't move. Not even when he reaches down and slips the black bag over my head.

THE NIGHTMARE

The waves are alive. Lifting me up, throwing me down, dragging me through the angry fizz of black bubble-wash till I'm snagged by the deep-water grip of the ocean. Suspended in the dark, a familiar chorus echoes all around me, low and sickening. The groan of a dozen hungry things. Flashes illuminate the water—from below, not above—and I see *them*. The white-fire eyes. The great, yawning mouths. A glowing, heaving mass of tentacles streaked with lightning, reaching out to grab me. The force of the rising swell pushes me back to the surface and tosses me around like a toy. I steal a breath at the crest of a monstrous wave . . . and scream.

But there, in the distance. Something I'm sure I've never seen before. A giant rock rising from the whitewash. A small island. I kick toward it even though it's a mile away, even though I'm already being forced back, thrown down, sucked under the waves again.

Forced back to the place where the monsters dwell.

THE MAN WITH THE BLACK BAG

These blankets stink of sweat and smoke. I feel like I've been sleeping for hours, days, months. My arms are too heavy. I can barely wipe the drool from my chin. I yawn and rub the sleep from my eyes. I'm sprawled beneath a statue of a man with a bull's head.

A pair of goggles hangs from its horn. *His* goggles.

I jump up, fists raised and ready to fight.

The man isn't here.

I'm in another candlelit room. No snow, no wind, just four stone walls and a door chocked open by a big metal bucket. My hand has been re-bandaged. An odd thing for a kidnapper to do. Come to think of it, how can I even be sure I've been kidnapped? Yeah, the man black-bagged me, but at least he got me out of the snow. He saved my life, really.

There's a bucket chocking the door open, filled with something black and goopy-looking. It reeks so much I have to hold my breath when I nudge the door open a little wider. The hallway beyond isn't very long. There's a T-junction at the far end. The candles are already lit.

Is the man coming back? Do I want him to? He could help me find Dad. Or at least point me in the right direction. Or he could turn my skull into a breakfast bowl. I flip between splitting and staying a billion times, and then I hear it. Footsteps.

The Man with the Black Bag's coming back.

I figure I should lock the door between us while we come to some sort of agreement, preferably one that involves me not dying. Problem is, I can't find the key. Can't remember if it was in my hand or my pocket when I passed out. Did he take it? What do I do if he did?

Keep it safe, Winifred said. *I have returned it to you, and with you it must stay.*

I rummage through the blankets at the bottom of the statue, just in case. Thank all that's good and shiny, it's here, buried down the bottom.

The door creaks open behind me.

I grab the key and duck behind the statue just in time.

The guy's taller than I am. Big but lean, as if every bit of fat has wasted away from his body, leaving only muscle and bone. He isn't even a man. Not really. A guy, sure, but only a few years older than me, tops. He's dressed in torn, dirty rags. His almost-beard and shag of black hair are flecked with specks of melting snow. He reminds me of a wild animal—the kind you definitely don't want to be trapped in a room with.

This is how I'd like things to go down:

I say, "Who are you?" He says, "Someone who can help you." I say, "You've seen my dad?" He says, "Gray hair? Yea tall? Big red cloak? Well, tonight's your lucky night, friend! He's resting down the hall, right next to the door back to Bluehaven. I can take you to him now if you like." Then we high-five and skip the hell out of this place.

This is how things *actually* go down:

I say nothing, stay not-so-hidden behind the statue. He smears some of the bucket-gunk onto his shoulders. I gag from the rancid stench. He sniffs. Scratches his balls.

Has he forgotten I'm here?

I clear my throat, even cough out a little *ahem*, and the guy finally looks at me. Or through me. Kinda hard to tell. I want to say something tough like "Don't try anything stupid, I know karate," but what I end up saying is "Are you wearing my boots?" because I've just realized the jerk's wearing my boots. He's even cut off the ends so his toes can poke through.

"Hey." I step out from behind the statue. "Give me back my boots."

"Not yours," he says at last. "Mine now."

I don't know what to say to this, so I ask the question I should've opened with in the first place. "Who are you?" The guy keeps staring. "Where did you come from? Thanks for getting me out of the snow and all, but seriously, I can't believe you ruined my boots." Nothing. He doesn't even respond when I get all polite and say, "My name's Jane, what's yours?" It's a shame, because I've always wanted to meet a stranger. Someone who doesn't know my name, who's never heard of curses. And here I am, still being treated like a leper.

I decide not to take it personally. What I do instead is throw the guy's goggles at him. They bounce off his chest and hit the floor. He picks them up and stuffs them into his pocket. I brace myself for an attack, but it never comes. He just slides the seedy bucket across the floor with his foot and says, "Wipe it on your clothes. Hides your scent."

"Excuse me? I'm not wiping anything until—"

"Just cleared our tracks in the snow. I'm leaving now. Don't try to follow."

"Wait a second, pal." I point at him to show I mean business. "I've just had a really bad day. Or, like, couple of days. I'm not sure what time it is. The point is, my dad's missing and I'm not letting you leave without—hey!" He's leaving. "Fine. Have it your way. Go."

But I can't let him go.

I leave the blankets and the bucket of poo and follow him into the hallway. "Come on, you can't just leave me. I'm looking for my dad. You might've seen him. Gray hair? Yea tall? Big red cloak? No? Well, I've been wandering around in here for hours and hours."

"You'll get used to it."

"I don't want to get used to it. Look, you've clearly been in here a while. Maybe you could give me some directions. You owe me. You shoved a bag over my head."

"You could've been dangerous."

"What makes you so sure I'm not?"

"You squirm in your sleep."

Damn nightmares. "Look, judging by your personal hygiene, I'm guessing you haven't had much people-time lately. Why not show a bit of human decency while you can, huh?"

I plead and beg for three corridors and one flight of stairs. No matter what I say, I can't turn the Guy Who Won't Stop Walking into the Guy Who Just Might Stay. I compliment his almost-beard. Say "please" more times than I can count. Then I get angry and call him a jerk. That's when he lashes out and pins me to the wall. He glares at me, but not for long.

"Your eyes," he says. "They're—"

"Yellow. Got a problem with that? You know, yours aren't exactly . . ." Actually, his eyes are pretty incredible, for a guy and all. Big and dark. Somehow, they seem older than the rest of his face. "Okay, so your eyes are kinda cool, I'll give you that, but—"

"Shut it." The guy leans in so close our noses are almost touching. I tell him to let me go. He says, "What are you gonna do?" So I knee him in the balls and he staggers back.

I straighten my tunic. "That."

The guy groans. "Don't. Follow. Me. You stay." He opens the nearest door and the candles in the hallway beyond flicker on.

It's time to play my final card. Now or never. *Keep it secret*, Dad told Winifred, but it's all I have.

"You're trapped in here, right? Looking for a way out? I can help you. I have a key."

The guy freezes, one hand stuck to the doorknob.

"A key?"

"Yeah," I say, but I'm already wishing I hadn't because now he's turning around, staring at me with a hungry look on his face.

"Show me."

I take the key from my pocket. The guy tries to play it cool but I can see his fascination plain as day. His eyes twitch. His mouth hangs open. "Where did you get that?"

"Doesn't matter where I got it. It's mine."

"Yours." He wrenches his eyes away from the key. "Where'd you say you came from?"

"I didn't. But I come from an island. An island called Bluehaven."

"Bluehaven." He says the word slowly, trying it on for size. Is he happy? Sad? About to flip out? I don't think he even knows. For a while, he doesn't say anything at all. Feels pretty awkward, really. Then he clears his throat. "Your father. You followed him in here?"

I nod. "Kind of. He was maybe an hour ahead of me? I need to find him as soon as possible. He's sick. You don't want to tell me who you are or where you come from? That's fine. But this key has opened every door I've tried so far. Help me find my dad and you can have it. Once we find the gateway back to our world, you can use it to find yours."

But even as I say this, a tiny voice in my head asks, *Why?* Why go back to Bluehaven? We're in the place-between-places, after all. Me and Dad could go anywhere, to any world. Pick a gateway, any gateway. Hell, we could find our home. Our *real* home.

We could even find my mom.

But what about Violet? What if the next world's worse than Bluehaven? What if Dad really did have to leave our home because the people there hate me, too? What if Mom died long ago? What if *that* was the reason he left? What if, what if, what if?

It's all too much.

I tuck the key back into my pocket to cover the fact that my hands are shaking. The guy's been staring at it all this time, enchanted, but he snaps out of it now, takes a breath.

"So," I ask him, "do we have a deal?" I don't get a nod, but I don't get a headshake either. "Good. Go get your dog and we can start searching right away."

"What dog?"

"That dog." I point through the open door behind him at the ugly mutt that's been watching us for the last few seconds down the hallway. "What, it isn't yours?"

The guy turns around. Makes a sound like kittens dying. The dog takes a few steps forward, and I realize it isn't a dog at all. It's too big, too muscly, more like an over-sized boar. It isn't hairy, either, but covered in rusty metal plates from head to claw, stained bloodred and brown. No eyes. No ears. Just a wet snout and a set of long, razor-sharp teeth.

"Should've kept that bucket," the guy says. He quickly closes the door and the thing-that-isn't-a-dog snarls and barks. "Um. Run. Now."

TIN-SKIN TROUBLE

Heart pumping. Lungs burning. Bare feet slapping on the stone. My almost-friend might be bigger than me, but I'm just as fast. Turns out his name's Hickory. He finally told me when the not-a-dog broke through the door and started chasing us. No point keeping secrets now, I guess. We're sprinting along candlelit corridors, praying for another door.

"What is that thing? Where'd it come from?"

"Tin-skin," Hickory says. "Otherworld. No more questions."

We bump into each other as we round corners. A hard right. A left. There's a door up ahead, and it's about time, too. The Tin-skin's gaining on us, gnashing its teeth.

Hickory reckons the door's locked, tells me to get ready, but I already am. I grab the handle, shove the key into the lock and turn it. We dash inside and slam the door behind us as the candles flicker on. But the Tin-skin isn't giving up. It throws itself against the door again and again. Barking, snarling, scratching with its claws. I throw my weight against the door, ask Hickory for a hand, but he's gone all quiet behind me.

Because this isn't any ordinary room.

The floor, walls and ceiling are covered in square stone plates, each about a foot wide. Every slab has a symbol carved into it. A circle-within-a-circle, a bird-looking thing, a star. Crooked lines and swirls and demonic, frowning faces. Hundreds of pictures, but no way out.

I wedge myself at the base of the door. "There has to be a secret passage, right?" The doorknob rattles above my head. "*Right?*"

Hickory just stands there, staring at the stone plates.

"Triggers," I think he says.

"I can't keep this thing out forever," I yell. The door cracks and splinters. "Hurry!"

Hickory moves carefully around the room, running his hands over the symbols.

The Tin-skin claws a gap through the wood above my shoulder, forces its snout through the hole, teeth chomping, spit drooling. Smells like rotting meat.

"Just pick one, Hickory," I scream. "Press them all!"

But he doesn't. He moves from symbol to symbol. Goes to press a lightning bolt. Stops. Heads back across the room and starts plotting again. I check the corner to my left. A skull on the wall. An eye on the ceiling. An almost-triangle-in-a-circle on the floor and—

"Wait," I shout. "That one over there. The circle with the messed-up triangle in it."

"Quiet," Hickory shouts, "I'm thinking."

"Trust me." The Tin-skin shoves its whole head through the door. "Push it!"

"We push the wrong one and we're dead. I think it's this one."

"The *snake?* Are you dense? When are snakes ever a good thing?"

Hickory shakes out his hands as if he's about to do the most groundbreaking thing anyone has ever done. He slams his palms into the snake plate.

It doesn't budge.

"Amazing," I say. "Now would you please press the damn triangle? It's the symbol on the key. Over there. Left corner." He goes right. "No, *my* left, idiot! You know what? Fine!"

I launch myself from the door. There's a crash behind me. I slam my fists onto the stone plate as hard as I can. It *clicks*, something else *clunks*, and a massive stone tablet above the door plummets down, sealing us in with a bang. Problem is, the Tin-skin's in here too.

"Ah," Hickory says. "Much better."

The Tin-skin growls, chomps its teeth. I scoot back into the corner and hear something through the wall. Hidden wheels turning. Cogs ticking over. An ancient engine getting louder, getting faster, shaking the room.

The Tin-skin's spooked. It takes a step back.

Then the machine, whatever it is, stops.

Silence fills the room. I look at Hickory. Hickory looks at the Tin-skin. The Tin-skin barks, and I know it's gonna strike. It launches forward, I close my eyes and—BAM—a square column of stone shoots up from the floor, pinning the creature to the ceiling in a wreck of twisted metal and splattered blood. Guts dribble down the column.

I get to my feet, puff a strand of hair away from my eyes. "Well, that was lucky."

BAM. A second column shoots from one wall and slams into the other. BAM. A third drives down from the ceiling, smashing into the floor. More and more columns spear the room, slamming into their opposing stone plates and staying there. Hickory swears and calls me names as he ducks and dodges. I swear and call him names back because it isn't my fault.

"Turn it off," Hickory shouts, but I can't see the symbol from the key anywhere else, just lion heads smashing into lightning bolts and arrows pummeling alligators.

But there. Over in the far corner of the room. One column's moving much slower than the others, grinding upward at a snail's pace. And there's no stone plate above it. Must've slid into the ceiling when I set off the trap. A black hole big enough for us to squeeze through.

Our way out.

"There," I point and shout.

Hickory doesn't hesitate. He dives, rolls and leaps across the room as the columns shoot out faster and faster. He reaches the corner, jumps to the top of the slow-rising column, and pulls himself up and out of the room in one swift motion.

The exit glows as the candles up in the next room flicker on.

"Okay." I psych myself up with a deep breath. "Easy as pie."

I'm nowhere near as graceful as Hickory. Where he

dived, I trip. Where he rolled, I tumble. Where he paused and plotted, I panic and plunge ahead. BAM—I dodge left. BAM—I jump right. BAM—I drop and slide as BAM! BAM! KA-BLAM!—three columns slam down behind me. Candles are smashed from the walls. Columns criss-cross and crash, filling the empty spaces, but I'm nearly there. I grab the edge of the slow-rising column and haul myself up. It's a tight squeeze, but Hickory yanks me clear just in time. The column seals off the room below. I smile and laugh. Hell, I even consider spinning round and giving Hickory a hug.

But something isn't right.

The hands that grabbed me haven't let me go. They're pinning me onto my stomach and they can't be Hickory's because he's kneeling in front of me, arms raised in surrender.

Stop struggling, his face is saying, *don't do anything stupid*, but now I can feel the cold barrel of a gun sticking into the back of my neck. So I do something stupid.

"Get off me," I grunt, shouting, wriggling, grabbing at the gun. "Let—me—go."

Heavy breathing at my ears now. A flurry of insect-like *click*ing and *clack*ing. The hands flip me over and I'm staring up at a soldier—no, two soldiers. They're both impossibly tall and lanky. Carrying rifles. Wearing glassy-eyed gas masks. Skintight suits of dirty, patchwork leather stitched head-to-toe. One of them dangles a chain with a round shackle at its end. The other tilts his head curiously at me. Points his rifle again, ready to fire.

Until Hickory whistles.

The soldiers look at him. I look at him, too. His hands are still raised and he's still on his knees, but one of them has moved.

Now it's resting on a stone-slab trigger.

The soldiers *click* and *clack* and raise their guns, but Hickory's already shifting his weight. Already diving onto his stomach as two giant blades spring from each wall and slice the chamber clean in half. I clench my eyes shut and turn away as the two soldiers hit the ground in four pieces. When I open them again, Hickory's lying right beside me, face flat against the stone, a lone dimple creasing his cheek.

"You're welcome," he says.

THE WAY THINGS ARE

Hickory raids the dead men's pockets, keeping this, discarding that. Bullets. A knife. Strips of dried meat that he sniffs and throws away. Me, I'm huddled in a corner, keeping clear of the big black puddle leaching across the stone. I feel sick. Can't stop staring at the soldiers. Their top halves look like spilled sacks of sausage and their bottom halves are twisted a meter away, legs akimbo.

"Well," I say, "this is traumatic."

One of the bodies makes a noise. A tiny pop. A bubble of escaping air.

The chamber seems normal enough. One open door. A dozen candles on a claw-like chandelier. I can't even see the slits in the walls where the blades quick-as-blinked, but I can see the stone trigger poking up from the blood puddle. No way I'm standing up in a hurry.

Hickory keeps looking at me. Whenever our eyes meet he quickly turns away.

"Got lucky," he says after a while, and points at these little symbols carved into the stone beside the door. A tiny arrow. Two wavy lines. A cross. "I've been in this room before."

"You carved those?"

Hickory nods. "Directions. Secret signposts."

"Right," I say. "Yeah, lucky." I nod at the corpses. "Um. So who are they?"

"Not who. What." Hickory picks up one of the soldier's arms. The leather's wrapped around it like a second skin. Brown and stained. He whips off the glove and I gasp. Three fingers, not five. Way too long. Gray-speckled skin. "Leatherheads. Foot soldiers. Very bad." Hickory kicks the collared chain coiled beside the other corpse. "For the Tin-skin."

"That thing was their *pet?*"

Hickory nods. "Tin-skins and Leatherheads—trackers and snatchers."

"Snatchers. You mean they were gonna take us somewhere?"

"To the fortress."

"Wait, there's a fortress in here?"

"Big one." Hickory picks up half a rifle. Both were sliced clean in half by the blades. "Shame," he mutters, and throws it aside. I figure he's gonna expand on the whole "big fortress" thing, but he just shuffles back against the wall and sighs. Maddening is what it is.

"Okay," I say. "I've heard a lot of stuff about this place over the years, but I'm damn sure I've never heard anything about Tin-skins and Leatherheads and—and big fortresses. Not to mention the gigantic corroded gateway leaking *snow* all through the place. You can't tell me that's normal. Hickory, what the hell is going on in here?"

He considers for a moment. Stares at the Leatherheads. Glances at me.

"Step where I step," he says, standing up. "Stop when I stop. I tell you to run, you run. Tell you to hide, you hide. We get separated, stay put, wait till I find you."

"Hang on, what?" I get to my knees, still wary of the blades. "Where are we going?"

"Somewhere safe." He heads for the door. "Show you something on the way. Be quick, be quiet. Worse things than Tin-skins, traps, and Leatherheads in here."

"Oh, that's comforting," I mutter, crawling around the blood puddle.

I follow Hickory down grand stone staircases. Across rooms filled with statues. Past arches that open onto balconies that look over vast pillared halls that seem to stretch on forever, all of it thick with candle-flicker and a feeling we're being followed. Hickory moves like an animal on the prowl through these winding corridors of stone, stopping now and then to check out his secret symbols carved into the walls. More arrows. A tiny eye. Little squares and crosses. He mumbles to himself, keeps shaking his head. Clearly, he isn't used to having company. He seems conflicted. Keeps glancing back at me. I just hope he isn't debating whether or not to strangle me, steal the key, and leave. He doesn't speak to me. Doesn't answer any more of my questions. "How far is it?" "Did you hear that?" "What did you mean by *worse things?*" "Are we nearly there? Hickory?" All I can do is step where he steps, stop when he stops, and wish someone else was tangled in my puppet strings.

We walk and walk, and if it wasn't for the occasional blast mark on the wall or the odd missing candle, I'd swear we were going in circles. It's like we've done a hundred laps of Bluehaven. Then Hickory says, "We're close," and points up at a chandelier. There's an insect dancing around the flames. Moth-like but sparrow-sized. A flutter of purple and white.

"How'd that get in here?"

"Same way the snow did."

There are more moths down the next corridor. A yellow one on the wall. A big black one surrounded by a swirl of tiny white ones. And then there's grass on the ground. Real, lush, honest-to-goodness grass, golden brown under the candlelight, sprouting right from the stone.

"Manor draws it in," Hickory says. "Gives it life."

I take the lead, scrunching the grass between my toes. There's another gateway round the next corner, about the same size, shape and pale, tooth-like color as the one I came through from Bluehaven. It's flanked by a couple of flaming torches and covered in pockmarks like the gateway in the snow. Some are furry with brown moss, others have cocoons nestled in them. The grass at its base is dotted with tiny flowers, and none of them look bent or broken, far as I can make out. The scene looks undisturbed.

Dad didn't come this way.

"Are all the gateways made of stone?" I ask.

"Yep. Wooden doors just lead to different parts of the Manor."

"So . . . so is this the gateway to your world? Your home?"

"No."

"You don't sound so sure." I look at Hickory then, as if seeing him for the first time. His old-man eyes sitting in his young-man's face. Suddenly it all makes sense. "You can't remember where you came from, can you? Hickory, how long have you been in here?"

"Long enough to forget," he says.

I turn this over in my mind. At first, the idea of forgetting Bluehaven doesn't seem so bad. But then I think about Dad and Violet. Forgetting Bluehaven would mean forgetting them too. Hell, I miss them both already, and it's only been—what—one night? One day?

"Can you remember anything?" I ask. "Family? Friends?"

"My name," Hickory says. "Nothing more."

I'm about to ask him why he isn't a wrinkled wad of skin slumped over a walking stick—scratch that, a mummified corpse—but then I remember something Winifred said about the Manor. *Time can do strange things in there.* Hickory must know what I'm thinking because he holds his arms out and says, "Manor gives life," with a bitter edge to his voice.

"So . . . so what's wrong with it?" I ask, nodding at the gateway. "Why's it all . . . holey?"

"Dying."

"The gateway's dying?"

Hickory shakes his head. "The Manor."

"The Manor can't die," I say, as if I have a clue on the subject.

"Can die. Is dying." Hickory looks around at the walls and the ceiling and the gateway like he wants to kiss them and stab them at the same time. "The snow. This grass. Not meant to be in here. Any of it. Gateways are failing, see? Otherworlds creeping inside."

"Why are the gateways failing?"

Hickory's face darkens. "Roth."

I swear the torches flicker when he says it, as if the flames themselves are frightened. "What's a Roth?" I ask.

"Not a what. A who. The boss. The bad guy. Sneaked inside the Manor somehow. Marched his army in, too. Tin-skins. Leatherheads. Trucks, tanks, and guns. They built the fortress. Started tearing everything apart. The Manor's strong, but that much evil?" Hickory shakes his head. "It can't handle it. Not forever. Roth's been here a long time. Too long."

"As long as you?"

"Nobody's been here as long as me," Hickory says, but he isn't bragging. Far from it.

"I'm sorry," I say, and I mean it, too. "But . . . why did Roth bring an army in here?"

"Why do you think?"

And it hits me. "He wants to take over an Otherworld. He's spoiled for choice in here. He could conquer any world he wants."

"Yes. And no. He got *into* the Manor. But the Manor's not letting him *out* again. Gates don't just open for anyone, see? The Manor chooses. Always. Who goes, who stays."

"So he's stuck here, like you."

"Like *us*." Hickory nods at the gateway. "Try it."

"I don't think I should," I say, and then, because Hickory's eye twitches, "Okay, sure."

I step up to the gateway and touch the honeycombed stone. Nothing happens. There's no grinding stone. No burst of sunlight or breath of fresh, Otherwordly air. There's just the soft flutter of the moths, the crackle of the torches, the heavy silence of the Manor beyond.

It's a dead end.

"Way I see it," Hickory says, "the Manor's out of balance. Crying out for help. Letting people in to stop Roth, not letting 'em out again because it can't risk him tagging along."

"So there are other people in here?" I step back from the gateway, scratching absent-mindedly at an itch in my injured palm. "People from different worlds?"

"Hundreds," Hickory says. "Lost people. Scared people. Can't-get-home-again people. Roth captures anyone he can."

"He tries to get them to open their gateways," I say. "The ones they came through."

"Takes 'em out, one by one. But the gateways never open." Hickory kicks at a mound in the grass, then bends down and starts tearing it up, unearthing something gray-brown and moldy from the tangle of roots. He picks it up. Spins it, tosses and catches it. "Tin-skins get a feed."

It's a mangled human skull.

I kick it from his hand. A reflex motion. Not super respectful, I guess, but neither's being tossed around like a juggling ball. Two corpses and a skull in one day. Some kinda record. "And, um, if a gateway finally does open?"

"Roth enslaves an entire world."

The evil wasps buzz in my gut again. "Listen, that all sounds horrible, but this," I wave a hand at the golden grass and the moths and the foul skull, "this isn't my problem. I came to get my dad, and that's all I'm gonna do."

I half-expect Hickory to look at me like I've kicked a baby, but he just smiles and heads back down the hallway. "My place. Very close. We rest. Get supplies."

"Supplies for what?"

"Long walk. Very far to Roth's fortress."

"Wait a second." I hurry to catch up. "You want us to go *toward* the bad guys?"

"You said your dad's sick," Hickory says casually, as if he's commenting on the weather. "If he's sick, he's slow. If he's slow, he's already been captured."

And that's how he does it. That's how Captain Bad News shakes my already upside-down world to the core. There's no easing me into it. He shoots the words at me, rat-a-tat.

"How do you know that? Hey!"

I punch Hickory's arm. He spins around like he wants to pin me to the wall again, but I raise a finger this time, cock my knee, ready to fire. *Uh-uh.* Hickory thinks twice, backs up.

"Manor's infested. Leatherheads everywhere. Everyone's caught at some point."

"You haven't been caught." My voice is shaky, but

the words still slap Hickory in the face, and that's when it dawns on me. He knows the way to the fortress because he's been there before. "Wait a second, you were caught? When? How did you get away?"

"With great difficulty," Hickory says, and it pretty much seals the deal. I have to trust him, even if he is a thousand-year-old shoe thief who collects buckets of poo.

I have no choice.

"How long does he have?" I can't help glancing back at the skull.

"Depends how many other prisoners there are. Where he is in line. But I'll take you to him, find your gateway home. It probably won't let you out, of course, but that ain't my problem." He sets off down the corridor again. "Soon as we get there, the key is mine."

HICKORY'S HIDEOUT

I think we get to wherever it is we're going pretty quickly, but I can't be sure. We could've been walking for hours. Images of Dad being beaten and tortured by this Roth guy keep swirling through my mind. Worst-case scenarios'll be the death of me one day, I swear.

"So this is it?" We're standing in front of a dark hallway. "This is your hideout?"

"Not quite," Hickory says.

"What happened to the candles?"

"Got rid of 'em. Good cover. No talking."

Into the darkness we go, and it's the sound of Hickory's footsteps I'm following, the counting under his breath. When he hits thirty he turns right. When he hits seventy he veers left. When he hits eighty-two he stops walking altogether and I run into his back.

"You hear that?" he asks.

A cry for help—no, a howl—far down the corridor, back the way we came.

"Tin-skins," Hickory says. "Pack of 'em. Picked up our scent. Move."

The counting comes faster now. Ninety-three. One-twelve. One-thirty. The howling gets louder behind us and there are other noises too. Rattling chains and barking.

"How much further?" I ask.

Then I trip over. Scrape my knees and hands, feel my palm tear open again. I picture the base of the Sacred Stairs, my bloodied handprint on the stone, but there's no quake this time, no furious tide. Just Hickory feeling for my arm, pulling me back to my feet.

The squeak of an opening door. He pulls me inside.

"Don't move," he says, slamming the door shut behind us. "Not one step."

Rummaging down to my left. A clunk and scrape. A wooden plank sliding into place.

He's reinforcing the door.

"Will it hold?" I ask, wincing at the throbbing pain in my hand.

"Won't need to." The pop and rattle of an open jar. That familiar, eye-watering stench. A slopping, slapping sound. "Smell scares 'em. Blocks our scent. They'll run right past."

"What is that stuff anyway?"

"You don't want to know," Hickory says.

The Tin-skin pack storms past the door, rattling the handle. I want to turn and run but I stand my ground. And just when I think it's over, when the main pack rumbles out of earshot, I hear something else. Sniffing, slobbering, the clack of clawed paws on stone. A squeak of metal-on-metal. A lone Tin-skin has stayed behind. It's pacing just outside the door.

"Hickory?" I whisper.

"Wait," he whispers back. "Don't. Move."

Something warm trickles down the fingers of my left hand and I remember I'm bleeding. I adjust the bandage, ball up my fist, and hope to hell the scent of the rotten goo is as much of a repellent as Hickory says. There's another bark, another howl, and then nothing. The lone Tin-skin grunts and trots away, leaving me and Hickory alone in the dark.

"Okay," Hickory says. "Hands on my shoulders."

"What?"

"Put your hands on my shoulders. There's only one way across."

"Across what?"

Hickory curses, fumbles for my arm. Hands me the empty goo-jar. "Hold it out to your side. Drop it." I ask what's going to happen when I do and he says, "Just do it," so I do it.

I stretch out my arm, drop the jar and wait. And wait. I never hear it land.

"What is this place?"

"Told you. My place. Big maze. Many paths."

I slide a careful foot left and then right, feel the rough edges of a thin stone bridge with my toes. "What's down there?"

"No idea. Too far down to see. Found this place a long time ago." Hickory grabs my hand and slaps it on his shoulder. "Step where I step—"

"Stop when you stop. Got it."

The path goes on forever, zigzagging left and right. Hickory knows it all by memory. He counts out his footsteps in whispers, starting from zero whenever we make a turn. I don't even try to keep track. I'm as good as lost, being led over nothing, into nothing.

"Hold tight," Hickory says after a while. "Nearly there."

Turns out Hickory hasn't taken all the candles. I can see a bunch of them now, floating in the darkness ahead like a tiny cluster of stars. Shapes emerge from the gloom the closer we get. Enormous, empty chandeliers above our heads, row upon row of them. Other bridges, supported by immense stone columns stretching down, down, down into the darkness. And there, directly under the candle-light ahead, a crooked shack slapped together on an island of stone.

The center of the maze. Hickory has built a home in here.

I let his shoulders go, trusting my own eyes once again. I've left a trail of blood all down his back. I consider apologizing, but it's not like his shirt was pristine to begin with.

"Hey," I say instead. "Nice place."

The shack looks sturdy enough. Seems to be constructed from torn-off Manor doors and salvaged scraps of wood. Broken crates and barrels. He's even decorated the place. An old shield hangs beside the door. A line of stones on strings dangles from a tiny window. Bottles, flasks, and piles of golden coins are scattered all over the place. More jars of black goo. Weapons, gas masks, machetes. A strange compass lies discarded at my feet.

"Used to collect stuff. Things people left as they passed between worlds."

"You never saw anyone?" I ask. "Tried to follow them out? People from the world I just came from used to walk through the Manor all the time—a lot of this stuff's probably theirs." I nudge the compass with my foot. The needle won't stop spinning. "But you're lucky you didn't follow *them*. Bluehaven isn't a nice place. Better than here, I guess. No offense."

Hickory stares at his shack with a sick kind of look on his face. "Used to hear people. Track them. Always too late. The Manor never let me near them."

"What do you mean?"

"Doors lock. Rooms shift."

"The rooms *shift*?"

"Sometimes."

"*Sometimes?*" I can't believe I'm hearing this. "How can the rooms shift? How can you find your way back to Roth's fortress? How can you find anything?"

"Carved my symbols on the walls," Hickory says. "And rooms can't shift if doors are left open." He jabs a thumb back the way we came. "Always chock it open when I leave. Don't worry, they always shift back." He shrugs. "Eventually."

A DIFFERENT WINDOW

I remember the bluebird. It came one afternoon. Dad
was lying in the tub I'd dragged to the center of the
room, soapy water up to his chin. He watched the bird
as it hopped along the windowsill and pecked at a spider. I sat and watched beside him. The bluebird bobbed
around for a minute, chirping and singing, filling the
basement with music. When it flew away, Dad made
a sound, an almost-laugh. It was the first time I'd ever
heard him do that.

I made up a song about it afterwards called "Bluebird
in the Basement." Sang it for days. Still give it a run every
now and then. I'm pretty sure it's Dad's favorite.

Now I'm looking out a different window, nursing my
crook hand, curled up in a corner of Hickory's hideout
with a bundle of rags for a pillow. It's a tiny shack, but he
cleared me some space when we stopped inside. Packed
and stacked things, threw things out the door. I just stood
beneath the open hatch in the ceiling, soaking up the light
from the chandelier above.

"Sleep," Hickory said when he'd finished. "We leave

in the morning." I asked how we'd know when it was morning. He said, "When we wake up."

I told him we should keep moving, get what we need, and go. He closed the hatch in the ceiling, took off his shirt and lay down on his own bed of rags in the corner opposite mine. "Rest," he said, turning over to face the wall. "Need strength. Only way to survive."

He hasn't moved since then, but I can tell he's awake. Sleep in a shared room long enough and you can always tell when someone's awake. It's all in the breathing.

There's just enough candlelight coming through the window to see the scars and burns on Hickory's back. Whip lashes and hot pokers, I reckon. Roth and his goons really went to town on him. Once again, I think of a wild animal. Tired, wounded, resting in a cave.

I want to ask him about the things they did to him, about everything he's been through, but how do you start a conversation like that? Before I stumbled into his life he sat here in this shack with no one to talk to, surrounded by junk left behind by people with better lives. People with memories to savor, tales to tell, places to be. I think about him following sounds and voices, running for his life, the Manor screwing him over at every turn. Always the questions in his head. *Where did I come from? Why is this happening? Why me?*

It dawns on me then. We have a lot more in common than I thought. Replace the shack with a basement, the Manor hallways with Bluehaven streets, collecting junk with scavenging rubbish, and it's as close a match as you're ever gonna get.

The Manor has ruined both our lives.

I had sunlight, though. Not much of it, but enough. I could walk under the sky, breathe fresh air, talk to Violet. I had Dad. Even though I've always felt alone, I guess I never was. Not as alone as Hickory. Hell, I've finally met someone worse off than me.

"Hey," I say. "You awake?" And when Hickory doesn't answer, "Helllooooo."

He tells me to go to sleep again. I tell him I can't because my dad's been captured by an evil army. Also, I slept a bunch when a certain someone black-bagged my head.

"I just wanted to say I know what it's like." I sit up. "Being alone. Not knowing about your past and all. I don't know where I was born. Which world I came from. I don't know what's wrong with my dad. He's been sick all my life. And I've never met my mom. Don't have a clue where she is. Don't even know if she's alive or dead. I know it's hard, though, the not-knowing. Really hard." Hickory says nothing. "Well, that's it. So, um, goodnight."

I lie down again, wish I could start over, but then Hickory says, "Bluehaven. What's it like?" I get the feeling he's wanted to ask for a while. Rare details of an outside world.

I'm not sure where to start. "It's an island. With houses, farms, and people. Idiots, mostly." I wonder how much I should say, but before I can even think of a lie—anything to make my life there seem slightly normal—the truth slips out. "They hate me."

I have to wait about ten years for Hickory's response. "Why?"

Here we go, I think. "They call me the Cursed One. And it turns out I am. In a way. I mean, I'm not *cursed* cursed—not possessed or anything, I just—it's hard to explain."

So I explain it. Everything. From the townsfolk's obsession with the Manor to the Night of All Catastrophes. From my life with the Hollows to Atlas slicing open my hand. I tell him about the quake I caused. About the Manor waking up. About Dad running up the Sacred Stairs. I tell him everything Winifred told me in her study, unload a lifetime of baggage, and it feels great. Unbelievable. Therapy is what it is.

"Winifred pushed me down the hole," I say, sitting up again. "Can you believe that? Dropped a bomb down after me, too. Anyway, I made it to the gateway and—well—here I am." I huff out a deep breath. "Boy, that felt good. So what do you reckon?"

I wait and I wait. Hickory doesn't tell me what he reckons.

"Stay here," he says instead, and when he leaves the shack, I catch something shining on his cheeks in the dull glow from the candles outside. The trace of a tear. I wasn't expecting this. Am I supposed to say something? Keep my trap shut? I don't even know *why* he's crying. Do I ask him? What if it makes things worse? Then I get an idea.

"Hickory?" He stops just outside the door, the scars on

his back frowning at me. "You can keep my boots. You were probably gonna keep them anyway, but I won't ask for them again. They're yours. For helping me."

There's a long silence, but then he speaks. Softly. Quietly. Two words he probably hasn't said in a very long time.

"Thank you."

HUNTED

The cold water. The shape-shifting waves. The little island, closer than last time, but still well out of reach. I try to swim toward it, but another wave whips me up and throws me through the black bubbles to the deep, deep down. There's the eerie, underwater groaning again. The crackles of lightning in the depths that sear white shapes into my eyes. The glowing monsters are waiting, watching, unfurling their tentacles, ready to strike.

But this time I'm not alone.

Dad's here. A woman, too—my mom, I'm sure of it. They hold me. Kick at the tentacles. Take me back to the surface and swim as hard as they can, away from the island.

A white flash and we're out of the water, clear of the storm.

Dad's running through the Manor with me in his arms. Mom's by our side. Dad charges through a door and turns around in time to see Mom trip over. He runs back to help her, but the door slams shut between them. When he opens it again, she's gone. We're looking at an entirely different room. He screams, and the dream changes.

The Manor sharpens all around us, every detail becoming so much clearer. The joins in the stone-block walls. The grain of dark wood on the door. It's like I'm waking up inside the dream. Conscious, but not in control. Dad's scream echoes down the corridor and I travel with it, weightless now, bodiless, no longer in Dad's arms. I'm flying down corridors and around corners. Through archways, doorways and halls.

Another flash. There's water again—water *inside* the Manor—a half-flooded corridor, like a river—but I'm flying *over* it this time, alone, speeding past two enormous statues holding swords, soaring over rapids and a big flooded hall. I fly over the edge of a waterfall—I'm the one screaming now—and plummet down to the surging whirlpool at its base.

I plunge into the water, swallowed by darkness.

Let go, a voice whispers. A woman's voice. Mom's voice, I can feel it.

I cry out to her. Water fills my lungs. I'm choking, drowning, and then—

Then I'm back in the shack, wet with sweat and shaking on the floor. But I still can't breathe. Hickory's leaning over me, hand clasped over my mouth, breath hot on my face, whispering things. I try to fight him off me until I finally work out what he's saying.

"Calm down. Be quiet. They've found us." Hickory nods as if to say *Got it?* so I nod *Got it* back.

He lets me go.

"Tin-skins or Leatherheads?" I whisper. I can't see anything out the window.

"Both," Hickory says, ruffling through an old chest now, stuffing ammo into his pockets. "They'll break through soon."

"Are you sure?" And then I hear it. A thud in the dark. "How much time do we have?"

"Long enough. Maze'll keep 'em busy." Then he says, "No idea how they found—" and stops because he's just grabbed his shirt, noticed my blood staining its back. "What's this?"

"Um. I dunno."

"Is this your blood?"

"Maybe. Yes. I kind of opened the cut on my hand when I fell outside your door. But you said the black stuff—"

"Puts 'em off. Smell enough blood and they'll brave it." Another thud echoes through the dark. Hickory shoves his head into his shirt and glares at me. "The Tin-skin that stayed behind went to get its masters. And you've bled a nice trail right to us by the look of it."

Hickory grabs a rifle as the sound of gunfire echoes through the maze, followed by a whole lot of barking and howling. The Leatherheads have shot their way inside.

"Out the back," he says, throwing me the rifle. "Shoot anything that gets close."

"Right," I say, "shoot," but what I'm thinking is *How does this thing even work?*

There are stacks of jars, barrels, and chests behind the shack, all filled with the black goo, far as I can tell. I may not be able to see any Tin-skins out there in the darkness of the maze but I can picture them all too clearly, frothy-mouthed and snarling, clawing their way over the network of stone bridges.

We're being hunted.

I glance back at the shack. Hickory's rounding the corner behind me, slinging a knapsack over his shoulders. He's carrying a wooden club. "Middle one," he says, pointing the club at three thin stone bridges a little to my right. I can see two tiny flickers out there in the dark. Torches lashed to a chandelier.

"Is there another door out there?" I ask. "Another way out?"

"Locked door," he says. "On the far wall. Never been able to use it before. Hurry now." He swings the club and smashes the jars, kicks over chests and topples barrels, coating his little island, his home, in the rancid black stuff. "*Go*," he shouts.

I walk quickly but carefully, rifle slung over my shoulder, heading for the lights. Hickory follows with a small barrel in his hands, spilling a trail of goo in his wake.

"Bit late to cover our scent, isn't it?" I almost over-balance on the bridge. Pause for a second, find my footing. "It'll lead them right to us."

"Counting on it," Hickory says. "Move."

The bridge gets wider the closer we get to the pool of torchlight, eventually turning into a second, smaller island directly beneath the chandelier. No wall. No door. A dead end.

"Where to now?"

Hickory dumps the last of the goo, throws the barrel over the edge, and pulls a bundle of rope from his rucksack. Rope with a mangled piece of metal tied to one end. A grappling hook. He swings and snags it on the chandelier, pulls it tight. "We climb."

"And once we're up there?"

"Swing to the next one."

The Tin-skins have found the shack now. About twenty of them, I reckon. Frenzied, ravenous, darting around the island and tearing the place apart as if it were made of twigs. Wary of the black goo but slipping through it nonetheless. I grab the rope. Grit my teeth as my left palm throbs and burns. Climb and clamber up through the bars of the chandelier.

Then my stomach drops.

One of the Tin-skins has found the trail of goo.

"Um. Hickory?"

The Tin-skin barks and bolts right for us, leading the whole damn pack. Some of them slip, yelping, over the edge. Others get knocked over in the rush.

Most never miss a step.

"Shoot," Hickory grunts. He's only halfway up the rope.

I shift on the chandelier. Fumble the rifle, take aim.

Squeeze the trigger and—*click.*

"Crap."

"Shoot it," Hickory yells. He gets a hand onto the chandelier. "Shoot it now!"

"I'm trying!" I squeeze the trigger again—*click, click*—but it's useless. The Tin-skin's about to leap for Hickory's legs so I throw the damn rifle instead. It *whooshes* as it flies. Clatters on the stone and trips the Tin-skin up. The sucker goes howling into the darkness.

"Got it," I yell. "Hickory, I got it!"

But Hickory doesn't look impressed when he hauls himself up beside me. He just looks from the skid-marks below to my empty hands and back again. "Where's the gun?"

"Uh . . ."

"You *threw away* our only gun?"

"I had to stop the damn thing somehow, didn't I?"

"Just—" Hickory grits his teeth, "swing."

We throw our weight together, pushing forward with our legs and leaning back, swinging the chandelier. The Tin-skin pack crowds onto the island beneath us. Barking, jumping, snapping at our butts and heels. The next chandelier emerges from the dark with every forward swing.

"Get ready," Hickory yells, plucking both torches from the chandelier. "Get set."

The "Go" never comes. A bullet ricochets off the chandelier, and we duck.

The Leatherheads have come to play.

There's a whole troop of them stalking around the shack now, guns blazing and *pa-chow*ing, the glassy eyes of their gas masks glinting with every flash and bang. They *click* and *clack* at each other, the trunks of their gas masks amplifying every sound.

Click-click-clack-click-clack.

"Was this part of your plan too?" I shout.

"Is now," Hickory says. He drops one of the torches as we swing forward over the island of Tin-skins once more. "Jump!"

We launch ourselves into the air, hit the cold metal of the next chandelier along and swing again with the force of it, the platform behind us erupting in a blaze. Turns out the goo doesn't just stink—it's flammable, too. The Tin-skins yelp, squeal, and smash into each other, leaping into the dark to flee the fire. It burns back along the path quick as gunpowder, heading right for the Leatherheads, the shack, and the stack of explosive goo.

The Leatherheads scatter, glassy gas-mask eyepieces alive with reflected fire. The whole platform's engulfed in seconds and Hickory's shack explodes moments later, lighting up the dark. A handful of Leatherheads go flying, but we don't hang around to watch the show. We swing together, count together, and when we jump, we jump as one, chandelier to chandelier. The remaining Leatherheads shoot when they get the chance. From our left, our right, at our backs. We cop bruises and scratches, knocks to our heads, but every successful landing comes with a sense of exhilaration. A feeling of triumph that numbs the pain.

The Leatherheads are falling behind. We're getting away.

THE GRIP

"Sorry your house exploded."

"Don't be," Hickory says after a while. "Just a cage in a cage."

He's trying to figure out where we are from his symbols carved into the intersection a little further down the corridor. I tried to read them, find some method to the madness, but they might as well be chicken scratches. Now I'm hanging back, keeping watch.

We only just made it out of the maze alive. Swung down from the last chandelier, unlocked the mystery door on the far side of the maze and bolted through as bullets peppered the walls all around us. As soon as I locked the door behind us, everything fell silent.

No more gunfire. No more Leatherhead *clicks* and *clacks*. Slowly, carefully, I opened the door again and gasped.

The maze had disappeared.

Hickory was right. The Manor rooms really can shift. There's nothing behind us but an empty hallway now. I've left the door ajar so the rooms don't shift back, and kept the key at the ready just in case. I can't shake the feeling we're about to be attacked again.

"You gonna tell me what the gooey stuff is now?"

Hickory sighs, shifts the pack on his back. "Scum."

"Scum from what?"

"Specter."

"And what's a Specter?"

"Big, scary beast made of bright, white light."

I frown. "A beast made of light? You mean, like, a ghost?"

"Not a ghost," Hickory says, "but yeah, looks ghostly, I s'pose."

Great. As if we didn't have enough weird things trying to kill us.

"No idea which world it came from," Hickory adds. "All I know is I never wanna go there. Scum gets left behind whenever it flies through a wall. Only thing Tinskins and Leatherheads fear apart from Roth. I find deposits now and then. Scrape 'em, collect 'em, store 'em. Starts off clear but goes black over time. Accidentally dropped a candle in some once. Burned my eyebrows clean off. You know how long it takes eyebrows to grow back?"

"No, I—"

"Long time. Ages."

I triple-check the door behind us. Creak it open a little wider. The hallway's still the same. Long and empty, nothing but gray stone and flickering candles.

Still, I shudder.

"You're pulling my leg, right?"

"Nope. They really do take ages to grow back."

"I don't care about your eyebrows, Hickory. I'm talking about the Specter."

"Oh."

"You've actually seen it?"

"Oh, I've seen it, all right." He crosses the corridor to another set of symbols. "Sucker caught me one day. Came outta nowhere. Just the one in here, far as I know—thank the gods."

"How can something made of light *catch* you?"

"All predators got their tricks. Snakes spit venom, spiders spin webs." Hickory pauses a moment. "Specter gets inside you. Right through your eyes. Feeds on your fears. It doesn't last long—I mean, it *feels* like it does, but . . ." He shakes his head, struggling to find the words. "You're paralyzed, but you don't know it 'cause your mind's taken to a different place. A place where your nightmares come to life." He swallows. "I call it the Grip."

Hickory goes quiet then. I consider asking him what he saw in the Grip—what form the nightmares of a thousand-year-old guy take—but then I figure it's probably one of those things people like to keep to themselves. I know I would. The thought of being trapped in my nightmare makes me sick, what with the water and the tentacles and the island that doesn't get any closer and all. I reckon I'd die of fright. On the other hand, it'd mean I could see *her* again. Because it was her, wasn't it? My mom, right there in the water with me and Dad—and after that, running through the Manor with us, falling behind. It had to be.

Let go, she told me, but why?

If only Hickory hadn't woken me up. Maybe I could've seen or heard more.

I clear my throat. No point dwelling on that now. "How did you get free?" I ask instead. "How did you stop it?"

"I didn't," Hickory says. "The Specter just . . . released me. When I came to, I saw it hovering over me, like a flash of white-hot steam. I felt it watching me. Waiting." Hickory stares down the corridor, as if he can still see the damn thing floating there. "Monstrous thing. Huge. I was sure it'd Grip me again—finish the job—because I'm sure it could've broken me, sure it could've killed me—but it didn't. The Specter turned and flew away."

"Maybe it thought your nightmare was boring," I suggest. "Or maybe it was full."

Hickory ignores me. "My body was weak. I could barely move. I felt like I'd been in the Grip for a lifetime, but the embers of a fire I'd made before getting caught were still smoldering beside me. I was only out for an hour or so. Took me a long time to recover, though. The Grip never really lets you go." He blinks the bad memories away. "You ever see a big white light, Jane, you run. You run as fast as you can and you don't look back."

"You reckon we'll run into it on the way to Roth's place?"

"Knowing our luck?" Hickory shrugs. "Probably. But I hope not."

Another question pops into my head. "Hickory, why are you doing this? You want to get out of here, you want the key—I get that—but you could've just stolen it. You could've ditched me way back. Why stick around when you know how dangerous this is?"

Hickory ignores me, scratches at his almost-beard and nods at the symbols on the wall. "Good news is we're a long way from my hideout. Bad news is we're still a long way from Roth's fortress. Nine long marches, maybe more. If we take this corridor here—"

"Hickory." I stand in his way. "I need to know. Why are you helping me?"

His eyes meet mine, but only for a second. "Manor's taken everything. Honor's one of the few things I have left." He steps around me. "I'm helping you because I said I would."

LEECHWOOD HALLS

There are no clocks to judge the passing of time in here. No day or night skies to track suns, moons and stars. All I have is the ache in my shoulders and the lead in my feet.

Nine marches, Hickory said. I think he meant nine days. We haven't even finished the first yet and I reckon we've already walked the length of a mountain chain. Door after door, room after room, upstairs and down. Long corridor after long corridor, the slabs of stone cool and smooth underfoot, undulating slightly now and then. We barely speak. Have to change our route three times on account of the Leatherheads. A whole troop marching beyond a closed door. One standing guard at an intersection. A handful skinning some sort of animal carcass five stories below us in the center of a pillared hall. Hickory plots a different path each time.

It's exhausting, but the strange thing is I never get hungry or thirsty. At first I think it's adrenaline fueling me, but then I figure there's no way I'd be this tired if that were the case.

"I'm not hungry," I say as we descend a tight, spiral

stairwell. "Or thirsty. But I haven't had anything to eat or drink in ages."

"Manor gives life," Hickory says again.

"So you haven't had anything to eat or drink in, like, forever?"

"Eat or drink when I find something worth eating or drinking. Stray animals from Otherworlds. There's a river in here, too, you know. Water flowing through a gateway. Long way away. But you don't *need* to eat or drink. Manor sustains you. Keeps you going."

"I tried some snow. It's kind of like eating and drinking at the same time."

I'm actually enjoying this, shooting the breeze and all. I'm about to ask if Hickory wants to play a game. Twenty questions or something, I dunno. But then we reach the bottom of the stairs and freeze because we're standing at the edge of a forest. An avenue of thick, autumnal trees soaring right up to the high, vaulted ceiling, stretching as far into the Manor as we can see. The tree trunks are gnarled and twisted, their branches like crooked arms. Thousands of tiny spores hover in the air, floating up, drifting down, settling on the branches and the crimson leaves and the tangle of tree roots on the floor. They glow like little specks of moonlight in the living, breathing silence of the wood.

I draw in a deep breath, smell the dying leaves. Something sweet, too, like honey.

"I'm guessing this isn't supposed to be here," I say.

Hickory nibbles a fingernail, shakes his head. "Another

gateway must've started failing since I was last here. Been a while. Long while."

"But it's okay, right? I mean, they're only trees."

Hickory nods slowly, deep in thought. "No choice anyway. We have to go through."

We move quietly into the forest, ducking under the branches and their red, star-shaped leaves. Some of the glowing spores cling to our clothes and hair. If I didn't know any better I'd say we'd stepped out of the Manor and wandered into a night-time glade. The tree roots are so jumbled it's impossible to tell where one ends and the next begins.

"So pretty . . ."

The further we go, the wilder the forest becomes. Grayish vines hang from the branches. We clamber over piles of moss-covered rubble. Fallen chunks of ceiling. Go past gaping holes in the walls and floor that open onto other overgrown corridors and halls, the stone torn apart by tree roots. The forest seems to have spread just like the snow.

We move on instinct alone, as if we've walked this path before. A voice, my voice, buzzes through the back of my mind, telling me to slow down, go back, get out, find a different path, but it's drowned out by a feeling, a desire, a different voice that tells me to keep going. Every breath fills my body like a warm mist that smokes the evil wasps away. I'm not even worried when we come to a dead end. Neither is Hickory. We just grab the branches of a tree growing through a hole in the floor and start climbing down.

The air's even sweeter down here. A bolt of energy crackles through my body and I feel like I could take on every Tin-skin and Leatherhead all by myself. Their leader, too.

"Hey, Hickory," I say. "Tell me about Roth."

"Boss," he says, watching a spore dance over the back of his hand. "Bad guy."

"Yeah, I know, but what's he like?" We turn a corner. I splay the pretty, red leaves with my fingers. "You've seen him, right? Is he tall? Do you reckon I could take him? If I had to fight him, I mean." Hickory tells me to relax, so I tell him I *am* relaxed—I really, *really* am. "Still want to know, though. What does he look like?"

"You want a face to hate. Think it'll make it easier, but it won't. Not this face."

"Why not?" I ask. And then a bit louder—but not too loud, no, never, because this place is so peaceful and the air's so nice I could marry it. "Hickory, why not?"

He throws me something from his knapsack. "Don't say I didn't warn you."

It's a mask. No, a half-mask—the bottom half—carved from a strange white stone so smooth and shiny it almost feels like glass. A big crack runs across the nose at the top of the mask and down the left cheek. There's a thin slit between the lips for breathing. Buckles and leather straps hang from its edges, jingle-jangle. The underside's thick and bulbous in places, as if the half-mask's not meant to just fit over someone's face, but *in* it too. Like it's meant to plug some holes. A missing nose and a lower jaw.

I was wrong. It isn't a mask at all.

"It's a prosthemni—" My tongue fumbles the word. A chuckle swells in my belly but I swallow it back, lick my lips, try again. "Prosh—pr—prosthetic! It's a prosthetic face."

Hickory nods. Is he swaying or is it me? Maybe it's the trees.

I shake my head to lose the dizzy, but the dizzy don't go.

"It's his breath," Hickory almost-shouts. He stuffs the half-face back into his knapsack, but when he swings it over his shoulder the cheeky pack slips from his hand whoopsie-daisy, disappears down a hole. "Oh. Not good. Needed that."

I can't bury the chuckle this time. It shudders up my gut and out my gob so hard I have to steady myself on a nearby tree. "S'okay, Hickemy. We'll come back later!"

The red leaves go flappy now, which is weird 'cause there's no breeze, but there must be a breeze 'cause the spores are swirly too. We stumble down the forested hallway and that mosquito in my head tells me to stop again, go back, why was Hickory hiding Roth's face in a bag anyway?

"Hey Mickory, what'd you mean it's his breath?"

"Rotted his face away! Tha's why Leatherdeads and Tin-shins cover 'emselves up. Wrap 'emselves in dead skin and scrap metal. Roth's breath burns 'em!"

"His breath is *poisonous*?" We leap over a big, big tree root. "How can anyone live with poisonous-est breath?"

"He's immortal, tha's how."

165

"You mean he can't die? Ever?"

"Never."

"Wow," I say, "but that's—that's impossible," and Hicky spreads his arms out at the forest, wide like a big bird, as if to say *What do you call all this, then?* I tell him he makes a marvelous point. "Why didn't you tell me this before, though? It's, like, *info*, you know?"

"Didn't want to scare you. Are you scared?"

"Bah! Scared in a place like this? But hey, listen— immortal, huh? What if someone swung a sword at his neck?" I swing an imaginary sword, *sha-wing!*

"Broken blade."

"What if—hey—what if they pushed him off a really high cliff?"

"He'd hit the bottom. Climb back up. Track 'em down."

"What if they shot him in the head? No—the eye!"

"Shoot him anywhere. Wouldn't change a thing."

"No fighting. Got it. We'll just have to—hey, Dickory—we'll just have to sneak in and out of his fortress. Quiet-like. We could even dress up! In disguises! Nobody'll ever suspect a couple of trees to stage a prison break, will they? No way! Know why?" I pull a tree branch down as I pass it, let it flick back up behind me. "Everybody loves trees!"

We come to a spiral stairwell that's all slippery with tree roots and moss. It smells so sweet down there it's ridiculous, which is why we throw ourselves in, go *wheeeeeeeeee* all the way down, round and round. When it's over I want to do it again but I can't 'cause I'm laughing too much.

We move through this new bit of forest arm in arm, singing and skipping through the trees. We're both singing different songs, but I love it 'cause I'm singing one I made up ages ago called "The Coconut Son" and it's one of Dad's favorites, and Hizzory's is a song about seeing some girl called Farrow again. The mosquito in my head yells at me. Stuff about the fake face and the trees. It tells me to turn around, run away, but if we do that we won't get where we're going and it's beautiful down here, it really is. S'more a swamp than a forest now and the ground's all smooshy-wet, sticky too, and the glowing spores are everywh—*cough*—I think I just swallowed one. I clear my throat, and the mosquito shouts *Jane! The face! Why was Hickory hiding the face, idiot?* So I think, *Fine, already!*

"Why'd you—hey, Lickory. Hate to interrupt your Farrow song—lovely voice, by the way—but why'd you have Roth's face in your bag?"

"Can't tell," Hicky sighs loudly. "Big secret. You'll hate me if I tell you!"

"Couldn't hate you, Hickemy. You're my best friend. Always have been. Except for Violet, o'course, but she's a kid. Does that still count? Yes! You're my *second*-best friend!"

"Bad second-best friend. And you let me keep your boots and errything!"

"Okay." I clap my hands, *bang!* Trip on a tree root, keep walking. "Tell you what. I'll tell you one of my secrets, and you tell me yours. Same time, like."

"No!"

"Ready?"

"M'kay."

"On three. One, two, four!"

We shout our secrets out at the very same time, and it's so great it's wonderful, it sounds like "I've—I'm—never been—kidnapping—kissed—you."

"Brilliant," I say. "See? That wasn't too hard, was it? Bit of a load off, really. I've never been kissed and you're— wait, what'd you say again?"

"I'm kidnapping you."

"Oh." Warning bells *ding-a-ling, ding-dong.* "You're kidnapping me?"

"Uh-huh, 'fraid so. Leading you into a trap. Turning you in!"

"But what about my dad?"

"Lied. He's probably dead already! That mask I had. Remember that? It's like a calling card. Proof of allegiance and all. Means I'm a bounty hunter. For Roth."

"Roth? *That* guy?" I shake my head, swipe a branch. "But the Tin-shins. The Leathermeds. You blew 'em up!"

"Couldn't let *them* take you in. Take all the credit then don't get mine! After the trap, I thought, 'Why drag Jane kickin' and screamin' if I can get her to come along easy,' see?"

I dunno what to say. I look at Hickory and Hickory looks at me and I want to run away from this traitor-guy, from Roth, from that smell that don't seem so sweet no more, but then the leaves flip-flap again, a thousand red flags waving, and my body feels light but heavy at the same time, like I'm floating in a dream. I want to rest, that's what I want. The mosquito goes, *Run, idiot! Fight! Get away!* But I can't run, too tired, and I can't stay mad at Hickory either. He's my second-best friend, and it's nice down here, it really is.

All I need is a nap.

"Got no choice," Hicky yawns. We float side by side, sludgy-trudgy. "Sorry."

"S'okay."

"Roth wants the key. I gotta give it. Gotta keep my promise."

"Exactly," I say. "Promise is a promise!" And I laugh, because it really is funny when you think about it. I'm being kidnapped. and I really don't give a damn.

THE FLOWER IN THE DELL

The floor's different now. Our feet sink ankle-deep in dark red sludge. I trip on a rib cage, go splash, slop and tingle. I want to rest, need to sleep, but no, no, no, not yet.

"We're here," Hicky says, and he's right, we've arrived.

It's an intersection. Big one. The forest's floor-to-ceiling thick all round, but not in the center. All the tree roots go dippy-downy like a dell, a bowl, a big sunken bed.

"Look," Hicky says. There's a single flower down in the dell, lonesome-like and yellow. Unfurling. Uncurling. I want to touch it, but Hicky slips into the dell first. "Mine."

I start to follow him, but then I hear something down the next corridor. Figure I should check it out because maybe it's another flower. I slip round to the right, swing on a branch, *whoosh!* But I don't see no flowers, just some people-shaped things on the ground. I want to go back to the dell, but the warning bells are raging, *ding-a-ling,* DING-DONG.

Look closer! Snap out of it!

"M'kay, mosquito." I focus, take a breath and— "Oh, that's not good."

The sight's a sledgehammer, knocks the fog from my brain. There are hundreds of them. Everywhere. Leatherheads piled in stinking heaps or strung up in the branches. Masks ripped away, jaws broken, forced open by the tree roots snaking round their necks, into their mouths, down their throats. The trees are feeding on them from the inside out.

No, not *trees*. Tree. It's one enormous plant. That's why we haven't seen any bodies till now. We're at the center. The core. We're in the damn stomach.

I cover my mouth. Back away from the gray-fleshed corpses with their beady little eyes staring blankly. Two hang to my left like sacks of meat, roots trailing from their mouths. Another's down in the sludge to my right, wrapped in vines, but it isn't dead yet. It blinks, twitches, makes that *clicking* sound in its throat. The root moves in its mouth, just an inch, going deeper. The leaves flap and flutter. I trip on a leg and topple back into the sludge. It tingles and burns. Acid. Some sort of rotting body soup oozing down into the dell where—

"Uh-oh."

I spin around. Hickory's in the center of the dell. Crawling through the muck.

Reaching for the flower.

"No," I shout. "Hickory, don't—"

But Hickory does.

He plucks the flower and the forest comes alive. I stumble, trip and roll down into the dell, the ground a writhing mass of tree roots and rotting corpses. Hickory's already half-buried by the bubbling sludge, roots snaking around his chest and arms, pulling him deeper.

He just stares at the flower in his hands, slack-jawed and dumb.

"Hickory, move!"

I throw myself into him. The roots snap. We roll through the sludge. Bile rising, eyes watering, skin tingling, turning numb. The roots wrap around my ankles, Hickory's wrists. We're surrounded by skeletons and gas masks and machetes. I grab one and start hacking.

"Don't hurt 'em," Hickory says.

I cut him free and slap him hard, and even though it seems to break the spell, I slap him again anyway because I might've been off with the fairies but I remember what the jerk told me a minute ago. I should leave him here—let him die—but I still need him.

"Run," I shout, and shove another machete into his hands.

We scramble out of the dell, cutting a swathe through a new corridor. The tree roots and branches swipe, whip and tangle. We sprint our hearts out. My machete's lodged in a thick, swinging branch, and ripped from my hands in a flash. The ground rumbles, the walls crack and crumble. We dodge rocks and boulders, duck through a hole in the wall, but the forest's here, too. Hickory slices a swooping branch clean in half. Sap splatters like blood. With a groan, screech and crack—*crack*—*CRACK*, an enormous tree branch slams down across the corridor ahead, blocking our path. I leap from a fallen boulder. Hickory springs from another swinging branch.

And the vines snatch us up mid-air.

They loop and tangle round our limbs and chests. They squeeze. Hickory swings his machete but the vines take that, too. I'm flipped upside down. Blood rushes to my head. The branches stop swinging, the forest stops swaying, and all I can hear is the *ka-thump, ba-dump* of my heart. A tree root curls up my arm and around my neck, snaking over my chin. I grit my teeth as hard as I can, but the root prods at my lips. This is it. This is the end. Dad's lost forever and I'm gonna die upside down, hanging next to a stupid liar who—

"Help . . ."

Hickory's voice. A wheeze that becomes a choke that means a root's sliding into his mouth too. Mine slips through the corner of my lips. I choke and gag and then I see him. A man. Running through the forest with fire blazing from his hands. Headed right for us.

THE BOUNTY HUNTERS

Scratch that. The worst thing about being known as the Cursed One is that when you're just minding your own business trying to track down your missing father in a never-ending labyrinth full of shape-shifting rooms and evil, butt-ugly creatures, you can somehow end up being drugged by some spores and half-digested by a freakin' tree.

I'm covered in gunk and leaf-litter from head to toe, bruised and beaten. The bandage wrapped around my injured hand looks and smells like soiled toilet paper. My muscles ache terribly, but my cuts don't hurt a bit on account of the numbness—the only upside to being covered in the stomach-sludge of a carnivorous plant. Who would've thought?

I'm in a cage with wheels again, but this one's made of metal and isn't being pulled by a horse, it's being pulled by the biggest freakin' guy I've ever seen. Even his muscles have muscles. He's shirtless and bald, and he's so tall his head almost touches the chandeliers. His bare feet sound like claps of thunder on the stone. He hasn't been whipped like Hickory, but another cracked prosthetic face dangles from his belt.

I'm gonna hug the first stranger I meet who doesn't have it in for me. I really am.

My key is in his pocket. The jerk nicked it from mine as soon as he dumped us on safer ground and threw down his torch. I was too weak to stop him, to even lift a hand, but I saw the look on his face when he found the key. Triumph and wonder, and some kind of sadness, too. He said something to me in a different language, something soft. Even placed one of his massive hands on my shoulder and smiled.

Then he threw us in the cage.

Hickory's as filthy and beat-up as I am. Shag of black hair like a bird's nest. He tried reasoning with the bounty hunter for the first hour or so. Told him they were on the same side and everything. "Had the mask, but I lost it," he said. "First to be given out. You taking us to the fortress? Huh? Big place, black gate? Yes? Roth won't be happy you stuck me in a cage. You'll see. Was taking the girl there myself. Maybe we could take her in together, huh?"

The bounty hunter never said a word.

Now Hickory's sulking in the corner, hands tied behind his back, same as mine.

"Honor's one of the few things you have left, huh?" I whisper to him.

"Don't get pissy with me just because you trusted the wrong guy," he says quietly.

He's right, of course. I should've known better. Me of all people.

"Why?" I ask him. "Why didn't you just take the key and leave? What does Roth want with me? I was *given* the key. That doesn't mean I know anything about it. And I really was gonna give it to you when we got my dad back to Bluehaven. I wasn't lying."

Hickory says nothing.

"Why side with Roth anyway? How long have you been working for him? And—what—he wants it so he can find more gateways? You seriously reckon he'll hand it over to you once he's finished with it? He doesn't exactly sound like the sharing type."

Then again, what do I know? I can't trust anything Hickory has told me, except for the stuff in the forest, when we were both high as kites and the truth seemed like a glorious thing.

"Where do you come from?" I ask him. "You remember. I know you do."

Hickory's staring at the bounty hunter's back now. At Roth's cracked and dangling half-face. "Wouldn't believe me if I told you," he says at last. He turns away, lies on his side, and maybe it's the way he was looking at the mask, but suddenly all I can think is: *What if Hickory comes from the same world as Roth?*

"Fine," I say. "But I'm getting my boots back. Soon as our hands are untied."

Hickory kicks them off and nudges them toward me without turning over. They look filthier than a couple of squashed toads. "All yours," he says.

I decide to leave them be.

The bounty hunter sticks to the main corridors. The cage is too wide to fit through any of the regular doors anyway. Hours seem to pass. We don't run into any unfriendlies, but they've certainly left their marks. Scattered bones. Spent cartridge shells. Torn scraps of leather and crumpled bits of tin. Stains and claw marks on the walls and floor.

I don't sleep on our "rest" stop. Hickory does. Passes out right away, as if his conscience is clear as water. I just sit beside him, watching the big bald guy. He's sitting cross-legged on a threadbare mat he pulled from some sort of compartment under the cage. At first, he mumbled and hummed for a while, something soft and deep and sad. Now he's shaving. Gliding a dry blade across the curve of his head, down his cheeks, his chin.

I was six when I started shaving Dad's face. I nicked one of Mr. Hollow's old razors, sat Dad down by the tub, cut away at his out-of-control beard with a pair of shears and then lathered soap over his cheeks and chin. I was afraid I'd cut him so I asked questions and imagined answers. "How much soap? That much?" *Perfect.* "Do I hold it like this?" *No. Like this.* "And I just drag it down like—whoops. Sorry." *Smooth strokes. Don't rush.* "Okay. Smooth—sorry! This is hard." *You'll carve my face off if you keep this up. Take your time, Jane. We have all the time in the world.* And so we sat there on the stools, taking our time.

Where is he now? What's he doing? I can't ignore the possibility that Hickory was telling the truth about him being taken prisoner. Or worse, that other thing he said.

He's probably dead already!

"Please let me go." My words hang in the corridor, hollow and lifeless. "I don't know what Roth wants with me. I don't know anything about the key."

The bounty hunter strides up to the cage, reaches down into the compartment again and pulls out an old, crinkled photograph of a smiling woman holding a baby. He talks to me, and although I still can't understand him, there's no mistaking the tone. Desperation. Sorrow. Part of it even sounds like an apology. And I understand. He doesn't want to do this. He hates being inside the Manor as much as I do. He's just trying to get home to his family.

"You don't need to do this," I say. "We can stop him. Roth. I don't know how, but—"

I'm silenced by a door slamming somewhere ahead, maybe in the next corridor.

The bounty hunter puts the photo back into the compartment and pulls out a whip, lets it trail behind him as he stomps off toward the sound. I don't waste a second. As soon as he disappears around the corner, I slam myself into the cage door and kick Hickory awake.

"What?" he mumbles. "Wassapnin?"

"He's gone," I say. "But probably not for long. What's the plan?" Hickory frowns at me. "I'm guessing you always have a plan, Hickory. How do we get out of here?"

"We?" he says, like it's the dirtiest word ever invented.

"Yes," I say, "*we*." I try hitting the door again, but the lock's too strong. "Look, I hate you and you hate me, but we're in this together, whether we like it or not."

Hickory takes a moment. "Get back to you on that one." I start to protest, but he nods down the corridor. The bounty hunter's already coming back with something— no, some*one*—slung over his shoulders. "We've got us a free ride. Relax. Plenty of time to escape."

The bounty hunter opens the cage and slings his latest catch inside. A guy roughly my size, I'd say. Boots, tight-fitting pants and a long indigo cloak. Hood pulled down over his face, hands already tied behind his back. The bounty hunter locks the door again, glances at me, packs away his mat, picks up the chain, and starts hauling the cage.

Hickory nudges me with his knee, nods at the newcomer.

I shuffle forward, reach out with my left foot and carefully lift the hood with my toes. The guy has a big black scarf wrapped around his face and head, like those people you see in pictures walking through deserts. Only his eyes are visible, closed and long-lashed.

Wait a second.

I shuffle back, look at the shape of his body again.

That's when I realize our new cell buddy isn't a guy.

It's a girl.

THE HALL OF
A THOUSAND FACES

She's watching me when I wake up, catlike hazel eyes fixed on mine. I sit up straight, clear my throat, wipe away the drool trailing down my chin. I'm not sure how long I've slept, how far we've travelled, but Hickory's asleep again. The bounty hunter's still hauling the cage, sweat shining on his shoulders under every passing candle. I wonder if I squirmed much in my sleep. Could the girl tell I was drowning with my parents, about to be taken by the tentacled monsters with white-fire eyes? Did I cry out with Dad when Mom disappeared? Did I make a noise when the dream shifted, when it became something *more*, and I went flying through those flooded corridors of the Manor, down that waterfall into the cold, black whirlpool?

Let go. Mom's voice came to me again, but I still can't figure out why.

"Hello," I say to the girl. Maybe I've spoken too quietly. Maybe she speaks a different language. All she does is narrow those eyes a fraction. I lean a little closer, speak slowly. "My name's Jane Doe. What's yours? Uh. Your name? Do you—can you understand me?"

Nothing.

I reckon she's about my age. I can see bits of dark hair beneath her scarf. She doesn't look frightened at all. Wary, yes, but not scared. And her eyes really are flat out—

"Pretty."

The word just pops out, and Hickory's woken up just in time to hear it. He turns over, chuckling like a damn monkey. I don't even know if monkeys chuckle because I've only ever read about them in books, but if they do I bet this is what they sound like. I tell him to shut up, and he does—right away—but not because of me. The bounty hunter's watching us.

Nobody says a word for the next billion hours or so. I get pins and needles down my arms because they've been tied behind my back for such a long time. My skin isn't numb anymore. All my cuts and bruises ache again. I count doors to pass the time. Dream up escape scenarios. Grand exhibitions of strength and bravery, things that would impress the girl and show her I'm the kind of almost-woman who always takes control. She's still watching me.

"Don't think she likes you," Hickory mutters, and I think he's right. I'm me, after all. Jane Creepy-Eyed Doe. What I need is a hat or something. One that says *Not a monster, just misunderstood.* I could wear it all the time. People like hats, right?

When the cage finally stops again I figure the bounty hunter's having another rest, but he just stands to the side and gestures at the archway ahead. The room beyond is long, slightly wider than the corridor we're in now, and the walls are covered in carved stone faces, floor to ceiling. Horned faces. Fanged faces. Screaming, snarling, laughing faces. The bounty hunter holds a finger to his lips, steps right up to the archway. He claps his enormous hands and—*pfft! pfft! pfft!*—the room comes alive. Darts, shooting from the mouths on one side of the room to the mouths on the other. He yells—a quick burst of sound— and the darts shoot back.

Another finger to his lips, and the meaning's clear: don't make a sound.

Before we can protest, he picks up the chain and hauls us slowly into the trap. The stone faces with their darthole mouths scroll by. I wince with every squeak of the wheel beneath me, but it's obviously just quiet enough. One sneeze though, one cough, and—

"No," Hickory whispers three-quarters of the way across.

I shush him. The girl kicks me because my shush is just as loud. The bounty hunter freezes—we all do—but the darts never come. The bounty hunter walks on, the cage resuming its slow *squeak, squeak.* Hickory nods frantically at the archway ahead. There's a mark above it, a blotch of paint on the stone. A three-fingered Leatherhead handprint.

You'd think it'd be a relief, clearing the booby trap and all, but the moment we're free, Hickory says, "Stop. Don't. You can't take us there."

The bounty hunter ignores him.

Hickory snaps and throws his weight against the side of the cage.

I wonder if he's acting, if this is all part of his escape plan, but then a cold lump grows in my throat. "We're not there already, are we? At the fortress? You said we had plenty of time."

"He isn't taking us to the fortress," Hickory says. "Not yet. He's taking us to—"

The bounty hunter shoves his fist into the cage, knocks Hickory out cold.

"Sit back," the girl tells me. "Everything's under control."

I stare at her, mouth gaping, and that's when the platoon of Leatherheads storms through the corridor and surrounds the cage. When the bounty hunter holds Roth's prosthetic face high in surrender. When every gun turns on the girl, on Hickory, on me.

THE PRISON CAMP

We're marched on foot into a big chamber, mouths gagged. There are cages everywhere. Metal spikes. Coils of barbed wire. Hundreds of people imprisoned. Tin-skins growl and gnash at us from their pens as we pass. Mangled bones rattle around their paws, picked clean. The air reeks of burnt coal, sweat, and stale pee. Leatherheads drag crates and bodies back and forth through the camp. Prisoners cower. The smoke-stained Manor ceiling looms high above it all, glowing a dirty red from the furnaces below. It's a nightmare.

We're thrown into the nearest cage. A dozen or so people are huddled in the middle. Two of them are kids. The gate's locked behind us, and an old man shuffles over and unties the girl's hands. Mine too. We take off our gags and thank him. He merely nods and bends his creaking bones over the third new arrival, Hickory, still groaning face-down on the floor.

"Not him," I say. "He's one of them. A bounty hunter."

The old-timer doesn't say anything, but he can obviously understand me because he leaves Hickory strung up.

Even gives him a little kick as he shuffles back to the huddle of prisoners.

Our bounty hunter's watching us from afar, uncaged, free. He isn't gonna let me out of his sight. There are other hunters, too. Some of them strut and glare at anyone they can. Others look just as worried as us prisoners and shy away from the Leatherheads whenever they pass, weapons not drawn but always at the ready. Some of them are women, most are men. Some wear rags and loincloths, others elaborate robes or dresses that might have been a sign of wealth and power in their home worlds, but in here don't mean squat.

I shake out my hands, rub my wrists. "What is this place?"

And then I see him, sitting in the huddle of prisoners not three meters away. My breath catches. The word I want to say more than any other forms deep in my belly and rises to my throat like a warm pulse of light but I can't say it, daren't say it, because it can't be. It's a trick, a dream. But the cloak, the stooped shoulders, the scraggly mop of gray hair . . .

"Dad?"

My voice sounds tiny, like a child's. Filled with hope but hesitation too, because I've imagined this moment a gazillion times, and it's already clear that something's wrong.

It's Dad, without a doubt. But he doesn't look happy to see me.

His face is cut and bruised. His eyes are wide, lips

trembling. I tell him it's okay, everything's okay, but when I step toward him he backs away and says, "Don't."

He's talking.

I mean, *actually* talking.

To me.

"Dad," I say, "it's me, Jane," but he jabbers nonsense over my voice and starts stumbling from one side of the cage to the other, waving his hands around like a nonsensical person.

I run to him. The other prisoners scatter. The girl tries to stop me, but I shake her off. I grab Dad's shoulders and try to calm him down, and he tackles me. Pins me to the floor. I can't move, can't breathe. I'm staring up into a face I know so well but don't recognize at all. Tears sting my eyes, but when I squeak out his name again I see it. The fire in his eyes burns out. He winks at me, forces a sad smile, and dimples crease his dirty, stubbled cheeks.

"We don't know each other," he whispers. "We can't. Stay away from me. I love you."

A gun fires somewhere. A warning shot. Dad calls me a stranger, shouts it, tells me I'll regret it if I come anywhere near him again. Then he scuttles over to the other side of the cage, and all I can do is lie here. Trying to breathe. Trying to think. Drawing blanks.

INTO THE GIANT'S MOUTH

He's there. Right *there*. Sitting in the corner of the cage. He hasn't so much as looked at me in about an hour, but every time I get to my feet and take a step toward him, he shakes his head violently or says "uh-uh" really loudly.

Why doesn't he want me anywhere near him?

We don't know each other. The first real sentence I've ever heard my father say. *We can't,* the second. *Stay away from me,* the third and worst by far. But the fourth, *I love you,* this is the one I cling to. The one that means this isn't about what he does or doesn't want. He's keeping his distance because he feels he has to, and I need to trust that, trust him.

Hickory's been twiddling his thumbs ever since Dad tackled me. Legs crossed, head bowed, chewing on the rope in his mouth. Watching us both. He heard the things I said, knows the man in the dirty red cloak is my dad. But even Hickory's attention is being diverted now. The Leatherheads are bustling around the place, clicking their throats, lugging chains and shackles. The prisoners shuffle as far from the cage doors as they can. One man starts babbling and points at an archway across the chamber that the Leatherheads must've expanded, block by block, ages ago. A giant mouth in the wall, gap-toothed and yawning, belching puffs of smoke and steam. Something's about to happen. We're running out of time.

I huff out a breath, stand up. The bounty hunter watches me. Hickory, too. Dad glares at me, but I'm not walking to him, I'm walking to the girl. She's kneeling by the chain-link wall of the cage a few meters from him, scarf still wrapped around her head, meditating or something.

"Hi," I say, casual-like. "Um. How are things?" The girl's clearly unimpressed. I half-turn toward Dad, catch him in the corner of my eye. "Wow, that's great. Excellent."

"I didn't say anything," the girl says, but I'm already raising my hand.

"Just let me get this out. Are you listening?" I cough and bury a "Dad" in there to make sure I've got his attention. "I want to tell you something important. I came to rescue you. I know that sounds lame, being a prisoner myself, but it's true. I came to take you home. And I'm going to. I don't quite know how yet, but I'm working on it. We'll be okay. Okay?"

If the girl didn't think I was an idiot before then she sure as hell thinks it now.

Dad heard me, though, I can feel it, and that's all that matters.

Two Leatherheads unlock our cage and dump a bundle of chain attached to metal collars onto the floor. They point their rifles at the largest cluster of prisoners and wait.

The old man moves first. Slowly, painfully, he untangles the chain and clips the first collar round his neck. Then he holds out the jangling line and a thin woman with thinner hair does the same. One by one, the prisoners shackle themselves without a word. I wonder where they've come from. How long they've been here. Whether they have any secret plans of their own to escape. I doubt it. These are defeated people. They're outnumbered a hundred to one.

We, I correct myself. *We* are outnumbered.

Four collars left. Dad chains himself. I chain myself. The collar pinches the back of my neck, fastening tight. I have to help Hickory into his on account of his bound hands. When the collar clicks he shoots me a smile through the gag but his eyes are black and burning. One of the Leatherheads tries to force the girl into the last collar. She swipes away its hand, even blocks a retaliatory punch. The Leatherhead looks at its comrade, stunned more than anything, I guess. Before it can do anything else, though, the girl snatches the collar and clips it around her neck so calmly she might as well be fastening a necklace.

"Well, go on," she says, flicking her head at the cage door.

We're marched from our cage with the other lines of prisoners, chains rattling, headed for the archway across the chamber. Tin-skins snap at us as we pass.

"Where are they taking us?" I ask Dad over the noise. At first I figure he hasn't heard me, but then he half-turns and says, "Train."

"As in choo-choo?" I glance back at Hickory. He arches an eyebrow back. There's never been a train on Bluehaven, obviously, but I've read about them. Saw a picture once, too. Big metal things on long metal tracks. I'm pretty sure they're normally an outside thing, like snow and grass and forests. "What the hell is a train doing in here?"

Heavy boots beside me now. The bounty hunter's keeping me close. He's just as big as the Leatherheads, but he's probably as nervous as I am. I bet my key's still in his pocket.

I'm sure his family has never felt closer.

Another plume of smoke and steam hisses through the giant's teeth in the wall, curling up toward the ceiling. The chain gang in front of us disappears into the haze, and then we're swallowed, too. The air tastes bitter and tinny. Fire pits color the steam and smoke red. Drums and mine carts filled with coal take shape. A snarling Tin-skin on a leash. More Leatherheads loom around us, a forest of gangly, menacing silhouettes shepherding us into this new chamber.

And then we're through the smoke and steam.

Staring at the train.

It looks like a boxy caterpillar, stretching from one side of the chamber to the other, disappearing at both ends through more angry archways the Leatherheads have made. They must've burrowed through a thousand walls to lay the tracks. Blowing the Manor apart, hacking away at it stone by stone. They're still at it now, chipping away with pickaxes.

The train looks ancient, rusted beyond repair, but a grimy electric light shines in every carriage. The sides are covered in tiny rotted holes, sliding doors spewing gangplanks, and the occasional small, barred window.

It's another prison on wheels.

We're marshalled into a barbed-wire pen with another chain gang while the other prisoners are herded onboard, shoulders bent, hopes dashed. Two groups per carriage. Once their prisoners are sealed inside, the bounty hunters wander off to a carriage of their own.

"My gods," Dad mutters under his breath, shaking his head in horror at the train. "They've gutted the place. The tracks probably lead all the way to their master's lair."

"Roth," I say. Dad can't help it this time. He turns to me, shocked I know the name. I jerk my head at Hickory. "He was gonna turn me in before we got caught."

Dad glares at Hickory. Hickory just shrugs back as if to say *Can you blame me?* so I kick him in the shins. He's about to kick me back when the girl slaps him upside the head. I force a smile in thanks but choke a second later as our chain gang's marched out of the pen. The bounty hunter grips my shoulder as we walk.

Strange, but it's almost comforting.

I help Dad into the carriage. Old habits and all. He tries to shake me off, partly because we're supposed to be strangers, but also—I suspect—simply because he doesn't *need* my help anymore. Not the way he used to. I don't know how that makes me feel just yet. Amazed? Happy? Thrilled? Maybe, if I'm being honest, even a little sad and scared. All I know for sure is that he's still a little unsteady on his feet, and I'm fighting a decade of instinct to care for him, help him, look out for him. He's gonna have to put up with me bugging him for a good while yet.

The carriage smells even worse than the camp. There are stains on the rusty walls. Steel doors front and back. The side door screeches shut once we're all aboard. The bounty hunter lingers outside a moment, watching me through one of the barred windows. He nods, satisfied, and vanishes. I wonder if we'll stop at other camps on the way to Roth's. I hope so. Anything to buy us more time.

A horn blows. Steam blasts. The carriage shudders and squeals.

"This is my first train ride," is all I can say.

Dad's dimples flare again, like a couple of Manor candles. "Mine too, kiddo."

THE GUARDIANS

I finally get my hug. Three seconds and Dad holds me tighter than anyone has ever held me before. Now that Roth's goons are out of the way, he doesn't seem to care who sees. He says he's sorry. Tells me I shouldn't be here. Asks if my bandaged hand is okay, and inspects a few cuts and bruises. His voice is as scratchy as his chin, and he doesn't exactly smell like roses, but I'm sure I smell just as bad. We stink, we're trapped, and the collars are half-choking us, but neither of us cares.

We're together, and that's all that matters.

"I'm exactly where I'm supposed to be," I say. "Winifred told me—"

Dad pulls out of the hug. "Winifred Robin? She sent you in here?"

I nod, and a shadow passes over Dad's face, but I still can't help but smile because he's here, *really* here, and he's *looking* at me. There are so many things I want to tell him, want to ask him, need to say. For now, though, I can only get out one word.

"Dad . . ."

"I know, Jane," he says. He hugs me again. Tells me how proud he is, how brave I am, how thankful he is for everything I've done. When his voice breaks I'm terrified he's fading away again, falling back into his trance, but then he clears his throat and pulls out of the hug. "There's so much I need to tell you, but first I want to know how you came to be here."

The old man shuffles to the wall and sits down. The rest of us have to follow, dragged down by the chain. The thin woman. The two kids. All the scared but silent men and women who have their own horror stories to tell, I'm sure. Dad sits down, then me and Hickory and the girl. The other chain gang in our carriage does the same. It's noisy, crowded, hot and clammy, even with the wind whistling through the barred window and the rusty holes in the walls.

"Go on," Dad says. "What happened after I left Blue-haven? Tell me everything."

And so I tell him. Everything. About the hidden gateway under the catacombs. The snow. The Tin-skin in the booby trap. Hickory's shack and the explosive Specter-scum. The carnivorous forest and the bounty hunter. Dad death-stares at Hickory a few times, but keeps his eyes fixed on the floor for most of the story, nodding now and then. Nobody interrupts me. Hickory couldn't speak even if he wanted to, what with the gag and all. I think I've sent the girl to sleep. Her head lolls slightly with the not-so-gentle sway of the train. Actually, I'm kinda bummed she missed the bit about me saving Hickory back in the forest.

"Jane," Dad says. "Keep going."

"Sorry. Um. Well, that's it. We got through the dart trap and the Leatherheads caught us. Took us to the prison camp with the bounty hunter."

"And he still has the key?"

"In one of his pockets, I think. Dad, I'm sorry"

"It's okay," he says. "You of all people have nothing to be sorry about. Better he has it than a Leatherhead. We can get it back." The train rounds a bend. The lights in the carriage flicker. He shakes his head. "I can't believe this is happening. You know, I was actually happy when Winifred turned us over to the Hollows. We owe her our lives, I know, but I knew she'd never stop searching for answers—about the key, about *us*—and I knew whatever she found would only put you in greater danger." He sighs. "I suppose we never really escaped the Manor. Deep down, I think I always knew it would get you some day."

"Knew the Manor would get me?"

Dad nods, slowly. "We should have been there to protect you from the beginning, but you had to be the parent. No child should bear that burden. Elsa and I didn't—"

"Elsa?" My throat catches. I can barely form the words. "Is that . . . ?"

Dad's eyes fill with tears. He blinks them away, hard. Grabs my good hand and nods.

"I'm sorry, Jane, I—yes." He smiles. "Her name is Elsa."

My mother's name is Elsa. Don't reckon I've heard a more beautiful name.

This is the stuff heart attacks are made of.

I grab Dad's arm. "What's yours? Your real name, I mean."

"Charleston Eustace Grayson." He screws up his face. "The Third."

"Oh. That's . . ."

"Terrible, I know."

"Maybe I'll just . . . keep calling you Dad?"

"Please do."

"And mine?" Crap, it could be worse than *Charleston*. "Actually, you know what? I don't want to know. I'll stick with Jane." Right now, I've got bigger fish to fry. "Dad, where's Mom? Where did we come from? What happened to you? Why are you better now?"

"I am free," he says, "because I returned to the Manor."

"Free from what?"

Dad takes a deep breath. "I believe you two call them Specters." He raises an eyebrow, nods. "Quite an appropriate name, actually. Not bad at all."

I'm sure I've misheard him. "The *Specter* got you? I don't understand."

"There's more than one of them, Jane," Dad says. "And they don't come from an Otherworld, they come from the Manor. Or rather, a very powerful place *within* the Manor."

I glance at Hickory. He looks as shocked as I feel.

"The Specters are the guardians of this powerful place," Dad continues. "Two escaped because of what we did. Hunted us down. We would've tried to seal them back in but we had to think about you. Get you to safety. Then Elsa and I were separated. I tried to find her again, but . . ."

Dad swallows hard. "I found another gateway. It opened. I didn't want to leave Elsa—I thought I could get you clear and return to find her once the Specter had gone—but I was too slow. It caught me. I fell through to Bluehaven and collapsed at the top of the Sacred Stairs. The gateway sealed behind me. I felt the Specter, I don't know, *panicking* inside me. I don't think they can exist outside the Manor without a host. I told Winifred to keep the key safe and secret, but then the Specter settled. It had no way of returning to the Manor, so it stayed within me, its host, feeding on my fears, tearing me apart." He forces a smile, pulls at a strand of gray hair. "Gave me a new look too."

Hickory says something then. It sounds like mush through his gag, so I translate for the jerk. "He was caught by one a while back. Must've been that second Specter you mentioned. He said it took him to a place he calls the Grip."

When Dad looks at Hickory this time there's still hate in his eyes, but there's something else too. Understanding. An acknowledgement of shared pain.

"A waking nightmare," he says. "There were moments when I could see through my own eyes, but most of the time I was consumed by that white light. One that brought all my fears to life, made them real. Turned any happy thought or memory against me. I found Elsa in there after a while. She was caught as well for a time, back inside the Manor."

"What do you mean you *found* her in there?"

"The Specters are connected through this—this *Grip*, as you call it. Elsa was still being hunted inside the Manor.

Couldn't run forever. She was Gripped. Not permanently as I was. In that place, that realm of nightmares, we were together for a while."

Just a while. Not forever.

"What does that mean?" Suddenly the carriage feels even smaller, the rusted walls closing in. "Dad, is—is she alive or . . ." I can't bring myself to say that other word.

He wipes away a tear, which pretty much rips my damn heart out. "I don't know, Jane. I never saw her again after that. She vanished from the Grip before we could say goodbye, but that doesn't mean the Specter . . ." He looks me square in the eyes. "She could've broken free. She was—she *is*—the strongest, wisest, most resilient woman I've ever known."

Could it be? Could Mom have escaped the second Specter somehow? Maybe it released her from the Grip, same as Hickory. Left her alone. She could still be in here somewhere, hiding from Roth and his army, surviving, waiting for us to come get her.

The carriage expands again, wider than ever.

Breathe. As thrilling as this prospect is, it's gonna have to wait for now.

"I saw others," Dad says. "Roth's soldiers mainly. Rarely—never for long—but I shared their nightmares, too." He nods at Hickory. "Probably even saw him in there once. They'd appear, vanish, and there I'd be, alone again. But something changed whenever a quake struck Bluehaven. The Grip would . . . shift somehow. The Specter was reacting to them. When Winifred took me to the festival—when your hand hit the Stairs—it went wild. The Grip cleared. I could see you. I wanted to go to you, but something had changed. It was as if . . . as if the Specter was being called back to the Manor, drawn up the Stairs. It knew the gateway was about to open. I couldn't stop. I was running, but I wasn't in control."

"And when you stepped back inside the Manor?"

"The Specter fled my body immediately, flew off into the Manor, disappeared. After all those years of suffering— all those years when you cared for me so brilliantly," Dad runs a hand over my hair, "I was free." Then he drags his eyes around the carriage. "*Was* being the operative word. You're lucky you entered the Manor through that second gateway. I was found by a whole platoon of Roth's soldiers right away. I was too weak to fight, to run."

"But why were the Specters after you in the first place?"

For the longest while, Dad doesn't say anything. Then he takes a deep breath.

"We opened it," he says. "The powerful, sacred place they're bound by the Makers to protect." And he traces a finger through the grime on the floor, draws the symbol from the key. "We opened the Cradle of All Worlds."

THE TRUTH ABOUT
JOHN AND ELSA

"The Manor goes by many names, and is known across many worlds, as are the people of Bluehaven. The history of our own world, Tallis, is littered with accounts of—"

I hold up a hand, need a second to let this sink in.

Tallis. Our home world is Tallis.

"Are you okay, Jane?"

"Mm-hm. Yep. Just . . . processing. Tallis, huh?"

"Yes."

I wanna know everything. What does it look like? What's the weather like? Can we go there when this is over? Why did we leave? Do they have coconuts there? There are so many questions they all get jammed in my throat and I end up just staring at Dad, wide-eyed, mouth flapping slowly like a fish drowning in air. He waits for a bit, then clears his throat.

"Um . . . can I continue?"

"Please."

"Right. As I was saying, the history of Tallis is littered with accounts of mysterious strangers coming to aid us in our greatest time of need. The Hundred Year Plague. The Reign of the Winter King. The Uprising of 1312. Many had forgotten the stories. Most believed they were myths, legends. But not us. Elsa and I had devoted our lives to finding the lost gateways of old—to proving not just the Manor's existence, but the Otherworlds', too. Ancient texts, scrolls, documents—we scoured them all. Gathering information, plotting potential gateway locations, to no avail. Other historians thought it was all a waste of time. We were ostracized."

I know what this word means. "People chased you with knives too, huh?"

Dad frowns. "No, I meant—I meant people laughed at us. Called us fools."

"Oh. Right, yeah. That isn't very nice either."

He sits straighter, narrows his eyes. "Somebody chased you with a *knife?*"

"Yeah. Um. I never told you that. It's okay, though. Good sprinting practice."

Dad clenches his fists. "Right. We'll deal with that later, shall we? Where was I? Ah, yes. Well, everything changed on our expedition down the river Tallin. Elsa had finally gained access to an ancient text belonging to a local warlord—look, it's a long story. Very dangerous and exciting. The point is, she translated the text, cross-referenced it with a load of other information and maps we'd gathered over the years, and found us a gateway. I'm talking actual coordinates. We were close. I couldn't believe it. I hadn't even wanted to go on that particular expedition." Dad forces a sad smile. "Elsa was pregnant, you see. Three months."

"Oh," I say, buzzing at my appearance in the story, albeit in fetus form.

"'We're not turning back,' she told me. 'Not now.'"

Dad falls silent, lost in the memory. The train chugs round another bend.

"So you went and found it," I say.

Dad nods, slowly. "Deep in the jungle. A day's journey downriver, hidden in a valley of limestone pinnacles. A stone door in a shallow cave. We stood there before it, unable to move, unable to speak. Then we moved as one. Touched the stone. The gateway opened."

"You entered together? You broke the Third Law."

"I think the Three Laws were created by the people of Bluehaven, long ago. As far as I'm aware, they exist nowhere else—certainly not on Tallis. So, yes, we entered the Manor together. Found ourselves in a candlelit corridor. It was like stepping into a dream."

The gateway closed behind them. They never saw their home again.

Mom and Dad walked. Corridor after corridor, hallway after hallway, rooms and chambers shifting behind them as they went. They encountered no booby traps. Had no idea what kind of nightmare they were about to walk into. Then they saw it, touched it, another gateway that opened onto a different world with two suns. One small and white. One large and orange. They were standing at the base of a cliff, looking out upon a dune sea.

"Arakaan," Dad says. "A desolate world. Ruined. Decayed. Roth's world."

Bitter air blasted their lungs dry. The gateway sealed when they stepped out of the Manor, indistinguishable from the cliff face. Bullets sprayed the sand at their feet at once. They tried to run, but found themselves trapped in a net, watching as a troop of Leatherheads rappelled down the cliff and surrounded them. The gateway was obviously no secret.

"Someone must have used it before. Perhaps Roth saw them leave. Maybe he tried to leave with them but was a moment too late. Either way, it was clear he'd been waiting a long time for the gateway to open again." Dad's voice gets a little shaky now. Even after all these years, the memory still scares him. "We were bound. Gagged. The soldiers— Leatherheads, as you call them—sent up a black flare. We didn't know it, but that was the signal for Roth to come. Day turned to night. The temperature plummeted. We were given no blankets. No food or water." He trips over the start of his next sentence, tries again. "We felt him before we saw him. The air turned sour. We felt ill, as if struck by a sudden sickness. Roth is no man, Jane. He's a walking disease, contaminating the very air he breathes."

"Is that why he wears the mask?"

"He wears the mask out of vanity. I think his was a handsome race. Strong and proud, now all but extinct. I don't know how he came to be the way he is. What-ever happened, he's now an abomination of his former self. Rotten to the core, but still very much immortal. I fear even the Specters are powerless to stop him. I never saw him in the Grip. Not even his mind can be broken."

"What happened to his people, then?" I ask. "Were they immortal too?"

"If they were, somebody obviously found a way to kill them. Maybe *he* found a way to kill them. Roth, the last of the immortals. I think he'd like the sound of that."

The thin woman's trying to comfort the two kids now, talking to them, patting their heads, wiping the tear-streaked grime from their cheeks. I think they're in shock. A man from the other chain gang's sobbing quietly to himself, nursing an arm that's clearly broken. Several more have gone to sleep. All these people from different worlds forced together, trapped and terrorized by Roth. I clench my fists so hard it hurts my injured hand.

"And when he came to you that night in Arakaan? What did he say?"

"Well, technically he didn't *say* anything. He doesn't have a mouth."

"Oh, yeah. So, um, how does he talk?"

"Roth has no need for speech. He pokes around inside your mind. Reads you. Drains your thoughts. You can't stop it, it's—" Dad shakes his head, can't find the words. "We pleaded and begged. He just stood there. Reading us. Breaking us down. Telling us in our minds what he wanted, his voice like ice, scraping around inside our skulls."

And what he wanted was to get inside the Manor. Roth dragged Mom and Dad back to the gateway. When they refused to open it, he pulled a couple of curved, sickle-like blades from his cloak. Held one of them to Mom's neck and traced the other down to her belly.

Dad didn't hesitate then, not for a second.

"I let him in," he says. "I touched the rock and the gateway opened again. All this—" he waves a hand at the carriage and the other prisoners, "is because of me."

He looks so helpless, so sorry, like he's about to cry. A man with the weight of a thousand worlds on his shoulders. I grab his hand and squeeze it tight. Tell him it wasn't his fault—*isn't* his fault—that anybody would've done the same. Roth gave him no choice.

Dad squeezes my hand back, a simple gesture he never used to be able to do.

"It all happened so fast," he almost-whispers. "Roth marched his troops in. Hundreds of them. They constructed a thick, metal frame inside the gateway to keep it open. Turned corridors into roads. Drove in tanks and trucks. Disabled booby traps. Started building a fortress in the first large chamber they found, starting with a brand-new cell for us. Months passed before Roth came for us again. About six months, to be precise. He came when Elsa was in labor. When we were most vulnerable. He knew I would do anything to help her."

"He wanted you to show him the gateway back to Tallis," I say. Dad looks at me, puzzled and frowny-eyed, so I let his hand go and add, "That's why he takes prisoners, right? So they can lead him to more gateways. He ruined his own world so now he's looking for another."

Dad shakes his head. "Jane, Roth doesn't want to conquer *one* world. He wants to conquer *all* of them. And to do that he first needs to conquer the Manor itself." Dad taps the symbol drawn on the floor between us. "He's looking for this, Jane. The Cradle of All Worlds. It's the core of the Manor. The first chamber created by the Makers—a chamber with one purpose: to house and protect a source of immense and unmatched power." Dad pauses, takes a breath. I swear I can hear a drumroll somewhere. "The Cradle Sea."

The vibe in the carriage changes at once. The old man looks at us. Hickory closes his eyes as if he's just swallowed something bad, like this is the one thing he didn't want me to hear. Even the girl twitches, and I wonder if she's really sleeping.

"A sea," I say. "You mean, like, an ocean?"

"Yes."

"Sorry, I just have to . . . get my head around this." I hold out my hands, like I'm lifting a really big ball. "The Cradle of All Worlds is a really, really, ridiculously big chamber." Dad nods. "In the center of the Manor." He nods again. "With an entire *sea* inside it?"

"Precisely."

The first thing I think is, *That's ridiculous.* The second thing I think is, *Crap, my nightmare, could it be?* The third thing I think is, *No way, move on, forget it*, but then Dad says, "I heard you, Jane. Even in the Grip, I was listening. All those times you spoke about your nightmares. All those nights you cried out in your sleep. I know you had the drowning dream most of all."

"It isn't a nightmare, though, is it?" I say after a while, and suddenly it feels so obvious. How could I not see it before? "It's a memory."

THE GATEKEEPER, THE
BUILDER, AND THE SCRIBE

"How much do you know about the Makers, Jane?" I make
a noise, somewhere between a huh? and an oh, still trying
to come to terms with the fact that the most terrifying
place I can possibly imagine actually exists. It's real, and
if what Dad says is true then I've really been there, tossed
around by those waves, nearly drowned in that water,
which means the tentacles of crackling light are real, too.
The yawning mouths and white-fire eyes. The Specters, I
suppose. Guardians of the Cradle.

You ever see a big white light, Jane, you run, Hickory told me.

Turns out I already have seen one. More than one. I've
seen dozens of the damn things, writhing and crackling in
the deep, reaching out to get me.

They're real.

But what about my other nightmares? The ones I had
back on Bluehaven. All those terrible things I've seen and
heard in my sleep. The men, women and children in danger. Strangers being chased, crying out for help, dying.
They can't be memories, so what are they?

"Jane? The Makers. How much do you know about them?"

"Um." I shake my head. "The Makers. I know they were gods. There were three of them. Supposedly they built the Manor."

"Not supposedly. They did. In the beginning. And by beginning I mean *Beginning*. As in the very, very, very, very, *very*—"

"Beginning with a capital B," the girl says. "We got it." Dad, Hickory and I turn our heads. She opens her eyes and shrugs. "What? Keep going." She rests her head against the wall, closes her eyes again. "We haven't got all day."

"Right," Dad says, "well." He looks around the carriage. "How do I explain this? Yes. Okay. Think of a stack of paper, Jane. A stack bound in string. A thousand pages. And each page represents a different or alternate dimension with its own suns and moons and stars."

"And worlds."

"The Otherworlds, yes. A thousand dimensions existing separately, but layered on top of each other, all held together by the string. The stack is fixed. Secure. Stable. Pick it up, throw it around, leave it outside all day, the pages stay together. But if you cut the string—"

"The wind can blow them apart."

"One gust. One breath."

I look up at the window across the carriage and the dots of candles whipping by outside, the stone walls a blur. "The Manor's the string."

"Exactly. The Makers created the Manor to fill the gaps between the worlds. To bridge and bind them together. You see, in the Beginning the dimensions were spinning uncontrollably, the worlds within them violent, uninhab-. itable places unable to sustain even the smallest glimmer of life. They were realms of the gods. Lands of chaos." A smile flicks the corners of Dad's lips. "And then Po came, a god who could see things the other gods could not. A network of portholes linking the dimensions together. A tangle of threads branching out like the strands of a spider web. Po travelled along these threads, visiting the different dimensions and their worlds. She met Aris, creator and shaper of stone. Nabu-kai, a wise and powerful god with the gift of foresight. He could see every future in every world. All three of them believed it was time for the reign of the gods to come to an end, to let life spread and prosper in every dimension, but it was Nabu-kai who knew how to do it. He had been waiting for Po and Aris. Had already seen the wonder they would create.

"So Po took Aris and Nabu-kai along the threads, and in that place-between-places they forged the Manor together. Aris built every wall, every chamber, every trap. Po made every gateway and connected them to the Otherworlds. And Nabu-kai—Nabu-kai engraved the fate of all worlds into the walls of the Manor itself, and the destinies of those who would shape them. He saw all of our paths, Jane, and we walk them, whether we like it or not."

Nabu-kai. The one who left the symbol for Winifred. The one who gave her the vision.

"He's my least favorite one, then," I say.

"Don't hate the gods, kiddo. They're pissed off enough as it is." Dad smiles. "So, the Manor was finished, the Otherworlds calmed. But the Makers still had to contend with the Gods of Chaos, many with powers stronger than their own. So instead of fighting them, they tricked them. Spread word of the wonder they'd created and lured the gods inside to see it. Po opened every gateway, Aris channeled the gods directly into the empty Cradle and, once inside, the combined energies of every god clashed, swirled and transformed irreversibly into a pool of energy and light. The Cradle Sea was born, a force strong enough to lay entire worlds to waste. The energy and essence of the old gods bound together, forever, as one."

"And what happened to the Makers?"

"Well, they knew that in order for the age of life to truly begin, they too would have to join the fallen gods inside the Cradle. After sealing it from the inside, they poured their own spirits not into the Sea, but into the foundation stone lying at its center."

"The first stone laid down by Aris," I say, picturing the steep-sloped little island that started popping up in my nightmare ever since I stepped inside the Manor. "It's big, isn't it?"

"Oh yes. From there, the essence of the Makers has powered the core of the Manor and kept the Sea safe and secret ever since. Po, Aris and Nabu-kai. The Gatekeeper, the Builder and the Scribe." Dad taps the symbol on the floor. Traces over the almost-triangle again. "Three gods."

He moves onto the circle now. "At the center of their most sacred creation."

I frown at the almost-triangle. "Why's that line there curved inward?"

"I don't know."

"And the Specters? Where'd they come from?"

"I don't know that either. Perhaps the Makers fashioned them from the Cradle Sea. Perhaps they were Gods of Chaos spared by the Makers. A lesser order of gods chosen to watch over and protect them. All I know is, the Specters can't use the gateways or exist in the Otherworlds without a host, as I said—I wouldn't have been Gripped all those years if they could—and while they can pass through the walls of the Manor, I don't think they can pass through the walls of the Cradle itself. It's too powerful, even for them. Too protected. The two that chased us from the Cradle are trapped in here, like the rest of us."

I shift my weight on the butt-numbing floor, one cheek to the other. This is all so huge, so beyond me. I'm used to worrying about house chores, escape routes, and rowdy fisherfolk, not the Beginning-with-a-capital-B-of-all-existence. My head hurts.

"So what does all this have to do with the key?"

"Ah, now we come to it. The legend of the Makers told on Tallis finishes there, with the creation of the Cradle Sea. I believe the version told on Bluehaven is the same. Winifred spent many nights reading to us in the museum, Jane. The story never went beyond that point. But remember, the Manor is revered in many worlds. Some legends travel far and change with every telling. On Roth's world—on Arakaan—it is said that before the Makers sealed themselves inside the Cradle, Nabu-kai foresaw a great evil that would one day try to conquer their creation. And so the Makers forged a key. A key that, in the hands of someone pure of heart, would be able to unlock the Cradle and use its power to expel this evil from the Manor. At least, that is what Roth would have you believe." Dad glances at Hickory and the girl, both watching him intently now. "The truth is, there are three keys."

Hickory leans out from the carriage wall, as if something has pinched his back.

"Phwee?" he says through his gag. "*Phwee?*"

"Two keys hidden inside the Manor to open the Cradle of All Worlds—yes, your key is one of them, Jane—and a third key to control it. This is what Roth ultimately wants. The third and most powerful key the Makers left *inside* the Cradle—on the foundation stone in the center of the Sea. Control the third key and you control the Cradle. Control the Cradle and the power of the Makers is yours. The power to see all ends. To open any gateway. To channel the Sea anywhere you choose. Roth could hold every world to ransom. Destroy entire civilizations in the blink of an eye."

"And you knew all of this back then," the girl says. "When Roth came to you? When Elsa was in labor?" The accusatory tone in her voice bugs the hell out of me.

"No," Dad says. "But Roth wasted no time educating me. While Elsa cried out in pain, he pinned me to the wall, entered my mind and told me the story, showed me the symbol. He had spent months looking for the keys and the Cradle entrance to no avail. He could feel the Manor itself working against him. He believed that somebody with more noble and innocent intentions might have better luck. He had chosen his timing well. I swore on my life and Elsa's I would help him find the Cradle. And he let me go. He let me help her."

I nearly jump out of my skin when I hear this. "So I was born here, then? In the Manor?"

"Yes, Jane," Dad says, struggling to find the words, to get an answer out, "you were born in the Manor, but—"

A jolt in the carriage throws us sideways. Brakes squeal. Sparks fly past the windows. Prisoners shout and hold each other. My insides squirm. There's a *clank, clank, clank*, an exhausted bellow of steam, then we're all jerked back into silence. A heavy quiet fills the carriage, broken only by the distant barking of Tin-skins and the gentle tinkling of our chains.

"Why have we stopped?" I ask.

A woman from the other chain gang peeks out the window. Turns back, shakes her head, says something no one seems to understand.

"We're not there yet," Dad says. "We can't be."

Hickory's the first to panic. It begins as a stillness, a refusal to shuffle with the rest of us to the window. He says something over and over, "Wruff—wruff," getting louder, getting quicker. He backs away, into the girl, past the girl, yanking us all toward the back of the carriage.

213

He slips and pulls most of us down with him. Tries to free his hands.

"Wruff! Ruff! Roff!"

And then I feel it. A burn in the throat. An itch on the skin. A dizziness. I cough, and so does the girl. The old man clutches his chest and gasps for air. People rub their eyes, hold hands to their hearts and heads. I can hear prisoners crying in the other carriages. Banging their chains in protest. A carriage door screeching open and shut further up the train. The girl reaches over and pulls the rope from Hickory's mouth, and that's when the train starts its caterpillar crawl again.

"It's him," Hickory coughs. "Roth's on the train."

THE MAN WITH THE PORCELAIN FACE

Panic spreads fast. The other prisoners may not know who or what Roth is, but they know a bad feeling when it hits them. The screams further up the train sure don't help either. Some people are too scared to move. Others scramble round the sliding side door, as if scratching at the steel's gonna set them free. Never mind the nooses jangling round their necks or the chugging of the speeding train. They want off and they want off now. Dad tells them to stop, tries to calm them down. I kinda want to join them.

"Don't worry," Dad tells me. "We'll be fine."

"Oh, sure we will." The girl pulls a pin from her scarf, fiddles with the lock round the back of her neck. "We're stuck on a speeding train with a poisonous, immortal maniac who's been hunting you two for the last however-many years. What could possibly go wrong?"

Her collar tumbles to the floor. We stare at her.

"Now?" Hickory gasps. "You only pick the lock *now?*

"Waiting for the right moment," the girl says. A swish

of her cloak and she heads to the back of the carriage. "I'll catch you folks later."

"Wait," I yell. "Are you kidding?" Cough. "You can't leave." Splutter. "Help us."

"I am helping you," the girl shouts, but then she kicks open a small panel set low into the back corner, flicks her pin at Hickory and slips out into the wind.

"She left us," I say. "She *actually* left us."

A volley of rifle fire, further up the train. My imagination runs wild. Leatherheads mowing down prisoners. People clawing at the doors till their fingers bleed. A half-masked man striding through it all with blood sticking to his boots.

Dad grabs Hickory's collar, pulls him close. "Why is he here?"

"Untie my hands and I'll tell you."

Dad shoves him into the wall face-first and starts untying. "Talk."

"Not sure why," Hickory says. "Checking camps. Progress on the train line. Inspecting prisoners. Who knows? Maybe he felt a shiver down his spine when you two came back to the Manor."

As soon as the rope falls free, Hickory shoves Dad away and snatches the girl's pin from the floor. He sets to work on his collar, tongue wriggling between his teeth.

Dad grips my shoulders so hard it almost hurts.

"Listen to me very carefully. Roth won't have forgotten my face since our last encounter, but you were only a baby. He won't recognize you. No matter what Roth does to me, do not under any circumstances intervene. He cannot know who you are."

"What? No, Dad—"

"Don't flinch. Don't make a sound. Keep your head down and your eyes on your toes at all times. You don't know me, I don't know you. We're strangers, Jane."

"I'm not gonna let him touch you. We can pick the locks and get out of here before—"

Another round of rifle fire, louder than before. Closer.

"No time," Dad says. "And we can't go anywhere without the key."

"But the bounty hunter—he could've handed it over already."

"Nobody approaches Roth," Hickory says, still fiddling with the lock at his neck. "Big no-no. Bounty hunters'll be spreading through the train right now. Waiting for him to come to them. Ours will be here any second now—hand you and the key over together. Means we'll have a minute or two to take him out."

"What, so you can hand us over yourself?"

"Plan's changed."

"Oh, so you're on our side now?"

The front carriage door unlocks, squeals open. We're all blasted by wind and noise. Our bounty hunter ducks inside, harried but resolute, long whip coiled in a white-knuckled fist. I shuffle back on my knees.

Hickory's behind me, blocking my path.

"Until I get what I want," he whispers in my ear, "yes." His collar un-clicks.

The bounty hunter shuts the door, strides toward me. He doesn't notice the girl's collar lying on the floor. Doesn't even glance at Hickory, which is his biggest mistake.

Hickory strikes. Rips the collar from his neck and tackles the bounty hunter round the waist. The tackle doesn't floor him—the punches and kicks don't seem to bother him at all—but Hickory's quick and crazy as a rabid dog. Every time he's thrown back he charges in for more. The fight doesn't last long. Hickory dodges a punch, leaps onto the bounty hunter's back. The bounty hunter throws his weight backwards into the wall, and our only hope of retrieving the key crumples to the floor. Conscious, but only just.

And our time's run out.

The forward door squeals again. A bunch of Leatherheads charge inside, heavy boots thumping, a stench to end all stenches hot on their heels. A rolling, toxic fog.

Roth.

The reek of him. A heat-shimmer haze of ash and rancid meat. A stain in the corners of my eyes. I sink to the floor with the rest of the prisoners, defeated by the mere presence of him. I couldn't look up if I tried. Bile rises in the back of my throat. It burns.

The door swings shut and there's nothing but the muted *clankity-clunk* of the train and Roth's death-rattle breathing. My skin crawls. My vision swims and blurs. The bounty hunter drops his whip, kneels in submission. Hickory flaps Roth a weak, apologetic wave from the floor. He's as screwed as we are, and he knows it. Roth growls in reply.

But then something catches his attention. His breathing quickens. Two heavy steps and Roth's boots are right beside me.

"Always knew I'd see your ugly mug again, Roth."

Dad's voice is a wheeze. Roth lifts him to his feet. The chain rattles and pulls at the collar round my neck, forcing me up to my knees. A thud tells me Dad's pinned to the wall. A stifled cry tells me he's in pain. Roth lets out a menacing, satisfied sigh. I want to stop him, want to fight him, but I can't get up. Can't even bring myself to look at him.

Dad's lifted off his feet. They start jittering, his toes tapping the floor, as if volts of electricity are shooting through his body, choking his screams. I will myself to stand up, to fight, but it's useless. Hickory's watching me, knows exactly what I'm thinking. He shakes his head, wants me to forget it, but I can't. I may not be able to fight. But I can talk.

"Hey." At first it's just a whisper, a croak. A coughing fit grips my lungs but I fight through it, force out the words, louder this time. "Hey. Crap-for-brains. Down here."

My throat's on fire. It just about kills me, but it works. Dad's feet stop dancing. He gasps, tries to catch his breath. Whatever Roth was doing, he isn't doing it anymore, and now his attention's on me. I can feel him watching me. Feel his eyes burning into my skull.

Hickory tries to drag the attention his way. "Don't worry about her," he says. "She's just a fool, lost her mind," but a Leatherhead smacks him with its rifle.

Dad collapses to the floor and Roth plants his boots

square in my blurry field of vision. I figure I'm about to get my very own case of the jitters, but then the bounty hunter talks. I can't understand what he's saying, but it's scattered with Leatherhead *clicks* and *clacks*, and it gets them all riled up. When the bounty hunter points at me I swear every rifle in the carriage does the same. Next thing I know a Leatherhead grabs me. I'm on my feet and choking in no time, eyes closed. Anything to avoid looking at Roth.

"Leave her alone," Dad splutters. "She's nobody. I'm the—the one you want."

A hand grabs my face. Five fingers, not three. Roth's hand, long-nailed and cold. His breath scrapes at my skin, unbearably close. I try to keep my eyes closed, but I can't.

The sight of Roth's face blasts them dry.

His half-mask, shiny-white and flawless. The air rippling between his fake, frozen lips, alive with heat and decay. The leather straps wrapped around his bald head so tight they dig into his skin. Skin that isn't wrinkled but stretched, gray-veined and mottled. And those eyes, perched above the porcelain like two bottomless pools. A cold, unseeing blue.

They capture mine. Trap them. Turn them inside out.

At least, they try to.

Something's wrong. I can see it written all over the top half of Roth's face. He wants to read me, but he can't. I can feel him probing, prodding, trying to open me up with his mind, but I can block him without even trying. It's like a reflex, a jerk of the knee.

And Roth doesn't like it one bit.

He releases me. Strides over to the bounty hunter, who's rambling now, still on his knees. I don't even need to speak his language to know what he's saying. He's worried he isn't gonna get his free ticket home. The poor sucker actually thinks he still has a chance.

Roth grabs the big man's face as he stands. The bounty hunter might be taller and bulkier but he isn't anywhere near as strong. They lock eyes and it's like what happened to Dad all over again. The bounty hunter twitches and jitters. The prisoners around him shrink into the walls. Hickory looks away. The bounty hunter convulses, bleeding from his nose, eyes and ears. It sounds like there's a dying animal trapped in his throat. You can almost see his life story pouring out of him, all of it gobbled up by Roth. His home. His family. Finding me in the forest with the key. I want to scream at Roth, tell him to stop.

But I'm already too late.

The bounty hunter's eyes roll back into his head. He hits the deck and Roth's on him in a flash, tearing through the big man's pockets, searching for the key. He turns the bounty hunter over, pats him down. Unsheathes one of two curved blades hanging from his belt and slices through the dead man's clothes. He can't find it.

The key isn't there.

And then I see it. A glint in Hickory's eyes. The flicker of a smile.

The fight was a ruse. He picked the bounty hunter's pocket.

Roth rounds on me again. I see the questions like ice

and fire in his eyes. *Where is it? What have you done with it?* I don't know what to say, what to do.

The Leatherhead behind me twists my arm, tries to force an answer out of me.

"She took it," Hickory says, pointing at the girl's empty collar. "Picked his pocket before she got away. I tried to stop her but she escaped through that panel down there."

Roth doesn't look at the panel, though. He approaches Hickory, who's rambling like the bounty hunter now. "Read me if you like, boss, but you're wasting time. Bet she's going for the brakes. Engine carriage. Probably there right now. I swear on my life, my soul, my—"

BOOM.

An explosion somewhere further up the train rocks the carriage. Makes the lights blink. We stumble for a second, but the rocking doesn't last long. We haven't been derailed.

We're speeding up.

Hickory flicks an eyebrow at Roth. "Told you."

It's all stations go now. Roth unsheathes his second blade and turns to the Leatherheads, one after another. He doesn't make a sound but they seem to know exactly what he wants. They scatter. Some through the forward door, some through the back. The Leatherhead breathing down my neck unlocks my collar. A different one frees Dad.

Roth shrinks us with his eyes.

Move it, they're saying. *And don't try anything stupid.*

ESCAPE

We stagger through the train, led by Roth, herded by our Leatherhead guards. Every carriage is the same. Blinking lights and human stains. Prisoners cowering in the corners.

Hickory has been left behind.

The Leatherheads open and shut doors for us as we go. Each time we're shoved into the roaring wind between the carriages I consider grabbing Dad and jumping, taking our chances with the fall. But even if we somehow managed to survive, Roth could just come tumbling after us. Then there's the matter of the key. We can't leave without Hickory.

"Where are you taking us?" Dad shouts. "We don't know where the keys are."

I'm sure I hear Roth laugh at this, or what passes for a laugh when your mouth's been rotted away. A guttural, rasping chuckle that makes you want to clear your throat.

Into another carriage now, and I'm trying to come up with a plan. We have to make sure Roth doesn't get his hands on Hickory and the key, but how? It's just me and Dad. There aren't even any prisoners left alive in this carriage to help us. I've never seen so much death.

And then I see the girl through one of the barred windows at the end of the carriage. A flash of her face and she's gone. But then a hand. Five fingers flashing twice. She said she was helping us, but what the hell does that signal mean? Hi there? Ten Leatherheads?

Ten seconds.

The train squeals around another bend and I make my move. Grab Dad and pull him down in the flickering light. A Leatherhead tries to grab us. Roth steps in, too, but the ten seconds is up. A metal canister flies through the window and clatters along the floor between the bodies. I throw myself on top of Dad in case there's an explosion, but an explosion never comes—at least, not one of fire. With a loud *pop*, the carriage becomes a cloud.

It's a smoke bomb.

Footsteps on the roof. The Leatherheads retaliate with a round of gunfire but they're firing blind. I crawl away from them, hauling Dad along with me, over and around the dead bodies, through the smoke and the noise and the gunfire all *rat-a-tat*.

The sliding side door screeches open. A gust of howling wind clears the smoke, and we're two sitting ducks. Thankfully, Roth and the Leatherheads are too busy worrying about the girl to pay us any attention for the moment. They edge toward the open side door. Don't even notice the grenade pop through the barred window behind them till it's too late.

This time there's an explosion. Me and Dad are far enough away to avoid being hurt, but the Leatherheads aren't so lucky. One of them is blasted clean through the open door. The other hits the side and gets sucked out a second later. Roth merely staggers, catches a handle, steadies himself and spins around. He advances on the girl in the window. She has a gun. Fires once, twice, three times, the blasts hitting him in the chest, the stomach, forcing him back, closer and closer to the open door. But it isn't enough.

I scramble to my feet and run at him, yelling, "Shoot him in the face! The face!"

The girl fires again and shoots Roth square in the mask. It shatters but he spins around before we can see the horror beneath. He's teetering on the edge now. I don't stop, keep running, throw the full force of my weight into his. As expected, it's like hitting a brick wall, but it's enough. I bounce back into the carriage. Roth tumbles out the door.

Just another blur.

When Dad helps me up, I'm a huffing, puffing wreck, sucking down the Roth-free air. "Don't you ever do anything like that again," he says, but he smiles and hugs me.

The girl swings down into the carriage, throws Dad a spare rifle. "Get a move on."

"Thanks for coming back." He pulls some kind of latch on the rifle, checks the sight-thingy. "You destroyed the brakes?"

The girl nods. "After I put the train on full-throttle. Raided their weapon cache, stole some explosives. Took out a carriage of Leatherheads too."

"Very good," Dad says, genuinely impressed. But he's missing the point.

"Good?" I say. "We need to stop this thing and get off it, not make it go faster."

The girl throws me a pistol. "I counted eighteen carriages, including the engine car. We're slightly closer to the back of the train so that's the way we go."

"Excuse me?"

"We climb onto the roof and run."

"You want us to run along the roof of a speeding train filled with bad guys? That's your big plan? What do we do once we get to the end?"

"Disconnect the carriage," Dad says. "Watch as the rest of the train speeds away."

"What about Roth?" I ask. "The fall couldn't have killed him."

"We'll have put enough distance between us by the time we get down there," the girl says. "We'll jump off the train and duck away from the tracks as soon as we start slowing down. Lose him in no time. You two manage to get the key back yet?"

"Hickory has it," I say. "He fought the bounty hunter. Picked his pocket right before Roth—well, I'm not exactly sure what Roth did to him. Fried his brain?"

"He can do that?"

"Yes, unfortunately," Dad says. "He gets inside your mind, he can tear it apart in no time. The good news is he doesn't already have the second key." I'm about to ask Dad how he knows this, when he says, "While he was reading me, Roth told me what he wants. The *keys*—plural. He's no closer to the Cradle than we are."

"Where's the second key?" the girl asks.

"Elsa has it," Dad says, and turns to me. "She survived a long time in here before the Specter found her. When we found each other in the Grip she told me—"

"Later," the girl says, "and not in front of me. Or anyone else. If Roth can read minds, the less we know about the keys, the better. Right now, we head up to the roof, stay low and move fast. We'll find Hickory and the first key as we go."

"Hang on," I say, "who put you in charge? Who *are* you?"

The girl shuffles her feet impatiently. After a deep breath she says, "It's me, Jane."

"You're gonna have to be more specific than that."

The girl undoes her scarf. Pulls the lower half under her chin and the top half back over her hair. It's dark and long and tied back in a braid. I stare at her and she stares at me and she looks so familiar it's ridiculous, but she can't be.

"Violet," she says, but I still say, "Violet who?"

She rolls her eyes. "How many Violets do you know, Jane?"

"One," I say. "And she's eight."

The girl steps back to the door. "Not anymore," she says, and swings out into the wind.

A CHANGE OF PLAN

So we're crouched on the roof of the train, hands and feet spread wide against the tilt and shudder of the carriage. The wind flaps our clothes and whips our hair and roars in our ears, trying to snatch us up and slam us into the Manor walls speeding by.

"Guns at the ready," the-Batty-Girl-Who-Thinks-She's-Violet shouts.

We move as fast as we can, keeping an eye out for low-hanging chandeliers and archways, ducking whenever they whoosh by. The candles and torches in the corridor keep trying to re-light themselves as we thunder past, but they don't stand a chance. Only the odd flash of sparks and the electric glow seeping from the train windows show us what's what.

The first jump's the hardest, even with the wind at our backs. One slip and we're train feed. The-Girl-Who-Can't-Be-Violet soars over the gap. Me and Dad make the jump together.

One down, too many more to go.

The train speeds into a new corridor. Chandeliers zip

by above our heads with a *shoom shoom zoom*. Another low archway and we're charging through a vast pillared hall. Torches flicker to life beyond the grip of the wind. We scramble on, the girl swinging over the edge of every carriage, looking for Hickory through the windows.

Dad says, "Where the hell is he?"

I say, "Maybe he's already down the back of the train, but *inside* like a normal person."

I don't think anyone hears me.

In the end it's Hickory who finds us, six or so carriages from the end. He clambers onto the roof ahead with the bounty hunter's whip looped round his shoulder, a gun in his hands and three Leatherheads hot on his tail. Dad and the girl raise their weapons, so I do as well. The girl shouts at Hickory, tells him to get down, and he dives. Rifles fire. My pistol *clicks*. By the time I've finished cursing the damn thing the Leatherheads have all been blasted clear.

Guns, I've decided, are the worst.

The girl smacks Hickory with the butt of her rifle. Dad punches him, takes his gun, and rummages through his pockets. Finds the key and shoves it into my hands with a quick "Don't lose it." I tuck the key back into my pocket and point my pistol at Hickory.

"What are you gonna do with that," he says, "throw it at me?"

So I throw it at him. Clock him a good 'un right in the face, too. He yelps and the pistol clatters over the side of the train. The girl glares at me.

I shrug. "It was broken anyway."

"*Stop* hitting me," Hickory shouts, clutching his nose. "We need to go. Now!"

Then we see them. A troop of Leatherheads climbing onto the roof of the last carriage. Running and leaping toward us. And there, rising and striding among them with his blades glinting like fangs: Roth. He must've grabbed hold of the last carriage after he fell. His clothes are torn, but he's wearing a new mask.

Needless to say, he looks furious.

"Run," Dad shouts, handing Hickory back his gun. "Go, go, go!"

We make like rabbits into the wind, heading toward the front of the train, back the way we came. The jumps are harder now. We have to take them at a sprint, and I can see Dad's energy is fading fast. I ask the girl if she has a new plan and she says, "Get to the front, the engine car, detach it, speed away," but Hickory shuts her down.

"Can't speed away," he shouts over his shoulder. "We're coming up to the spiral road."

"The *what?*"

"The spiral road." He spins around, tells us to duck. Blows away a Leatherhead that's popped up right behind us. "It's a—a—it's a road. In a spiral. Big one, going down. If the train takes it at this speed, even the engine carriage alone—"

"We'll derail," Dad says.

"We don't have a choice," the girl shouts. "We'll just have to figure out a way to slow down once we're far enough away from Roth."

"Oh, this'll end well," I mutter.

Leatherheads pop up in front of us, at our sides, swinging fists and machetes, snatching at our heels when we jump, carriage after carriage. Bounty hunters join the fray, streaming from their carriage up near the front of the train, blocking our path. Nobody shoots at us, though.

Roth still doesn't know where the key is. He needs us alive and kicking.

"Heads up!" Dad shouts, and the train speeds through another giant's mouth, clotheslining a bunch of unwary bad guys from our path. Chandeliers whoosh and whistle above our heads. We duck and dodge them, slowing down. Roth takes the occasional bullet, but never stops. He's taking his time because time is all he needs. He's gaining on us.

But Hickory always has a plan.

He unravels the bounty hunter's whip, spins around and lashes it out. Roth blocks the blow. The whip wraps around his forearm, and he just stands there, eyes blazing.

Hickory salutes him and smiles. "Sorry, boss."

He tosses the whip handle. It catches on a passing chandelier, snagging Roth like a fish on a line, yanking him back, taking out a whole line of Leatherheads behind him as the train speeds on. He doesn't manage to free himself till he's hanging over the last carriage.

He rolls and tumbles, clings to the end just in time.

Hickory's given us one hell of a break.

The train speeds into a different, high-vaulted corridor. We're on the second carriage now. Smoke and steam trails through the air around us from the engine car up ahead. Two more jumps and we're there. Dad's limping badly, soldiering on. The girl's holding her own in a fist fight with a bounty hunter, having lost her gun. Hickory sprints ahead and drops out of sight between the carriages. He's gonna separate them, and it's a good thing, too, because Roth's charging toward us now, bowling over any Leatherheads stupid enough to get in his way. He'll be on us any second.

The carriage jerks. We stumble. Hickory's done it. The engine car and first carriage are already pulling away. The girl disposes of her bounty hunter with a roundhouse kick, and the three of us make the jump, our longest yet. Dad cries out when we land on the first carriage, nearly slips over the edge, but I grab him. He's sweaty, shaking, face screwed up in pain.

"What's wrong?" I ask. "Are you hurt?"

"I'm okay," he says. "Compared to your singing, it's nothing."

"Okay, that's—wait, *what?* You hate my songs? 'Bluebird in the Basement'? 'Scraps for Tea'? 'The Coconut Song'? 'Rat Poo in the Corner on a Sunshiny Day'?"

"You're many things, Jane." He winks at me. "A great singer ain't one of 'em."

I've never been so insulted in my life, which is saying something.

"We'll discuss this later," I tell him, and he chuckles.

We clamber down to Hickory by the carriage door, us and the girl. Watch as the rest of the train slowly falls behind us. Three meters. Five meters. Sparks from a

dangling chain scatter along the tracks between the carriages. Seven meters. Ten. I'm about to breathe a sigh of
relief when we see him—Roth—coming right for us. Dad
and Hickory empty their guns, spraying him with bullets
that might as well be flies. The *rat-a-tat-tats* blast our ears.

"He can't make it," I say.

"He won't try it," the girl says.

But he does.

THE SPIRAL ROAD

Inside the carriage now. Some sort of armory, I think. We lock the door behind us just as the force of Roth's impact buckles the rusty roof above our heads.

He made it.

"Great," I say, "what now?" But nobody has a chance to answer because there's a noise outside, a whistling squeal.

Hickory says, "Uh-oh," and the train takes a hard, constant right, the force of the bend throwing us against the left-hand wall of the carriage. A blur of stone through the small, circular windows at our backs. Across from us, nothing but empty space. I leap-crawl toward them, fog the glass with my breath and wipe it clear again. "Oh, hell . . ."

We've hit the spiral road.

An enormous domed ceiling above us. A cavernous circular shaft below that's so wide and deep I can't even see the bottom. The train-tracked road winds down its side, past arches and doors, and the whole shaft's lit by thousands of torches flickering to life, looping around and down, getting smaller, getting hazier, till they're swallowed by the gloom. We're headed the same way. Already picking up speed, sparks flying. Hickory and Dad were right. We're gonna derail.

"You know, it really is a pity you destroyed the brakes," I tell the girl.

And that's when Roth swings down in front of the window.

He smashes his fist through the glass, grabs my tunic. The rancid air hits us and we choke and cough. My skin prickles. My eyes water. Dad tries to pull me away. The girl punches Roth's arm, but it's useless. He pulls me right up to the broken window, right up to his half-masked face, the air between us alive with his heat-shimmer breath. His icy eyes meet mine for just a second, and I can feel it. I know it. Somehow he knows I have the key.

I shove a leg against the wall and push. My tunic tears and we all fall back in a spluttering heap. Roth slips out of sight, back to the roof, heading for the door, but Hickory's already there, throwing his weight against it. The door shakes and trembles as Roth tries to pound his merry way inside. The grimy window shatters. The metal bulges. I'm about to leap over there when I notice a pool of blood on the floor. A dark red stain spreading down Dad's leg. A gash across his thigh.

A Leatherhead must've got him with its blade.

I try to help him but he swipes my hand away.

"It's nothing," he says, even though it's definitely something. "Go. I'm fine."

I throw my weight beside Hickory and tell the girl to hurry. She's searching through the crates stacked further down the carriage. She finds another gun, checks the ammo. The door shudders. The lock snaps off and rattles past our feet. Roth forces the door open, just enough to get an arm in. I figure we're all done and dusted when the girl shoulders her rifle and heaves something else from the crate. Loads it, rests it on her other shoulder and aims.

It's a freakin' bazooka.

"Move," she shouts, and me and Hickory dive clear.

She pulls the trigger the moment the door flies open.

The rocket blasts through the carriage, a loud streak of smoke.

Roth ducks just in time and it explodes on the wall outside. A deafening blast that rocks the carriage and topples Roth off the back. I cheer and shove a fist into the air, but then I swear because we haven't lost him yet. He's bouncing along the tracks, clinging to the dangling chain. Hauling himself closer, hand over hand, back toward the carriage.

Doesn't this guy ever stop?

"Come on," the girl yells, throwing the bazooka aside. She opens the forward door and we're assaulted by wind, smoke and steam. The chugging of the train. The whoosh-whistle of passing archways. There's a coal compartment on the back end of the engine car. The girl leaps onto it, turns back, leans down between the carriages and tries to disconnect them.

Hickory runs to help, telling us to move it or lose it.

I lend Dad a shoulder. We run-stumble after them as the train tilts dangerously, the right-side wheels leaving the tracks for a second before crashing back down. We bump into a barrel. Dad cries out, tightens his grip on my shoulder. Glancing back, I catch sight of Roth's hand reaching up through the sparks, grabbing onto the train. I pick up the pace.

We're almost there. Three meters. Two. We get to the door and Dad collapses. I try to pull him up, but he pulls me down instead. Shouts in my ear, "Jane. No."

"Yes," I shout over him. "You can do it. You have to." Roth's heaving himself up now, getting to his feet. The girl aims her gun at him, thinks twice. Aims it down between the carriages instead.

"Get your butts over here!"

She pulls the trigger. The chain snaps, cables fly. Both she and Hickory reach down to unlatch the carriages. I tell them to wait.

"Elsa," Dad shouts into my ear, but I can barely hear him over the noise. "When I found—in the Grip, she—a hiding place—river—of waterfalls."

Why is he talking? We need to go, need to jump. The pin's been pulled, jolting the carriage. We're slowing down, falling back. Hickory and the girl scream at us, tell us to jump.

Roth's charging through the carriage now, but Dad just pulls me closer.

"You need both keys—open the Cradle. Find Elsa's— only way—the second key."

He's saying goodbye, I can see it in his eyes. "No, Dad—"

"Get to the Cradle—slow you down. I love you, Jane."

Then he catches me off-guard. Cries out, stands up, lifts and throws me from the carriage with every bit of strength he can muster. I catch a glimpse of Roth leaping over a barrel. Of sparks and the spiral road speeding by. Of Hickory and the girl reaching out, grabbing me, pulling me onto the bed of coal. We fall back, a flurry of limbs and shouting.

Hickory has me in a headlock. The girl's arms are around my waist. I try to break free, but it's useless. We're already speeding away from the carriage. All I can do is watch as Dad turns around in that shrinking rectangle of a door to face Roth, and it's like I'm back at the base of the Sacred Stairs with the mayor holding me back, watching his men go after him with guns.

Only this is worse. Much worse.

Dad throws himself into Roth. I feel the fear, the panic, the anger swelling inside me.

The engine car trembles. I can feel the spiral road shaking beneath us.

I'm causing another quake. Another *big* quake.

And we're surrounded by stone.

That's when she does it. When the girl pulls out a knife and digs it into my bandaged palm, reopening the wound, spilling the furious tide. She grabs my left wrist with both hands and holds it over the back of the train. My blood catches in the wind. The pain's excruciating, blinding. Somehow I can feel every drop of blood hitting the spiral road, ripping it apart in our wake. Feel the stone bending the tracks behind us, making Dad's carriage sway—first toward the void of the spiral, then rocking back the other way.

It lurches, tips, derails. Crashes and skids along the outside of the road, smashing through pillars and archways, exploding through the stone.

Hickory pulls us back. We collapse onto the coal, and I catch a glimpse of Roth through my tears, leaping from the carnage with Dad slung over his shoulders. Through an upturned window, out of sight. Our little engine car sways, but sticks to the tracks. We chug on, careering down the spiral, away from the wreckage. I bunch my tunic into my fist, try to stop the blood, try to stop crying, but I can't. Roth still has Dad, and this chase ain't over yet.

That's the problem with spirals. What goes around comes around.

The road beneath the derailed carriage is littered with rubble and debris from the crash, and we're looping round the bend, already speeding toward it. Hickory and the girl yell, "Hold on," and we crash through fallen chunks of rock, through boulders, over scraps of metal. I'm thrown forward through the coal, my head hits something hard, and then—

Nothing.

SECOND INTERLUDE

NOT THE GIRL SHE REMEMBERS

Time does strange things in the Manor, Winifred told Violet before she climbed the Sacred Stairs. *Be patient with Jane. She will not have aged as we have aged. She will not have suffered as we have suffered. Nevertheless, she needs your help. Protect her.*

Violet locks the door now. Takes a breath. Turns and runs again. Her hands are shaking. Adrenaline, yes, but something else too. Winifred warned her about the first few kills, but she never said there would be so many. None of this feels real. The prison camp. The train. John. Roth. The Cradle and the keys. Seeing *her* again. Those eyes again. This strange hero of her childhood who left without saying goodbye.

Jane Doe in the flesh.

Hickory is behaving but Violet cannot take any chances. Jane is slung over his shoulders, bandaged hand soaked red, dripping a trail. Winifred once told Violet that Jane would be the greatest weapon she would ever use. And the most dangerous.

Spill her blood, she said. *But only if you are ready to face the consequences.*

Violet will need to dress the wound properly, sooner rather than later.

"Any idea where we're going?"

"Away." Hickory opens another door. "Anywhere. Fast."

They fled the train as soon as it had slowed enough to jump, just as the Leatherheads appeared, firing flares and rifles. All they can do now is run and hide. Violet prays the rooms are shifting. But she cannot forget the wildcard, the traitor, the fiend. Even if they outrun the army, she will still have to deal with Hickory. He may have fooled Jane, but Violet knows this trickster's secret. Knew it as soon as she saw him in the cage. Now she adjusts the coil of rope looped around her shoulders, a handy find from the engine carriage.

She considers her options. In the end, there is only one.

Detain and question, Winifred would say. *Take control.*

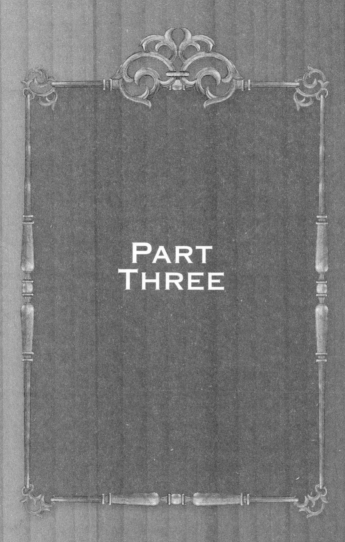

PART THREE

WAKING

Eyes open on the girl, leaning over me, wiping my cheeks with her sleeve. Blurry. Fuzzy at the edges. When she speaks it sounds like three people talking at the same time.

"Don't worry. We're off the train. We're safe."

We're in a candlelit room. A small chamber carpeted in black sand. I'm sweating and shivering, tongue tripping over words. Something about Roth taking Dad. How we need to find him, get him back, even though he said I'm a terrible singer and he never liked my songs.

I try to move. The girl grabs my shoulders and gently holds me down.

"Calm down," her voice echoes. "Try to relax. Hold this."

She tucks the key into my hand, just like Winifred did once upon a time. I manage to untangle a sentence then. Something about a door back home, I think. I'm not sure why.

"Rest," the girl says, and I sink back into the soft, soft sand.

Back to my floating cocoon.

THE FATE OF BLUEHAVEN

"We enter the Manor at will. We enter the Manor unarmed. We enter the Manor alone."

The girl's picking at a fingernail with her knife, sitting in the black sand that probably isn't supposed to be here, just like the snow and the grass and the hungry freakin' forest. She glances up at me, and I quickly pretend to inspect a tear in my tunic because I've been staring at her for a while, and I'm sure of it now: she's unmistakably Violet. Her eyes, her chin, the way she chews her tongue when she concentrates. But then there's, well, everything else. Her height, hands, and shoulders. The girl has boobs, for cripes' sake.

"Before you passed out again," she says, "you told me to prove I'm me. Asked what used to hang above our front door. The Three Laws. And if that doesn't convince you, I know you can't swim, you taught yourself to read and write, and you once made me promise not to tell anyone about the time my mom locked you out of the house, and you got stuck trying to climb back through the basement window because a stray dog started humping your leg."

"Oh." That's all I can say. Like I've just been told it's raining outside or something.

I try to stand, but my legs are too wobbly.

"Take it easy," the-Girl-Who's-Violet-After-All says. "You need to rest."

I swear and slip back to the sand. "How long was I out?"

"A few hours, maybe." She gouges a chunk of grit from her nails. Sniffs it and shrugs, flicks it away. "Do you remember what happened?"

"You mean do I remember derailing a train? No, not at all." I hold up my freshly bandaged hand. The sucker's definitely gonna scar. "I remember this, though."

"Yeah," I-Can't-Believe-It's-Violet says, "sorry about that. Ran out of options."

"Since when was slicing my hand open an option?"

"What was I supposed to do? Take on Roth with a coal shovel and a gun? I cut you to give us some time, and it worked. We got away."

The scene has played out in my head a hundred times since I woke up. Dad in the carriage, falling behind, left behind, slung over Roth's shoulders as the train crashes.

I lost him again. I can't *believe* I lost him again. Part of me wants to scream and shout and punch the walls, but if I start I doubt I'll ever stop. Besides, I'm too weak.

"You mean *some* of us got away," I say.

I-Still-Can't-Believe-It's-Violet finally stops picking at her nails. "Your dad chose to stay behind, Jane. He knew he'd only slow us down and he knows Roth will keep him alive so long as we're running around the Manor—so long as we're a threat." She flips the knife, tucks it into one of her boots. "We have the upper hand. We have the first key, not him."

I hang my head. As much as it kills me, I know Giant Violet's right. Finding the second key is the most important thing now. Getting to the Cradle before Roth. It's the only way to stop him, to save Dad, to save everyone, including ourselves. And it isn't just another needle-in-a-never-ending-haystack situation anymore, either. It's a race against an army.

"No sign of him, then?"

"Roth? No. We ran a fair way. I locked every door behind us. The rooms shifted at least once." Violet points at the door beside me. "That's locked, and we'll know someone's coming down any of those—" she points at three dark arches across the room, "if the corridors light up. I haven't got many bullets left but I'm pretty good with a blade. I'm sure we could use the odd booby trap to our advantage, too. And don't worry about Hickory." She nods at the glowing arch beside her. "Got him tied up down there, in front of another locked door. I roughed him up, but I think his ego's hurt more than any—okay, what is it? What's wrong?"

"Nothing."

"You look drunk. You're staring at me."

"Of course I'm staring at you. Listen to you. *Look* at you. You're all . . . old."

"I'm not *old*. I'm pretty much the same age as—"

"Me, exactly, which is a darn sight older than you were a few days ago. How is this even possible? Winifred said time can get all weird in the Manor, but this—this is just—" I plough my fingers into my knotted hair, "I dunno what this is." And then it hits me. "Oh crap, please don't tell me I've been away from Bluehaven for, like, ten years."

"Okay, I won't." Violet pauses for effect. "You've been gone six."

"*Six years?*"

"Calm down, Jane."

"*Calm down?*"

"And stop repeating everything I say. It's irritating. I'll explain everything soon enough, but right now I really think you should rest and—"

"Don't do that. Don't be like Winifred Robin. If you really are Violet then—then we're friends, right? So please, tell me. What happened back home after I left?"

Violet's expression softens. "Strange to hear you call it home."

I sink back into the wall. "Yeah. I guess it is."

Violet huffs out one of those *here-we-go-then* breaths. "The quake that struck during the festival. The night you left. It brought down a lot of homes, Jane. The fire that spread across the island destroyed even more. Broken stoves, they figured. Scattered embers. Many lives were lost. If Winifred hadn't taken control—"

"You mean she stopped Atlas? She beat him?"

Violet nods. "Right after you left, down in the cata-combs. Then she came and found me. Rallied everyone to fight the fire. After we'd all got it under control, she told people they'd got it wrong all those years. Told them you were on our side. That you'd left the island to help us, and if we stuck together, if we trusted you, then everything would be okay."

"She tried to get them to *trust* me?"

"Tried," Violet says, "and succeeded."

No way. "They believed her?"

"Some, yes. It didn't happen overnight. Atlas backed off for a few weeks, but when people realized the Manor wasn't going to open again anytime soon, he started telling people you must have fled to an Otherworld and kept cursing the island from there. He passed around orders to execute you on sight if you ever returned. He even tried to arrest Winifred and take over the museum, but we stopped him. Winifred locked him up."

"Wish I'd been there to see that."

"People were sick of listening to him. With you and John gone—sorry, but I can't call him *Charleston*—with the island still in danger, they found it harder and harder to blame you for everything. Winifred told us about her vision. Her instructions from Nabu-kai. With Atlas out of the picture, we came together and set about rebuilding the island."

"What about your parents? How are they?"

A coldness passes over Violet now. She doesn't seem to know what to do with her hands. "They kicked me out of home after you left."

"They *what?* Why? Because you stopped Atlas from killing me?"

"That. And other reasons. I don't care," Violet says, but any fool could see she does. "I moved into the museum with Winifred. I'm glad they kicked me out. They were horrible."

"Were? Oh no, Violet, you mean—"

"No. They're alive. I just haven't spoken to them in years. Only seen them a couple of times from a distance. As you can imagine, they've never embraced the idea of believing in you. I bet they're driving Atlas up the wall as we speak."

"Atlas? But I thought—"

"Winifred couldn't keep him locked up forever. She banished him to the other side of the island along with Eric Junior, Peg, and about a hundred others. Said if they were against you they were against everything the Manor stood for—even the Makers themselves. Didn't take my parents long to join them. They stick to their side and we stick to ours. Crop yields are pretty much the only thing we share, and even that's got tense. Landslides wiped out a lot of farms in the quake, but we managed to salvage some. Things were going okay, but—" Violet pauses a moment, unsure how to proceed, "Bluehaven's dying, Jane. A few years ago, the crops started to dry up. We can barely grow weeds let alone food, and the sea life's all but vanished. People are starving. I don't know how long Winifred will be able to keep the peace. I think whatever's happening in here, whatever Roth's doing to the Manor, it's catching up with our home, our world. All these weakened gate-ways . . . ours has started rotting away, too. The gateway down in the catacombs is still sealed, but Winifred says it'd be starting to rot as well. I think the Manor's trying to sustain itself by bleeding the Otherworlds dry."

I can't believe all this. Yeah, I've kind of always hoped something bad would happen to Bluehaven one day, but to actually hear it—to know it's been happening for so many years even though I've only been gone for, what, a few days?—it's too surreal to take in.

"Are you okay, Jane?"

"No. I mean, yeah. I guess. I just—six *years?*" I shake my head to scatter the questions cramming my brain. One refuses to budge. "Violet, what are you doing here?"

"Isn't it obvious?" she says. "I'm here to help you."

BEST-LAID PLANS

Turns out Winifred told Violet everything she told me the night I left, when they were heading off to fight the fire. Told her she'd need to help me one day, even gave her the exact date she would enter the Manor. She had seen it all in her vision. Sure enough, six years later, Winifred walked Violet to the Sacred Stairs and said goodbye. It was a perilous climb. Apparently the Stairs are in worse shape than ever these days.

"I've spent the last six years training to be your protector, Jane. Winifred taught me how to fight, how to shoot, how to survive. She even taught me how to drive."

"*Drive?* As in a car? There aren't any cars on Bluehaven. What'd she teach you in?"

Violet shrugs. "Theory. Mainly, though, she drilled me on archery. I'm deadly with a crossbow. I wanted to bring one in here with me, but—well—the Second Law."

"And Winifred never mentioned the Cradle or the keys?"

"First I heard about all that was from your dad," Violet says. "I'd heard the legend of the Makers, of course, but

John was right. The version we tell on Bluehaven is incomplete. I had no idea they left three keys behind. I never would've connected your key to the Cradle. I mean, there must be billions of keys out there in the Otherworlds. And you can't blame Winifred for missing the connection. The flashes she saw down in the catacombs showed her all the things *she* had to do. Her path alone. Setting your quest in motion, training me. If she does somehow know what's going on in here, she never shared it with me."

"Did she say anything about other people coming inside? Is she coming to help us?"

Violet shakes her head. "It was always going to be me. Only me."

Suddenly, she looks more grownup than ever. It weirds me out, but it makes me sad more than anything. The girl who used to run around playing tricks and burning caterpillars has turned into a teenager, an almost-woman, and for me it's been less than a week. I used to know everything about her. Now she's a stranger. Has the girl I used to know gone for good?

"I felt the Manor guiding me the moment I stepped inside," she says. "Guiding me to you. Only took me a few hours to catch up. All I had to do was cut ahead and wait."

"So you got caught on purpose?"

"Easier than tracking you from a distance."

"Why didn't you tell me all this stuff right away?"

"It was obvious you didn't trust Hickory. And I kept my face hidden because I figured you'd recognize me and freak out." Violet runs a hand through the sand, eyes

shifting every way but mine. "Besides, it was strange. Seeing you again. I mean, I always knew I'd see you again,
but when I finally did—I don't know. It's weird. Shut up."

"I didn't say anything."

"I know."

The mother of all awkward silences fills the room.

"So," I finally say, "what now?"

"You tell me," Violet says. "You're the one with the key."

I'm the one with the key.

"Okay." I ease myself up the wall and test my legs. So
far, so good. "Okay." I pace around the room, the black
sand soft between my toes. "Okay."

"Stop saying that."

"Okay." I swing by the candlelit archway beside Violet.
"By the way, you didn't accidentally kill Hickory, did you?
He's being awful quiet down there."

"He's fine. What's the plan, Jane?"

Yes. A plan.

"All right. Dad said we need both keys to open the
Cradle, so—so the plan's simple. We find the second key,
find and open the Cradle, get our hands on the *third* key,
then somehow use the power of the Makers to kill Roth
and his army. Or at least, you know, send them back to—
what was it, Arakaan?—wherever the hell they came from.
We save the Manor, save all the Otherworlds, get my dad
and take him home. Right?"

"Right," Violet says. "So how do we find the second key?"

And then I say it, the most unbelievably strange,

fantastic, terrifying-in-a-good-way sentence I've ever said in my whole life. "We find my mom." I start pacing again, getting the story straight. "Mom and Dad got separated after they found the Cradle, each carrying one of the keys. She was lost in the Manor, he was trapped on Bluehaven, but they found each other in the Grip. On the train, Dad said Mom was hiding somewhere. He said something about a river. I couldn't catch it all. Something about waterfalls, too, and—"

I stop in my tracks.

"I think I've seen it. I think I know where she is."

"What?" Violet stands up too. "How?"

"In my nightmare. I've always had them, Violet. All sorts of bad dreams, but this one's been changing ever since I stepped in here, as if I'm—I dunno—remembering more. My parents were in the water with me—in the Cradle Sea, I mean. We were being swept toward the foundation stone. It's big, like an island. A small island, though. And there were all these monsters under the water—the Specters, Cradle guardians. They were about to kill us."

"People don't usually remember things from when they were a baby, you know."

"Yeah, well, people don't usually cause quakes when they freak out, either. I'd never seen my parents in the water before. Or the foundation stone. *Or* the Specters. It was all new. And then we were back *outside* the Cradle. Mom and Dad were running, being chased by the two Specters that escaped, I guess. Or Roth. Maybe both. I saw them get separated, but then—then the dream changed again, and this new bit couldn't have been a memory because I wasn't with Dad *or* Mom."

I stare at the wall. Images from the dream tug at the backs of my eyes like pictures on strings. Spinning, slowing, slipping into place. "I was flying through the Manor. I saw the river. It isn't connected to the Cradle Sea or anything. I think it's water from an Otherworld, pouring through another weakened gateway." I turn to Violet. "I was flying *down* the river. I saw two big statues standing in the water. Then there were rapids and pillared halls filled like lakes, and a huge waterfall. And I flew down into this massive hall that had *more* waterfalls in it, and then—" I shake my head, try to shuffle another picture into place, "that was it. I hit the water and everything just went black."

I don't tell her about hearing Mom's voice.

That bit's just for me.

"And you're sure it wasn't just a *dream* dream," Violet says. "Made up."

"I know it sounds strange, but it felt—I dunno—different. It wasn't nightmarish at all. I mean, it wasn't nice—all that water, yuck—but now that I think about it . . . I reckon the Manor's been showing it to me for a reason. It *wanted* me to see it."

Violet doesn't look convinced.

"Look," I say, "everyone always talks about the Manor as if it's this living, breathing thing. The Manor chooses who stays, who goes. Draws you in. Guides you. Is it so impossible to think it might *want* us to get to the Cradle before Roth? That it might give us a nudge in the right damn direction? Trust me, Violet, I know it's a long shot, but I bet you my mom's hiding in that hall of waterfalls with the second key. In a cave or—or a secret passage or something. The Manor could be keeping her alive, keeping her young like Hickory."

Suddenly I'm sure of it. My mom is alive.

I reach out to hold Violet's shoulder in a reassuring way, but it feels weird so I kind of shove her instead.

She isn't impressed.

"Come on," I say. "It's something, right?"

She folds her arms just like mini-Violet—the same old sign she doesn't like what she's hearing. But then she puffs a breath through her nostrils—the same old sign she's giving in.

"You're right. Don't suppose you know how to *find* this river, though?"

"No," I say, "but I know someone who might."

I nod at the glowing corridor. Violet's face falls. "You want to take *Hickory?*"

"He's been to the river before. Told me so before we wandered into the forest."

"But we can't trust him. He's—"

"A lying, thieving jerk, I know. And believe me, I'd rather ditch the guy and never see him again for the rest of my life, but the fact remains—"

"Jane, he isn't who you think he is."

She's baiting me with this. There's something I've missed.

"Wait a second, do—do you *know* him?"

"Of course I know him. Everybody knows him. He really didn't look familiar to you at all? There are statues of him all around Bluehaven, or at least there used to be. The school was even named after him." Violet watches me, waiting for that spark of recognition. "He's Hickory Dawes, Jane. The first person to enter the Manor over two thousand years ago."

THE GREAT ADVENTURER

"You're from Bluehaven?" Hickory Dawes doesn't answer me, so I turn to Violet instead. "He's from *Bluehaven?* Our Bluehaven?"

"No, the other Bluehaven," she says. "Of course *our* Bluehaven."

I splutter a few *buts* and *hows* before settling on a *why*. "Why didn't he tell me?" And back to Hickory. "Why didn't you tell me?"

He's black-eyed and bruised, tied up between two man-sized statues in front of a locked door, knees planted in the sand, arms strung up and stretched out either side of him. He hocks a golly and spits.

Violet clenches her fists. Restrains herself. "He was one of the first settlers of Bluehaven. Part of the first group anyway. Says he can't remember the Dying Lands, and I believe him. He would've only been a small boy when the pilgrimage happened."

My mind flicks back to that classroom cupboard. My secret history lesson way back when. "They were fleeing some sort of sickness, right? A plague."

"The Unspeakable Plague," Violet says. "Not much is known about the sickness itself. Early Chronicle entries are light on detail, but we do know it killed millions of people. Cities and villages fell. Our world was wiped clean. Those who survived sought refuge across the ocean. Hickory's people found Bluehaven after a long, dangerous voyage. It was deserted. No buildings, no Outset Square, no Sacred Stairs. But they knew people had been there before. They found cave paintings in the tunnels. Drawings of a lone door standing atop the cliffs."

"The gateway."

Violet nods. "They scaled the cliffs, found the door, touched the stone, but nothing happened. Remains of an ancient temple, they thought. Gradually, it was forgotten. They set about building the town. Carving terraces. Cultivating fields. Living their new lives."

"And this guy?" I ask, nodding at Hickory.

"Well, the settlers may have been vague about the Dying Lands, but they were clear on the date the gateway first opened. According to the Chronicles, it happened sixteen years after their arrival, which means he grew up on Bluehaven. You would have been—what, Hickory? Eighteen? Nineteen?" Hickory doesn't respond. "Anyway, one day he wandered up the hill and never returned. A search party was sent out. A woman, Arundhati Riggs, found his tracks and entered the Manor too. Journeyed to the Otherworlds and returned. Everybody marveled at her tale. Over the years, more and more people were granted entry through the gateway. They built the Sacred

Stairs. The temple around the gateway—the Manor as we see it from Bluehaven today. And they realized the honor that had been bestowed upon Hickory. He was the first of thousands. The fact that he never returned only fed the legend."

She kneels down in front of Hickory.

"I always wondered what became of you," she says. "Even wrote a story about you once in school. And now I know. Hickory Dawes, the Great Adventurer. Liar. Thief. Traitor."

Hickory's eyes twitch. "Got me all figured out, haven't you, little girl?"

"Don't forget, this *little girl* beat you in a fair fight."

Hickory leans in toward Violet, straining against the ropes. "You call it an *honor* being trapped in here? Feeling every person you've ever known slip away from you. Forgetting faces. Voices. Simple things like the feel of the sun on your skin." He shakes his head. "That isn't an honor." He looks up at me now. "*That* is a curse."

"You still could've told me," I say. "You could've helped me. After we found my dad I could've taken you back—"

"To what? An island I don't recognize full of strangers? That isn't what I want."

"Then what do you want, Hickory? Huh? What exactly has been going through your head since you found out I had the key?"

Silence now. Surprise, surprise, Hickory Dawes doesn't feel like sharing.

Violet stands again. "His plan—if you can call it that—was to hand you and the key over to Roth, somehow fool Roth into showing him the entrance to the Cradle, then steal *back* the key and claim the Cradle for himself."

"Good plan," Hickory says. "Up to a point."

Violet ignores him. "John's story on the train changed everything, though. See, Roth let all the bounty hunters believe there was only one key, and that he knew the location of the Cradle already. I guess he figured it'd be easier to keep tabs on people that way. Didn't want anyone else getting their hands on both keys and beating him to the prize. When John said there were *three* keys, Hickory realized he'd been duped. That's why he didn't turn you in after he picked the bounty hunter's pocket—he knew he didn't need Roth anymore."

"You want the Cradle for yourself?" I ask Hickory. "Why?"

"That," Violet says, "he hasn't told me. But you heard him, it's obvious. He hates this place. He wants to unleash the Cradle Sea and destroy the Manor. He's no better than Roth."

"Better-looking than Roth," Hickory says. "Don't smell half as bad either."

I want to punch him. Square in the nose. "You heard what my dad said, idiot. The Manor binds the Otherworlds together—if it goes, they all go. You'd really kill every living thing in existence because of your beef with this place? You're sick in the head."

"Maybe," Hickory says. "Maybe not." He smiles.

"Now, are you two gonna get to the point anytime soon or are you gonna stand around and chat while Roth makes a more lifelike mask out of your pa's handsome mug?"

I step in to kick Hickory, but Violet pulls me back. I figure she's gonna give me the ol' *he's-not-worth-it* line, but all she says is, "I'll handle this." Quick as lightning, she grabs him by the hair with one hand and snatches the knife from her boot with the other. Holds the blade to his throat. "This pointy enough for you?"

Hickory coughs, grunts and grimaces. Then he cracks up.

"What's so funny?" I ask.

"You two. Acting all tough and in control when we all know you need me. Lost little ducklings want a guide to the river." He nods down the passage. "Voices travel far in here. Sorry to hear Bluehaven's gone to hell, ladies, but— hey—what can you do?"

"This should be easy, then," I say. "Do you know where we are?"

Hickory flicks his head at the statues either side of him. There are small symbols carved into their foreheads. Violet asks what they are. I shake my head in disbelief.

"Directions," I say. "Signposts. We're way back near your hideout, Hickory?"

"Different hideout. Old one. Carved these symbols a long time ago."

"And you know a path to the river from here?"

"Good path. Safe-ish path." He tilts his head my way. "Think you're right, by the way. Manor wants us to get to the Cradle before Roth." *Us*, he says, bold as freakin' brass. "Don't suppose you've asked yourself why, though? The things you saw in your dreams. Why the Manor showed them to you. More importantly, why you cause the quakes."

"Hickory." Violet tightens her grip on the knife. "Don't."

His face lights up. "Ah, so *you've* thought about it. Waiting for the right moment to tell her, huh? Didn't want to spring it on her till she got her full strength back?" Hickory *tut-tuts* at me. "Always the slow one, Jane. Been so focused on Violet's past and mine, you haven't even given a second thought to your own."

Violet pulls on his hair again, tilting his head right back. He swallows hard, bobbing his Adam's apple up and down above the blade.

"It's okay, Violet," I say. "Let him talk."

She backs off and lowers the knife. Hickory stretches out his neck, sighs dramatically.

"You and your folks went inside the Cradle. Swam in its waters without dying. Seems it gave you some sort of connection to this place. Maybe you swallowed some of the Cradle Sea. Maybe you made it all the way to the foundation stone and cut yourself on the rock. Maybe Mommy and Daddy let you hold the third key and you tried to swallow the thing—I don't know. Point is, your blood carves up stone." He lets the thought stink up the room for a moment. "Just like one of the Makers, no?"

The name slips from my lips before I can stop it. "Po . . ."

Hickory rolls his eyes. "Not Po, idiot. Aris. Shaper of

stone? Although who's to say there isn't a bit of Po in you as well? Maybe a bit of Nabu-kai, too. Who knows what you're capable of? I bet that's why Roth was having trouble getting inside your head on the train. Never seen that happen before."

Violet shuffles her feet. "I think he's right, Jane, considering everything John said. I mean, if Winifred had known you'd gone into the Cradle, if she'd known about the three keys, I'm sure she would have made the connection years ago but, well, she didn't."

I run a finger over my bandaged hand. Could it really be possible? Is that what Dad was trying to say before Roth got on the train? *Yes, Jane, you were born in the Manor, but the Cradle Sea infected you? A wave slammed us into the foundation stone and some of the Makers' powers stuck to you?* People on Bluehaven always treated me like I had some sort of disease, and maybe they were right. Maybe there is something inside me. Something abnormal. Jane Doe, Cursed One through and through.

"Anyway," Hickory says, "something to mull over on the way. Been a while since I've seen these symbols, but I remember 'em well enough." He tips his head to the door behind him. "You should see what's back there. Very pretty."

Violet's gaze lingers on me. She's waiting to see if I'm gonna freak out about the whole connection-to-the-Manor thing. I nod an *I'm okay*, but the truth is I'm not sure how I feel. Sick? Scared? Confused? All I know for sure is I need to get moving again.

"How far away is it? The river."

"Not far. Getting there's the easy part. River starts at a weakened gateway. Branches off into a thousand channels, many of 'em deadly. You saw it in your dream, Jane. Rapids. Whirlpools. Bet you didn't see the prison camps, though. More than a few. Leatherheads ferrying prisoners and supplies—very tricky. But I can help you. Most importantly, I can get us a boat."

I swallow hard. Far as I'm concerned, the boat seals the deal.

"How can we trust you?" Violet asks Hickory. "After everything you've done."

"You trust that I want to get to the Cradle as much as you." Hickory hauls himself up, grunting against the ropes, standing tall. "That I want to beat Roth even more."

Worst-case scenarios swarm. Tricks, traps, and back-stabbings. I'm beginning to think I'll never be free of this guy. The Great Adventurer. The Great Pain in My Butt.

"So," he says with a smile, "who wants to untie me?"

THE CRYSTAL CAVERNS

We're lucky the door opens inwards because there's about a foot of black sand on the other side. The candles and torches flicker on. My jaw drops. We're standing on the upper landing of a grand, two-story hall that's more beautiful than anything I've ever seen. There are crystals growing from the walls, hanging from the ceiling, sprouting from the sandy staircase right in front of us. White crystals, pale purple crystals, milky blue crystals. Some of them look like swords, others like mounds of coral clinging to the stone. And they're glowing.

"Told you." Hickory stretches and sighs. "Just imagine the world they come from."

"I'm just glad we've finally found something that isn't trying to kill us."

Hickory screws up his face. "Yeah, about that. Don't touch 'em."

"Why not?" Violet's on her guard. Ready to shoot, dive, and roll.

"Not like normal crystals." Hickory snatches a candle from its bracket and tosses it down the stairs into a patch of blueish daggers. As soon as it connects, they make sounds like cracking ice and grow several inches, right before our eyes. "They respond to touch. Anything but other crystals. Some of the corridors ahead are pretty choked."

"Pretty choked? Hickory, you said this path was safe."

"*Ish*. Safe-*ish*. And it is. Leatherheads steer clear, most of the booby traps have either been set off or jammed, and it's the most direct route to the river. Promise you that." Hickory nods at Violet's rifle. "By the way, no guns. Shatter a crystal, pieces go flying. Grow where they land. Blasted a piece into a Tin-skin's mouth once. Wasn't pretty."

"No shooting. Got it." Violet shoulders her rifle and raises her knife again. "But just so you know, I can throw this just as fast. Don't get any ideas."

"Yeah," I tack on.

I decide to lay some ground rules. I have the key. I'm the one who's been inside the Cradle before. It's *my* dad who's been captured. Sure, I've just found out I might have dead god juice swimming through my veins or a bit of foundation-stone grit lodged under my skin somewhere, and I feel like I'm gonna throw up any minute now, but I'm taking charge.

"Stay five paces ahead of us at all times, Hickory. You stop if we tell you to stop, you run if we tell you to run, you slap yourself in the face if we tell you to slap yourself in the face, and you speak only when spoken to."

Even Little Miss Stab-Happy gets a rule.

"While I'm at it, no more hand slicing." I wave my hands around my body. "All this right here—strictly off-limits to knives, spears, machetes, cutlery, anything sharp or pointy." The rule's met with silence, like she actually has to consider it. "Violet—"

"I just think that—"

"*Violet.*"

"Okay, okay, no more slicing."

"Promise."

She sighs, like *I'm* the one being unreasonable. "I promise I won't slice, cut, stab, scratch, or graze you for as long as I live. Now can we get a move on, please?"

There's so much sand on the stairs we pretty much slide down them, careful to avoid the crystals growing on the banister. The black sand is rippled down here, shaped by a long-forgotten, Otherworldly wind. Tiny dunes are heaped at every door. There isn't a footprint in sight. Most of the candles have been swallowed or ripped from the walls, but the crystals light the way. Hickory leads us down a corridor, passing through pockets of white, purple, and blue, even a stretch of pale, glittering pink. It's like walking through a treasure chest.

Apparently we're heading to a small Leatherhead camp at the start of the river, right at the base of the gateway, so we can make sure we won't miss the hall of waterfalls.

"Angry but brief," Hickory says when Violet asks what kind of welcome we can expect. "Only a few Leatherheads. Lightly armed. We take 'em out, pick a boat, float away."

We wind our way through the overgrown corridors, and I actually don't mind the crystals. I count them, look for shapes in them, wonder what would happen if I shoved a bit into Roth's ear, anything to avoid thinking about all the terrible things he could be doing to Dad right now. Torturing him, *reading* him, making his feet spasm and dance. Throwing him in some dark, cold, and lonely cell. Worse, a cell packed with Tin-skins. On top of all that, there's our upcoming river cruise to not-think about, and my possible connection to the Manor.

I mean, why deal with things you're not ready to deal with?

But I can't stay distracted for long. Hickory's already testing my rules. When I tell him to slow down, he walks right in front of me. When I tell him to speed up, he walks too far ahead. Worst of all, he spins around and screams at me right when I'm ducking beneath a crystal stalactite. Violet yells at him, but I keep my cool.

I know what he's trying to do.

"It's not gonna work, you jerk," I say, shoving him along. "Trying to scare me into causing another quake? Why the hell would you want me to cause one in here anyway? We're surrounded by stone, in case you hadn't noticed. Like, mountains of the stuff."

"I'm just curious, is all. What's it feel like when it happens?"

"It feels like shut-up-and-keep-walking."

"Like you're part of the rock? Does it hurt?"

I trip him up and he stumbles into a mound of white crystal on the wall. Only just manages to get clear before a dozen foot-long daggers stab the air. "Did *that* hurt?" I ask.

Once-Upon-a-Little-Violet steps between us.

"You," she points at Hickory, "leave her alone. You," pointing at me now, "watch the walls. If this stuff blocks our path we're screwed. And both of you, keep it down." Flick goes her knife. "Move it."

Hickory draws ahead, a little too far again, but I let him go this time. We enter a rose-colored corridor lined with statues, most of them covered by the crystals. They look like sparkling, people-shaped lumps. I decide to see if I can hold my breath till we reach the last one.

"So what *does* it feel like?" Violet asks. I shake my head. *Nice try. Not gonna happen.* "You'll have to talk about it at some point, Jane. You can't ignore something like this."

"Not ignoring it," I wheeze without breathing. "Just don't want to think about it."

"You're being stupid."

"Probably. But I'm allowed to be." My lungs can't handle it. I huff and puff four statues from the end. "Look, I haven't even got my head around the fact that you're nearly as tall as me now. Actually, are—are you *taller* than me? Wait. No. See, you're wearing boots."

"Jane—"

"I need some time to think, Violet. I'm glad you're here. Really. Just let me get to the heavy stuff in my own time, okay?"

"Fine," she says.

But it isn't fine. Two seriously overgrown hallways later, when we're crawling on our hands and knees and I'm busy looking for animal shapes in the crystals, she's at it again. "This isn't just about you, you know. You're smack-bang in the middle of it all, true, but we're dealing with the fate of all worlds here."

"You're more annoying than you used to be."

"You're dumber than you used to be."

"Maybe I was always this dumb. Maybe you just forgot."

"Cut the crap, Jane. You have this power for a reason, so—"

"Don't call it a *power.*"

"Why not?"

"Because it sounds stupid."

"This . . . *ability,* then. You may not like it, but you can't deny we'll probably need to trigger it again at some point."

"Trigger it? No, no, no. No more slicing. I told you."

"But—"

"My *ability* has almost killed us twice in a few days. Well, twice in six years for you, I guess. But still." I want to turn around and look at Violet, but I'm still crawling and there isn't enough space between the crystals. "Or have you forgotten what happened at the festival?"

"Of course I haven't forgotten," she says. "But what if you could learn to control the quakes? You cause them when you get a bit . . . you know . . ."

"Crazy?"

"I was going to go with *emotional,* but yeah. And when your blood hits the stone during those moments, things really go nuts. It's like it *supercharges* the connection. But what if you could command the quakes without losing your mind *or* spilling blood? It could come in handy, Jane. I mean, you just derailed a *train*. You're a walking, talking weapon."

"It's too dangerous, Violet. You said it yourself, people died at the festival. That's on me. And you know what? It does feel like I'm part of the rock, and it hurts like hell. I feel it tearing apart, every crack. I can't control that sort of—that sort of—"

"Power?"

"Yes. I mean, no. I said don't call it that."

"But if you practice—"

"No," I say again, more forcefully this time. "Look, you say I can cause the quakes because something happened to me inside the Cradle. Fine. But *what* happened? Did we really make it all the way to the foundation stone? If the Sea's so dangerous, why didn't it kill us? Does my dad have the connection too? Does my mom? Will *she* be able to tell us how to find the Cradle entrance? Or what the hell we're supposed to do once we're inside it? I mean, does the third key switch on some sort of ancient machine?"

"I reckon so," Hickory butts in. "Bet there's some infernal contraption in there. Gigantic stone cogs. Paddlewheels to channel the Sea. Turn the key, pull a few levers—"

"The point is," I shout over him, "it's guesswork. We don't know, Violet. *I* don't know. Every answer we get just leads to more questions, and I'm sick of it. So no, I don't want to control the quakes. I don't want to have anything to do with them. No. More. Slicing."

"And if we run into the Specter that caught Elsa?" Violet says. "Have you thought about that? I mean, that was where she was Gripped, wasn't it? What if it's still there?"

"I don't—"

"And what about the fact that Roth read John's mind on the train? Huh? What if Roth saw the hall of waterfalls? What do we do if he's headed there right now along a different path? What do we do if there's a whole platoon of Leatherheads waiting for us?"

"I don't know!"

I shout the words so loudly it startles us both. I didn't realize we'd entered a new hallway. Didn't realize we'd stood up and stopped moving. This isn't like us. Not like me and mini-Violet, anyway. Sure, we could annoy each other, but we never argued about anything serious. Me and mega-Violet's a whole new ballgame.

We're still trying to work out the rules.

"I'm sorry, Jane, but the Manor brought me here to help you."

"So go beat up Hickory again or something."

"I heard that."

"Shut up, Hickory." I glance at Violet's boots. Can't help wishing they were little red ones caked in mud. Familiar boots. "Look, I know this is bigger than me and my parents. And maybe you're right. Maybe I do have this—this *thing* inside me for a reason. Maybe I will need to trigger it again. But if I do, I'll deal with it then. Right now, I need to stay focused on finding Mom, rescuing Dad, and taking them home—wherever *home* is for us now. Thinking about this any other way . . . it's just too much, kid."

I brace for another argument. Violet just stares at the sand. I set off again, following Hickory's tracks, and that's when she says it, quietly, almost to herself.

"Don't call me kid."

A TIGHT SQUEEZE

By *not far* Hickory obviously meant *really, really far* because I swear we trek for hours. The Manor feels less and less Manor-ish with every turn. Older, rougher, more like a cave system than anything. A mineshaft riddled with holes and fissures. Enormous pillars of milky blue crystals breach walls and crisscross hallways, skewering the odd Leather-head skeleton. Torn leather suits and gas masks hang from their bones.

We trudge through the sand in silence. Hickory deci-phers his symbols. Violet chews on her tongue. I think about Mom. Seeing her, hearing her voice, telling her everything that's happened. I wonder if she has my eyes. I couldn't quite tell from the dream. I even start a list of questions I want to ask her:

1. *Are you okay?*
2. *Do you recognize me at all?*
3. *How have you avoided being caught all this time?*
4. *Do you cause quakes when you go a little nuts?*
5. *Can I have a hug?*

6. *Do you like coconuts?*
7. *What happened after you were separated from us?*
8. *Do you still have the second key? Please say yes.*
9. *How do we find the Cradle?*
10. *How exactly do we get rid of Roth and save the Manor?*

I go through the list a thousand times and then I get all nervous about meeting her. What if she doesn't know who I am? What if she doesn't believe me? What if she isn't even there? What if the Specter broke her mind and killed her? What if Dad got it all wrong and—

No, I tell myself. She's alive. She'll be there.

She has to be.

I think about the Makers, too. Do I really believe everything Dad said about them? How they fooled the Gods of Chaos and created the Cradle Sea, paving the way for life in every world? Seeing and believing in the Manor isn't enough because that only proves the present, not the past—that the Manor exists, not how and why it was made.

How can I believe it when all I have to go on are stories?

Say you find a loaf of bread. You can touch it, smell it, eat it, but the bread alone doesn't tell you anything about the baker. Someone tells you it was an old man. Ten more people agree—a hundred, a thousand—but what if they're lying? What if they've all been fooled and the baker's actually a ridiculously talented donkey? Dad said some legends change every time they're told. What if the truth about Po, Aris, and Nabu-kai has been twisted into a lie?

What if the story's all wrong?

A stifling breeze kicks up that smells like rotten eggs. The black sand deepens, transforming entire pillared halls and corridors into undulating dune seas, all of it eerie in the crystal glow. One of the massive halls we pass is filled with crystals so big they look like gigantic, glittering trees. They make me feel as small as the specks of sand, but it's an awesome sight to behold, no mistake. Some of the corridors are filled with sand almost all the way up to the ceiling, and we have to shovel armfuls out of the way before we can squeeze through. It's exhausting work, made no easier by the crystal-laden chandeliers half-buried in our path, or the stinging grains of sand cast up by the wind. Violet tears strips from her cloak to wrap around our noses and mouths. Our eyes are left to fend for themselves. We only have to backtrack once when Hickory takes a wrong turn, but we have to wait at four intersections while he paces and tries to remember the way. The crystals have destroyed some of his symbols.

Getting there's the easy part, my butt.

"Admit it," I shout as we dig our way through another corridor, "we're lost."

He shouts something back that gets lost in the howling gale, but I figure it must've been "We're close" because we soon lose the wind entirely and find ourselves caught in a mini-avalanche. The sand slips away beneath us, and we tumble down into a small room.

Violet lands on top of me. Time snags us for a moment. We don't speak. She breathes into my face and

I breathe into hers, and it's weird because the wasps start swirling round my gut again, but they feel different this time, like they don't have dirty great stingers. They're just buzzing.

Why are they buzzing?

"Sorry," Violet says at last, scrambling off me so fast you'd think she'd landed on a giant slug.

Yep. She hates me.

"Nobody move," Hickory says.

We've come to a booby trap stalled mid-cycle. Huge metal blades and axe-like pendulums poke from the ceiling, walls and floor in varying heights and lengths, all of them overgrown with rose-colored crystal swords and daggers. Some of the blades are embedded in these massive pillars of white crystal, too, growing from floor to ceiling.

It's a frozen freakin' meat-grinder.

"Hickory, I swear to—you're the worst guide ever."

"We're exactly where we need to be," he says. "Just a little more crowded than it used to be." Mashed-up clumps of Tin-skin carcasses are skewered to the floor, walls and ceiling. There's barely a crawl-space to be seen. "Just gotta pick our way through. Carefully."

Violet unshoulders her rifle, ditches her cloak. "Forward is the only way."

The awkward moment between us seemingly forgotten, she takes the lead, crawling and sliding through the trap. Feeding her rifle through first, considering every move. I go next, and Hickory follows soon after. It's like we're moving through a giant, life-or-death game of pick-up sticks, twisting and contorting, helping each other through.

Stop. Careful now. Watch your feet. Little to the left.

Violet's free. A clean run. I'm squeezing through a dip in the sand when Hickory tells me to freeze. My back's about to nudge a crystal spear. He scoops sand out from under me till I can fit. I nod back at him. Hell, I even thank him. I also tell him he's still a knob, just to remind him where things stand, and that's when I smack my head into another crystal.

"Ouch," I say. "Uh-oh."

The crystal cracks and grows, dislodging a giant blade. I duck and roll as it swings. The blade smashes through a pillar. Crystals burst. Shards scatter and swell. A Tin-skin corpse goes flying, and the whole trap comes to life.

"Go, go, go," Violet shouts. As if we needed to be told.

Naturally, there's a lot of scrambling and swearing, but we make it. Just. I leap for a gap up high, narrowly avoiding an oncoming shaft of crystal. Hickory stays low, sliding under a blade. We hit the sand on the other side at the same time. But we're not safe yet.

Hickory yelps and claws at his hair. Something's growing on my back, stabbing like a hundred needles. I cry out, and Violet's on me in a flash, tearing a lump of crystal from my tunic and crying out herself as it pierces her fingers. The lump's as big as a melon by the time it hits the sand. Hickory's clump of hair lands beside it, now buried in a ball of white crystal, and they're still growing. We step back, trembling.

Violet shakes her head at us, sucking a drop of blood from her finger. "Unbelievable."

"I'd say that went pretty well," I say. My back feels like it's been scraped by a grater. Thankfully, it isn't bleeding. "I mean, you know. Could've been worse."

Hickory glares at me. "No more mistakes. Things are about to get tricky."

As if everything we've been through so far has been a breeze.

UNDERSTANDING WINIFRED

"You've gotta be kidding me."

We're standing at the edge of the biggest chasm I've ever seen. The cliffs are enormous, stretching into the gloom above us, below us, way off to our right. Open archways dot each cliff face, flanked by flaming torches. Dozens of thin stone bridges span the gap high and low. Crude and crumbling things. Many of them have collapsed entirely. The one in front of us only juts out a few meters and ends in a mound of glinting purple. Other pockets of far-flung crystals cling to the bridges and cliffs around us, glowing like lanterns in the dark. There aren't that many, though. The black sand and crystals have reached as far as they can for now.

This part of the Manor belongs to an Otherworld of water.

We're too high up to see the river flowing through the chasm. Even the torches down there are nothing more than misty orange smudges. We can just make out the gateway, though, lurking in the shadows way off to our left, hundreds of stories high but no wider than a house.

It's even more pockmarked than the snowy gateway was. Thousands of water jets stream through the rock in a constant shower of rain, feeding the unseen swell far below. The torches closest to the waterfall flare on and off, caught in an endless battle to stay alight.

"Hickory, how the hell are we supposed to get down there?"

"We climb."

"And you didn't mention this earlier because . . ."

"Wouldn't have changed anything. You wanted the quickest way to the river—this is it. Walls are pretty rough. Plenty of grip. Leatherheads fixed some ladders closer to the bottom." He puffs his bottom lip at me. "Don't tell me the little Doe's scared of heights."

"Heights, I can handle. It's what's waiting for us at the bottom that scares me."

"Don't worry," Violet says. "Fall from this height, you'll die the moment you hit the surface. Won't even get the chance to drown."

"Oh, that's comforting."

"You could always try quaking up a nice set of stairs for us."

"I'm gonna pretend I didn't hear that."

Violet shrugs. "Climbing it is. Hickory, you first. We move quick, we stay quiet, and we keep an eye on those archways. Any Leatherheads spot us, we'll be sitting ducks."

Hickory eases himself over the edge. Violet pauses. Chews on her lip for a second, lowers her voice.

"Hey . . . remember the time you had to climb up the house opposite Mrs. Jones's because she let her dogs loose on you? And she started throwing bottles at you, and I stopped her by—"

"Setting fire to her curtains through her front window," I say. "Sure. She threw rocks, though. I had bruises for weeks. That was only a few months ago actually."

"Oh yeah." She stares into space the way people do when memories come rushing back. "I suppose it would be for you." She shakes the memory away and starts climbing.

"Hey," I say, and her head pops up again. "Thanks for helping me back there. With the crystal on my back and all."

She actually smiles then. It's still sort of a sad smile— nothing like the beaming grin I used to see on mini- Violet—but it's sure as hell more than anything she's given me so far.

She opens and closes her mouth a couple of times, as if she wants to say something but doesn't know how. All she gets out is a "Jane" and an "I" before Hickory tells us to get moving, which kills me because once she starts climbing again all I can think is *Jane, I* what? Jane, I have a cramp? Jane, I'm sorry I was so pushy before? Jane, I like you?

No, shut up, brain, it's Violet.

Still. A thank you and a smile.

Progress is what it is.

Dad would probably freak out if he knew I was dan- gling over a gazillion-foot drop right now, but it turns out I'm the best climber here. Isn't long before I'm in the lead, testing hand- and foot-holds, finding the best line down. Climbing barefoot hurts after a while, but at least I can wriggle my toes into the cracks. I take us on a zigzag down, from archway to archway, so we can rest our arms and legs. The first few are blocked by crystals. The others are deserted.

"Hey, how long do you reckon the river is, anyway?" I ask as we check one of the corridors for a staircase, a ladder, some other way down. "Where do you reckon it ends?"

Hickory shrugs. "How long's a piece of string?"

"What string? I don't have any string."

"He means," Violet says, "he has no idea how long the river is. Personally, I don't think it has an end. It could keep flooding new parts of the Manor till it drains the world it came from dry. Or until we find a way to heal the Manor, of course."

"So it's underwater, right? The gateway. On the other side. What good is that?"

"It probably hasn't always been underwater," Violet says. "Otherworlds evolve. Rivers change course, sea levels rise and fall, people build dams and flood valleys. But you're right. That world's cut off to us now. Unless there's another gateway there."

"So Bluehaven isn't the only place with more than one way into the Manor?"

"Of course not. Winifred used two gateways in *The Crusade of Sallis-Ur*. Some worlds might even have three or four. Anything's possible."

We find a stairwell a little further down the corridor. Hickory says it should take us down a couple of levels at least, so Violet takes the lead, rifle at the ready. She tells us to keep it down but I'm getting a real kick out of chatting to her again.

"What's she like? Winifred, I mean."

"You know what she's like."

"No, I don't. We only hung out for, like, an hour. Didn't exactly have time to chat about our favorite things. You must know her pretty good by now."

"I don't think anyone really knows Winifred."

"You never talked about normal stuff?"

"Nope."

"You just trained."

"Yep."

"But you've read all her books—"

"Which detail the legend, not the woman. Most people bang on about themselves for ages in their Chronicle entries. How amazing they are. How they were worshipped like gods. Winifred sticks to the facts. Her actions and victories speak for themselves."

"Do you know how she got her scars?"

"Battles, escapes, close shaves. Booby traps and torture. You can't do the things she's done and come home unharmed."

"Do you really think she never saw all this coming?"

"I told you. She only saw flashes of her own path when she touched the symbol."

"Yeah, but what if she was lying?"

Violet sighs. "You still don't trust her. After everything she's done."

"Well, everything she's done hasn't exactly been trustworthy. I mean, she started all this, remember? If she hadn't handed me over to Atlas that day—"

"You'd still be back in the basement and Roth would've kept looking for the Cradle until every gateway fell apart and all the Otherworlds were destroyed."

"No, but—well—yeah, I guess," I say. "She should've told me you were coming, though." Violet glances back at me and I shrug. "Would've been nice to know, is all. I could've waited somewhere for you. We could've planned a proper breakout for my dad. Could've avoided so many bad things." I jab a thumb back at Hickory. "Like meeting this guy."

"I heard that."

"Shut up, Hickory," Violet says. "Everything happens for a reason, Jane."

I roll my eyes. "Ugh, don't you start. You sound exactly like her."

"You say that like it's a bad thing."

"All I'm saying is if I was her, I would've done things differently. I would've told me everything—told *us* everything—right from the beginning. Before the festival even started. She says she only saw her path in the flashes? Fine. But her path doesn't run along all on its own. Nobody's does. Our paths cross and collide, unravel side by side. Hers, mine, yours, Hickory's, Mom's, and Dad's. Not to mention the paths of everyone on Bluehaven. Winifred should've told us all exactly what we were in for. Made things easier for everyone."

The stairwell winds on. The candles on the walls flicker as we pass.

"Would you?" Violet asks after a while. Her voice is so quiet I figure she's talking to herself, but then she speaks up. "Would you do things differently? Say you were the one who touched the symbol under the catacombs. Saw flashes of the horrible things to come. But after them you saw something beautiful. You and John, happy and healthy in a new home. And if you knew this final, perfect vision could only come true after suffering through all the misery and hardship first, would you really do things differently? Would you change the path the Makers had laid out and risk that happy future, or would you let the bad things happen?"

I don't know what to say. She's right. I wouldn't just let the bad things happen. I'd do anything I could to make sure they did. Just like Winifred has.

"*Terrible but necessary, Jane.* Isn't that what she told you all those years ago in the boatshed, back when all this started? She said the same thing to me again and again. You may not like her methods, but you have to trust her. Even if she did see more than she's letting on, you have to believe there's a reason for all of this."

Freakin' puppet strings. Now it's my turn to sigh.

"Did she actually tell you she saw a happy ending?"

"No," Violet says. "But I choose to believe she did. Why else would she sacrifice so much? Why else would she still have faith in the Makers? So much faith in you?"

A question pops into my head then. Spills into the stairwell before I can suck it back. "Do you have faith in me?"

Violet leaves me hanging till we reach the bottom of the stairs and head back toward the chasm. "Yes," she says, but it's impossible to miss the silent *I guess* dangling at the end of it, clinging to the word like a shadow.

THE RIVER

"There she is," Hickory says.

We're lying on our stomachs now, beside another broken bridge, and we can finally see the river coursing between the cliffs far below. A crooked structure crouches in the shadows near the base of the raining gateway, built over the water, stretching between the two cliff walls, shrouded in mist. The Leatherhead camp. A haphazard network of rickety wooden platforms and ladders scale the cliffs either side of it, clinging to the rock, connecting the archways like some vertical maze.

"See? Cells down on the left. Quarters in the middle. Dock's over on the right."

I count five tiny boats tethered to the jetty.

"The place looks deserted," I say.

"Might be patrol time," Hickory says. "Or nap time. Either way there'll be guards."

He takes the lead again, climbing to the first of the wooden ledges a short way down. It's only a few planks wide. Fixed to the rock with rusty metal clasps and dodgy, knotted rope. We take each section one at a time. The platforms and ladders creak and groan.

"Careful," Hickory says. "Sometimes they post Leatherheads up these parts."

"How do you know so much about this place again?" Violet asks.

"Second hideout of mine used to be over there a ways." Hickory points at a bunch of arches further along the cliff. "Small place, nothing fancy. Way before the river came through. Figured if I was here I could keep watch on all the bridges. Better chance of spotting someone. Then Roth and his army came. Knew they were no good. Avoided them for ages. Gate rotted. Water flowed." He gets a good grip on the wall with one hand, lifts up his shirt with the other, revealing a particularly nasty scar on his side. "Then they found me."

"They shot you?" I ask.

Hickory nods. "Led 'em on a merry chase. Couldn't run forever, though. They dragged me down there. Tortured me. Kept me a while before carting me off to Roth's lair."

"And your life as a bounty hunter began."

"Look, I didn't *choose*—" he starts to say, but then the rope lashed around his platform snaps. He only just manages to get a decent hold on the cliff before the planks slip away and plummet down to the river, crashing through other platforms as they fall.

We freeze, eyes sweeping over the distant station. Every black window, every open door. The cages and coils of barbed wire. Still, not a Leatherhead in sight.

"They would've heard that," I say. "Surely."

"Keep climbing," Violet says. "And no more talking. Something isn't right here."

By the time we reach the bottom my arms and legs feel like jelly. My hands and toes like mangled crab claws. We're about fifty meters downriver from the station on a wider, sturdier platform that's only inches above the river. The others breathe a sigh of relief. Me, not so much. The water's black as ink, gurgling under the boardwalk.

We duck behind a couple of barrels on the board-walk, and Violet starts flapping all these hand signals. Fingers pointing, twirling, walking on air. When she's finished she waits for a pointy, twirly response, but me and Hickory have no idea what she means.

"Come again?"

Violet screws up her face, holds a finger to her lips. It's pointless, really, because even if there were Leatherheads here they'd never hear our voices over the raining gateway, especially from this distance. She starts the signal all over again, gives up three moves in.

"Forget it. You two stay here. Don't move till I give you the all-clear." She creeps along the boardwalk, edging closer and closer to the empty cages beside the compound, into the cloud of mist. I ask Hickory if he thinks it's an ambush.

"Not really their style," he says. "But I've been wrong before."

Violet steps inside the main two-story shack, disappears.

We wait, and we wait, the river gurgling away beneath us. Hickory taps his fingers on the barrel, sucks at his teeth and sighs.

I can't take it anymore.

"Come on. I'm going to help her, and if you want to make sure the key doesn't fall into the wrong hands you'd better come too."

Hickory tries to grab me, but I give him the ol' slippery fish routine and duck around the barrels. He swears at me but follows. I squish myself into the wall, stay as far from the water as I can. We step into the mist, past the empty cages, our skin damp and beady from the spray. All's dark and deserted inside the main shack. Barrels, crates, upturned benches. Half a broken stepladder's hanging from a hole in the ceiling, leading to the upper floor. There are half-a-dozen or so dead Leatherheads in here, too.

Slashed bags of bones, the lot of them.

"What happened here?" I almost-shout over the gush of the weeping gateway.

"No idea," Hickory says. "But it must've happened a long time ago." He picks up a gas mask by its trunk. An old skull clatters to the floor. He barely glances at it, runs his fingers round the neck of the mask instead. "Ripped clean off."

"By what?" I spot a severed hand in the corner. An inch of bone poking from a leather glove. I take a step closer to Hickory. "Specters can't do this, right?"

"Don't think so."

"So what did it, then?"

He tosses the mask aside. "Best if we don't find out."

Violet's in the next room, crouched over a pile of clothes or something in the corner. Claw marks scar the walls. Water drips from the ceiling. She spins around, rifle first.

My hands shoot up. "Whoa, whoa, it's us."

"You were supposed to wait for a signal."

"Felt wrong sending you in here alone," Hickory says. "Had to drag Jane along."

"*What?* That isn't true, you lying sack of—"

"It doesn't matter," Violet says. "Come take a look at this."

They aren't clothes in the corner. It's a mound of sodden—

"Skin," Violet says. She snags a bit on the end of her rifle, holds it up. The stuff's pinkish, translucent. "Something shed this. A creature, what, five feet long? Six? I think these bits," she jiggles one of the dripping sleeves, "are arms or legs."

"Do you reckon it killed all the Leatherheads?" I ask.

"Maybe," Hickory says. "Or killed some and drove the others away."

"These frilly bits here might be gills," Violet says.

"You mean it came from the water?" I say. "Through the gateway?"

"The holes are big enough for a fish egg," Violet says. "Or a tadpole."

A noise outside gives me goose bumps. A bird-like chirrup and a froggy croak gargled into one, followed by a tiny splash.

"Riiight," I say. "I guess it did us a favor, clearing this place out and all, but let's not hang around to thank it. Violet, did—please put that thing down, it's disgusting." The skin makes a wet, slappy sound when it hits the floor. "Did you check out the boats?"

Violet nods at the door leading to the dock. "Through there. We're good. First, I think we need disguises. Could buy us a few precious seconds if we're spotted."

We head back into the first room, pick the Leatherhead suits clean. It doesn't take us long to clad ourselves in the foul-smelling strips, ill-fitting as they are. We wrap them over our clothes and bare skin, help each other tear and tie them off. We forget about the gloves because they're way too big, with too few fingers anyway, but we grab a gas mask each. I make sure there's a gap in the leather round my waist so I can get at the key in my pocket.

"Brilliant," I say once we've finished. "We look nothing like them."

"Believe it or not, this isn't the first time I've tried this," Hickory says. "Long story. Didn't end well." He shakes his head. "We're way too short, for starters."

"There must be Leatherhead children out there somewhere," Violet says. "Maybe they'll just think we're kids."

"Technically, we are kids," I say.

Hickory flexes his arms. "Speak for yourself."

We step outside onto the dock, into the downpour. Scan the river. The coast is clear. No bad guys. No pink-skinned creatures. Nothing but the churning black water.

Hickory and Violet figure the boat on the far side of

the dock's best, where the water's slightly calmer. The motor's all smashed up like the others but the sides aren't as dented. They go on about it like it's a real find, but as far as I'm concerned the thing looks like a metal coffin. We can only find one oar so Hickory rips up a plank from the dock to use instead.

Violet unties the boat, holds it steady. I take a step back. Creepy as the shack may be, leaving this place by boat suddenly seems like a really bad idea.

"What if I fall in?"

"I'll jump in and get you," Violet says.

"What if we all fall in? And get sucked down one of those whirlpool thingies."

"Then we hold our breath and hope for the best."

"But what if we get sucked down a really long stairwell or a hallway and—"

"Comes down to this," Hickory says. "Do you want to find your mom or not?"

Oh, hell. He's right. I hate that he's right, but he's right.

There are three seats in the floating coffin. Benches front, middle, and back. I plant myself in the middle, hands gripping either side, gas mask in my lap. Hickory holds the boat as Violet takes the front, facing forward. The boat lurches and sways. I clench my eyes shut and pretend I'm sitting on a rocking chair. Back in the Hollows' basement. Anywhere on dry land.

"Tell me when we're about to cast off," I say, eyes still shut tight.

"Jane," Violet says after a while. "Look at me."

"Can't."

"Why not?"

"I'm busy."

A sheet of icy water drenches my back. I yell and spin around, ready to punch Hickory—and see the Leatherhead station shrinking into the distance behind him. The current's already spiriting us gently through the chasm, beneath the bridges and the corridors and the colored dots of crystals glowing like stars high above. Hickory smiles at me.

"Now," he says, "let's go find that key."

DRIFTING

The chasm branched off into three corridors a while back. I chose the middle one, a gut feeling more than anything. We cruise in silence under a vaulted ceiling, weaving between the chandeliers hanging just above the surface. Pools of reflected candlelight ripple as we pass. Drips and drops echo from the surrounding archways, all of them black. Violet steers when we need it, but the current does most of the work, a swift and steady thing.

Hickory's sleeping now, curled up beneath the broken motor. I'm beginning to think he made the river sound extra dangerous just so we'd be sure to bring him along for the ride. Apparently we have a good few hours before we reach the next Leatherhead station.

I keep my eyes peeled for anything that looks familiar, something I might've seen in my dream. Nothing stands out. I make adjustments to my suit, which is tight and clingy in all the wrong places. Try on my gas mask. Unsurprisingly, it smells terrible.

We drift on down the river, and I decide to start another conversation with Violet. Partly to stay calm but also because she catches me staring at her twice and you can only compliment someone's rowing skills so many times. I quiz her about Bluehaven, and she seems happy to answer. No, she hasn't worn red boots in years. No, there hasn't been another Manor Lament since I left, but Atlas probably holds his own to mark the occasion. Yes, all the fisherfolk still hate me, and Eric Junior's probably most definitely still a jerk.

Speaking of jerks, I also ask her about Roth, because I've been thinking.

"There's gotta be a way to kill him, right? Everyone says he's immortal, but *something* hurt him. Or some*one*. He isn't exactly a picture of health, you know?"

"I don't know, Jane," Violet says, stifling a yawn.

"I bet my mom's worked it out. All that time in here? She'll be able to help us for sure. You wanna hear the questions I'm gonna ask her? I've culled it down to ten."

I only make it to five before Violet interrupts me.

"Do you really think she'll be there?"

"Yeah," I say, "I really think she'll be there."

Violet dips her oar into the water. We skirt round another chandelier. "I'm really sorry to say it, Jane, but— but I don't. And I'm not convinced the key will be there either."

"Why? All this everything-happens-for-a-reason talk and you reckon the Manor just—what—took me on a mental scenic tour of the river for the fun of it?"

"I didn't say I don't believe there's a reason for this. I just don't want you to pin your hopes on Elsa being there, that's all. She split a long time ago, and this is a dangerous place."

"She didn't *split*. Besides, Hickory managed to survive in here."

"By joining the bad guys." Violet shrugs. "Kind of."

"Oh, so you think my mom's a bounty hunter now?"

"No, Jane." She rests the oar across her lap, twists around to face me. "Okay, you said you saw a couple of statues, and then you went shooting down the river over rapids and across lakes and down a big waterfall and then everything went black."

"Yeah. So?"

"So you're terrified of water. What if everything went black because you got scared and—and woke up before it showed you exactly what you were supposed to see? What if you only saw the *beginning* of the path? And don't forget about the Specter. Elsa was caught. Gripped. You need to prepare yourself in case—well, in case—"

"She isn't dead, Violet," I say. "I know it. She'll be there, and the key will be too."

Violet turns her back on me again. I figure that's it, game over, we'll never talk again, but then she tilts her head and says, "We never used to argue this much, did we?"

"Not really," I say. "I mean, there was that time you set fire to my bedsheets. That was a fun way to wake up."

Violet laughs. "I'd forgotten about that. Well, you'll be glad to know I have those impulses quite under control now, thanks to Winifred."

"Oh no. What did you do?"

"Nothing."

"Come on, tell me. What happened? Let me guess. You set fire to her study? That nice weapon case she has in there. Or—wait—you didn't set fire to the Great Library, did you?"

"No," Violet almost-shouts, as if that's the most offensive thing I could've said. Then she clears her throat and says, "Okay, yes, but it was only a small fire."

"Why the hell would you set fire to the library?"

"I didn't mean to do it. Okay, I did, but—so it was about a year after you left. We were doing some research, and it's always so dark down there, so I figured I'd lash a few torches together and make a really *big* light—just so we could read better, of course—"

"Of course."

"And then the torches kind of—"

"Exploded?"

"Right. Because I guess I poured a little too much oil over them."

"Accidentally."

"Yes. Accidentally. Absolutely accidentally. I didn't burn myself, but the books around me weren't so lucky. Winifred came running down the aisle, put the fire out with her cloak, and it was fine. Well, not *fine*. She punished me. Fifty laps jogging around the library. It's a big place, remember, and I was only nine at the time. I wasn't allowed to touch anything with an open flame for a whole year."

"Wow. So all the candles and torches in here must be

doing your head in, huh? Lighting up and snuffing out all around you. Magic fire. A pyro's dream, right?"

"I'm not a pyromaniac," she says, a little too forcefully. "I'm fine. Completely cured. Nothing to worry about at all." She twists around again, dumps the oar in my lap. "Here."

Oh crap. "You want me to row?"

"It's easy, Jane. We drift too far to the right, you paddle on the right. We drift too far to the left, you paddle on the left. The current will take care of the rest. You can do it."

"Yeah, no probs." Big probs. Many probs. I wouldn't trust me with a toy boat in a bathtub. "I'll just row the boat. Down the creepy black river. And not drown us."

"Yell out if there's any trouble. I haven't slept in days. Need a rest."

Violet tucks herself into the space at the front of the boat, curls up like a cat. I grip the oar and straighten up. I can do this. I have to do this. She watched over me after I got knocked out on the train.

"Okay," I whisper. Eyes forward. Be at one with the oar. Little dips, left and right. Let the current do the work. "Jane Doe. Captain Doe. Row, row, row your boat, gently down—"

"You okay there, *Captain?*" Hickory says behind me, and I almost pee my pants.

"Damn it, Hickory. I'm good. Fine. Everything's— crap, what was that?"

"Calm down. I just moved back to my seat."

"I am calm. Completely calm."

Hickory sighs. Dips his makeshift oar into the water. "If you say so."

The river flows, the Manor rolls on by. All those empty archways leading who-knows-where, hiding who-knows-what. Violet doesn't stir. Poor girl's fast asleep already.

"I think it's sweet, by the way," Hickory almost-whispers after a while.

"What is?"

"You and Violet."

"Me and—wait, you were *eavesdropping?*"

"We're in a tiny boat. Hard not to. But I think it's great. You're a girl, she's a girl—"

"You're an idiot."

"Hey, don't take your frustration out on me. If you like her, just—"

"I don't *like* her." I check to make sure Violet's still sleeping. Praise the Makers, she is. "Not like that. It's Violet, for cripes' sake. I don't think about her that way."

"Then why'd you tell her she was pretty?"

"What? I never told her—" Oh no. I did tell her she was pretty. In the bounty hunter's cage. I'd forgotten all about it. "But. But she had that scarf. I didn't know."

"Don't worry," Hickory says. "Best to get these things out in the open."

"Just—" I clench my fists, lower my voice, "shut up and row."

We pass another chandelier and I briefly consider stabbing my face with a candle. I can't believe I told her she was pretty. I mean, it's *Violet*. But wait. No. Maybe she didn't hear me. It was noisy in the cage, right? Squeaky wheels and all? Maybe she thought I said *pity*. As in, *Gee, it's a pity you got captured.* Yep. That's what I'll tell her if she ever brings it up.

"I think you're right, by the way," Hickory says. "About your mom. She'll be there."

"Yeah, well, you're not going anywhere near her. New rule. You have to stay six feet away from her at all times. Actually, you're not even allowed to look at her. Or the second key. And as soon as we find her, you're out of here, pal. Banned from the group."

"Banned from the group?"

"Yep. Banished. We won't need you anymore. My mom can lead us to the Cradle entrance. *She* can help us open it. *She* can help us cross the Sea to the foundation stone in the center, and when we get there, the third key will be ours, not yours. You've lost already."

I can tell Hickory's watching me. I feel his cold gaze boring into the back of my head.

"You're wrong about me, you know," he says.

"Oh, so you're *not* a lying, conniving jerk? You *don't* want the Cradle so you can tear the Manor apart? You *didn't* kidnap a bunch of people and take them to Roth's lair? By the way, how many people died because of you, do you reckon? Rough estimate, huh?"

This shuts him up. I glance back, expecting another death stare, but he's gazing down at the water instead, lost in the reflected candlelight. He actually looks sad, and I feel like I'm seeing the real Hickory again. The Hickory

I haven't seen since the shack, when I told him all about my life on Bluehaven. No lies. No glib remarks. Just a deflated, broken, lonely guy.

"How, then?" I ask him. "How am I wrong about you?"

He snaps out of his daydream, shakes his head. "Forget it."

"No," I say. "I want to hear it. I mean, it must be exhausting, Hickory, keeping up the whole Mystery Guy Act. Just tell me. What's the big secret?"

But I've lost him again. He just paddles, here but not here, eyes glazed in a thousand-yard stare. I wait. And I wait. Then I let it go, too tired to play these games.

We paddle together in silence. Time slips away as swift and sure as the current. Violet sleeps.

Then, after who-knows-how-long, Hickory starts humming something. Soft. Sad. Somehow familiar. I don't think he even knows he's doing it. I know he'll stop if I turn around, so I sit tight, keep paddling, trying to figure out where the hell I could've heard the tune before. And it hits me. Suddenly, I'm skipping through the red-leafed forest again with Hickory by my side. I'm singing "The Coconut Song"—I still can't believe Dad hates my voice, but what does he know about music anyway?—and Hickory's singing about a girl.

A girl called—what was it? Willow? No, F-something. Fi—Fo—Fa—

Farrow.

I stop paddling. Hickory stops humming. Maybe he figures I'm onto him. I consider asking about the song, about the girl. Who is she? Who *was* she? A childhood sweetheart from Bluehaven? A girlfriend? Obviously, he hasn't forgotten *every* face from his old life, unless all he remembers is the name. I'm about to turn around, call him out, tell him I know something he doesn't want me to know—

But I miss my chance.

The boat glides round a corner and shoots down a few short rapids. The corridor's much wider now, and balconies dot the walls, streaming water. We pass under a rope bridge slung over the river. There's a dark lump tangled in the ropes.

A dead Leatherhead, caught like a bug in a web.

"Next station's coming up," Hickory says.

We fly through an archway, and I see them, standing either side of the river up ahead. Two half-submerged statues with their swords held high over the water, tips touching.

The statues from my dream.

"This is it," I say. "I saw this. This is what the Manor showed me."

The corridor ahead forks into three smaller passages.

I shake Violet awake. She sits up, alarmed. "What's wrong? Are we there?"

"Yep," I say. *Don't look at her, idiot, you told her she was pretty!* "Um. You'd better take this." I hand her the oar. "We need to go left. And we better hold on tight."

OPEN NIGHT AT THE
CASKET BUFFET

This surging broth. These pummeling waves. The roar of wind and water. We splash around corners, scrape along walls and shoot over staircase waterfalls—always that moment of weightlessness, a turn in the stomach, a yelp and sudden drop as we slap back to the whitewash, only to be carried swiftly away again. I'm terrified, sure, but focused too, the path to the hall of waterfalls unravelling so clearly in my mind it's like I'm back in the dream.

I know exactly where we have to go.

I shout directions, guided by feeling as much as memory. Hard right. Left. Straight ahead, nice and easy. We've only got one shot at this. If we miss a turn, there's no going back.

Balcony waterfalls soak us to the bone. We duck under toppled columns and slip around broken statues. Stone heads like boulders. Giant hands reaching from the water. We splash into a lake, and it's exactly how I remember it. An unseen ceiling. Pillars disappearing into darkness. A distant, gurgling roar, like a giant drain. There's a whirlpool in here.

"Head right," I shout. "Right, right, right."

The water's choppy. The whirlpool tries to suck us in, but Hickory and Violet steer us clear. We join a new current and make it to the far side of the lake in no time.

"That way." I point. "Third arch along."

And we're back to the rapids of the hallways and corridors. We're getting closer, I can feel it.

"Left, left," I shout, "we're nearly there," but as soon as the words leave my mouth we hit a stone head. The boat lurches. We spin, miss the turn, and shoot off to the right instead.

"Hold on," Violet screams.

We soar over another waterfall and hit the rapids again two seconds later. The force of it bounces me backwards. I should land on Hickory, but Hickory isn't there.

I look back. He's dangling from a chandelier above the falls—must've been flung up there as we shot over the edge. I can just hear him shout, "Wait!" over the roar of the rapids, but then we round a corner and he's gone.

"Duck!" Violet shouts.

A low arch. We shoot through it into darkness. The boat drops out from under us. We hold on tight, spinning round and round, down and down, slamming and scraping against a wall. It's a spiral staircase. We pop from the bottom like a cork from a bottle, skip along the surface like a stone. Shaken, drenched, and gasping.

This new corridor's wider, lit by a few torches on the wall. The water's calmer but just as swift. We call out to Hickory again and again. Scan the black water.

He's nowhere in sight.

That's when we notice the skins floating in the water. There's more snagged on the torch brackets just above the surface. A little further on, the water's thick with them.

"Uh-oh," I say. "Not good."

Violet points her rifle downriver, at the wall of darkness fast approaching. The torches down there have been ripped from the walls or swept away by the water. "Keep your arms and legs inside the boat," she says quietly. "Don't make a sound."

"But we have to head back somehow and pick up the trail to the—"

"*I said be quiet.*"

The darkness swallows us. The roar of the flushing stairwell fades to a growl, and I wonder why it is that whenever you need to be extra quiet your breathing gets extra loud.

A tiny splash in the dark. Something knocks the boat.

"They're here," Violet whispers.

Another two bumps rock the boat, and then we hear it. The soft chirrup-croaking all around us. Slippery, scraping sounds, too. I'd like to think we're safe so long as we stay in the boat, but the creature back at the station shed its skin on dry land, which means we're kids in an open casket. Snacks on a floating dinner plate. We spin around a corner in the dark. The current picks up again. A distant growl gets louder, probably another set of stairs ahead.

But first, three dots of light. Candles on a chandelier drifting closer.

Shapes emerge. Violet crouched up front. The empty candle brackets on the walls. And there, not far below them, the creatures. Dozens of them gliding through the water all around us, their tails like slithering snakes. We float under the chandelier and with the brighter glow comes the details I'd rather not see. Gills. A pinkish gleam. Swollen pouches of skin where their eyes should be. Flashes of teeth and claw and forked tongues flicking. Rings of strange frilly things around every neck. Webbed feathers made of skin that bristle and twitch.

Why aren't they attacking us? What are they waiting for?

Violet goes to hand me the plank—a weapon now, not a paddle—but it's unwieldy with the rifle. She fumbles it at the last second. The plank knocks her seat. Not much of a noise but more than enough. A creature leaps from the water and smacks, full-bodied, into the side of the boat. Then another, and another. We rock and almost roll. I clench my eyes shut and think *rocking chair, rocking chair,* but it doesn't help one bit. Then the biggest splash and thud yet rocks the boat—not side to side like the others, but back to front, up and down.

One of the creatures has leapt into the boat. It's sitting right behind me.

I can hear it breathing. Smell sour milk and rotting fish. I open my eyes and Violet's staring back at me, holding a finger to her lips. She points at her eyes and shakes her head.

It can hear us, but it can't see us.

She aims the rifle at the creature behind me. I lean forward, slowly, sticking a finger in each ear, getting ready for the blast. The creature's tail hits my side, snakes round my stomach. The breathing becomes a hiss, a snarl, and I shout, "Now! Shoot!" and Violet pulls the trigger.

The creature's blown from the boat along with my eardrums, but I can't worry about that now. The creatures attack from all sides, leaping from the water, trying to scramble aboard. We're surrounded by a frenzy of snarls and chirrup-croaks. Whipping tails and whitewash. Violet empties her rifle. I grab the plank and start swinging.

Don't notice the staircase until it's too late.

The boat drops away beneath me, dragging my guts down with it, but this time I'm not holding on. This time I go flying through the dark, about to take a swim with the creatures.

THE NEST

Staircase waterfalls are the worst, especially the several-tiered ones. I'm airborne. I hit the water. I'm airborne. I hit the water. Swept away, blasted out, dunked and tumbled again. I steal breaths when I can, but they're shallow. Water. Air. Water. Air. Water. Water. Water. Where's the air? The staircase must've ended. I'm being swept through a flooded corridor.

I need air I need air I need—

Air. Lots of it. I've been shot out into a pillared hall. I'm flying—flipping—falling down, down, down. I catch a glimpse of flaming torches. Wooden platforms. Another indoor lake rushing toward me. *Where's the boat? Where's Violet? I'm screwed. All alone.*

I hit the surface hard and shoot under, bubble-washed and dazed. I'm sinking, suspended in the dark, just like in my dream, but there's something different about this water, something strange. It's thick, soupy and warm. My eyes sting when I open them.

Something grabs my arm. I fight it, try to get away, but the grip tightens. Five fingers, not a claw. It's Violet. Her arm wraps around my chest. I can feel her legs kicking so I kick too, and before I know it we're half-sprawled over a low wooden platform, coughing and spluttering, wiping stringy bits of slime from our eyes.

I feel in my pocket for the key. Still there. Still safe.

"I don't suppose there's any point telling you to calm down," Violet says beside me.

The jetty's trembling. I'm causing another quake.

"Uh-oh. Not now . . ."

Gotta think happy thoughts, but I can hear the creatures all around us. Snarls and chirrup-croaks. They're dropping down the waterfall behind us, spilling from an archway near the ceiling, an upstairs gallery that seems to wrap all the way around the hall. One of the creatures lands on the back of our upturned boat. The rest dive into the muck and disappear.

We pull ourselves clear of the water, take in the scene.

A forest of pillars and jetties. A network of tall ladders and wooden platforms fixed like treetop balconies, multiple levels of them, sagging rope bridges connecting them all. Rotten wood. Frayed rope. Clumps of skin. Chandeliers glimmer in the darkness above. Torches burn on every pillar. The hall's enormous, but I can just make out a jumbled heap of cages, shacks and sheds built against the far wall, soaring right up to the gallery. We're in an old Leatherhead stronghold. Another abandoned station.

"Um." Violet's lost her gun. "Any bright ideas?"

"Head for the station," I say. "Don't get eaten."

We run. Creatures leap from the rotten broth, landing on the jetties left and right, their pinkish skin so pale it's almost see-through. They dart alongside us, behind us, tails stiff and pointed, webbed feathers bristling. Ten creatures. Twenty. A whole pack on the hunt.

The jetty splits into two paths. Violet takes the left. I want to follow, but a creature lunges from the water and snaps at my heels, so right it is. The jetty lurches. One of the pillars beside me cracks. A chunk of stone breaks free and splashes into the muck.

Happy thoughts, Jane. *Coconuts. Dad. Violet.*

Where is she?

The jetty sways. I leap for a ladder and scramble up as fast as I can. A rung snaps. The bottom half of the ladder falls away beneath me, but it doesn't stop the creatures. They leap from the collapsing jetty and climb the surrounding pillars like cats up a tree.

There's a platform above me. A rope bridge. I pull myself up and run. The bridge bounces beneath me, woven handrails swaying like skipping ropes. I find a long-dead Leatherhead slung over the platform on the other side. A machete still clutched in its hand. I pry it loose and hack at the ropes behind me till they snap. The bridge collapses, taking three creatures down with it.

But I'm not out of this yet.

The creatures keep on coming. Leaping from the water. Running along the other bridges. Climbing the other pillars. Streaming in from the arched gallery lining the walls.

The place is overrun.

I bounce and leap toward the station. Swinging the machete, cutting ropes. When I find myself cornered I climb another ladder to the next level up. A dizzying height. Catch a glimpse of Violet far below, swinging a torch, sprinting to the station. She's nearly there. The water all around her is tinged with red. There's something down there. Something *in* there.

Three bridges later, I'm on the final stretch, sprinting toward a doorway at the top of the station, creatures snarling at my heels. I want to run faster but the bridge is too unstable. I'm halfway across when the ropes make whipping sounds.

"Uh-oh."

I ditch the machete, hit the deck, and hold tight. The bridge splits clean in half right beneath me, and I swing—down, down, down—holding on tight. The creatures fall. My feet nearly hit the foul-smelling red slop, but a tangle of rope stops the bridge from swinging any further. I'm jerked back, dangling inches above the surface.

Not slop.

Eggs.

Millions of them. A mass of creature-spawn clustered in the water, all around the station, up the walls.

This is the creatures' home, their nest.

And we've run right into it.

"Not good," I mutter. "Very gross."

Violet shouts my name, already inside. I climb the fallen bridge like a ladder. One story, two stories, three. Reaching for the platform now, I grunt, haul myself up—

And come face to face with a set of snarling teeth.

A forked tongue. A bristling ring of webbed feathers.

The creature lunges. I drop back down and swing to the underside of the bridge. Some of the creatures below have sensed me again and they're leaping from the egg muck, climbing the ladder-bridge. I'm trapped. I look around for something, anything to help me.

There, a single rope dangling behind me.

And over on the station, one level down. Second floor. A window.

All I have to do is leap and swing.

The creature on the platform smashes its head through the wooden planks right above me, gnashing its teeth. I launch myself backwards, twist mid-air, grab the rope and swing, soaring over the egg-slop and the creatures snapping at my heels. Honestly, it feels amazing.

I miss the window, of course. Unfortunate miscalculation.

Instead, I crash through the wooden wall beside it— "Crap!"—and straight through the floor beyond—"Damn it!"—before landing in a heap one story below.

Violet's kneeling right in front of me, wide-eyed and open-mouthed, rattled as hell. "Hey," I wheeze.

"Hey," she replies. "Um. Perfect timing. Thanks." I stare blankly at her and she glances beneath me. "It was about to eat me."

I've landed on one of the creatures. Squashed it. Broken its neck. I yelp and scramble off it. "Well, that was . . ." Lucky. Accidental. A fluke. "I mean, yeah, I meant to do that."

"Of course you did." Violet almost-smiles.

A thump and chirrup-croak behind me. Violet's eyes bulge wide, and I spin round. Another creature's standing in the doorway. Hissing, bristling, ready to strike. It leaps into the room and—THWACK. Hits the floor, dead. My machete's lodged in its back.

A second later, Hickory dives into the room. "Shut the door, shut the door!"

Violet leaps forward and throws her weight against it, slamming it shut on two more creatures mid-pounce. I barricade it with a heavy metal crate.

The creatures pound the door. The wood cracks. Won't hold much longer.

Wincing, puffing, I help Hickory to his feet. "Not bad for an old man."

He grimaces. "You're welcome."

Violet wrenches the machete from the creature's back. "Follow me." We weave across the room, under the me-shaped hole in the ceiling, around the piles of junk. "Have to get to the gallery." She scrambles up a ladder in the corner. "Find a door and hope the rooms shift."

And so begins our scramble upstairs. Climbing ladders, opening trapdoors, slamming them shut. Dashing across rooms and barricading doors with barrels and crates. Nothing holds the creatures back for long. We slip on bits of egg muck. Wade through clusters waist-deep. By the time we burst out of the station onto the arched gallery, the creatures have doubled in number. They crawl over the roof, around the walls, hissing their tongues.

"There," I shout, pointing at the closest door. "*Go, go, go!*"

We sprint along the gallery. The door's locked, but my trusty key sorts that out in a damn jiffy. I shove the door open, step into the roaring darkness beyond—

And my toes feel nothing but air.

I'm teetering on the edge of something. Hickory and Violet pull me back from the edge just in time. We slam the door behind us and huddle against it, watching in wide-eyed wonder as the candles and torches flare to life all around us, lighting up the dark.

We're standing at the edge of another broken bridge, only a meter away from a hundred-foot drop. But we're not back at the chasm. We're in a tall, circular chamber. And there are waterfalls, dozens of them, pouring from arches and balconies below us, beside us and above us, some of them tumbling from such impossible heights they're merely sheets of fine mist by the time they hit the violent whirlpool of water surging around the bottom.

"This is it! We found it!"

The hall of waterfalls. We've made it at last, but where do we go from here? We're trapped. Stranded. There are no stairs leading from this cracked and slippery ledge.

The whirlpool far below spits and swirls. The door trembles at our backs.

The creatures aren't giving up.

I scan the archways for any sign of Mom, but the few that aren't gushing water are empty. The place is deserted. I shout over the roar of water. Tell her we're here—we need her—come out. I can feel the panic rising again. The ledge shaking and crumbling at my feet. The quake's building again. Violet yells at me, tells me to stop, but I can't.

"She's here! She has to be!"

The door shudders at our backs again. A claw slashes the wood between my head and Hickory's. He screams in my ear, "We need to go. Climb around the walls right now."

"We can't leave," I shout. "We need *her*, it's the only way."

More snarls and chirrup-croaks, way up to our right. Some of the creatures have found another way into the hall. They're twitching their webbed feathers at us from another broken bridge. One of them leaps onto the wall, starts crawling down toward us. Others follow.

But that isn't the worst of it.

Something else is coming, too.

There, far beyond the creatures. A pinprick of strange, white light—soft, crisp, and cold—shining from an archway at the top of the chamber, glowing brighter and brighter.

I stare at the light, captured by it like a moth to a flame. Is it Roth? A troop of Leatherheads? But then it comes, that dawning realization, like a kick to the guts.

This is something bigger. Something worse.

"Specter," Hickory says, shrinking away from the light. "No, no, no . . ."

Talk about a rock and a hard place.

The white light shines brighter, filling the hall. I expect the creatures to scatter, but they don't. They're still coming for us, leaping from ledge to ledge, scrambling down the walls. And why wouldn't they? They can't see the light. They have no idea what's coming.

"What do we do, Hickory?" Violet shouts.

I scan the empty archways again, my gaze dropping to the whirlpool once more, that swirling void. I know exactly what we need to do. Where we need to go. As much as I hate it—as much as I fear it—the Manor has already shown me the way. Violet was right.

My mom isn't here. This isn't the end of the path.

"We jump," I say.

I take Violet's hand in mine. Entwine my fingers through hers. I grab Hickory's hand, too, because he's come this far with us. Maybe he really is supposed to be here, after all. He nods at me. I turn and nod at Violet. Incredibly, in the face of so much danger, she smiles, outshining the Specter, filling me with a different kind of light, warm and glowing.

"See you on the other side, kid," she says.

And as the door crashes open behind us, we jump.

THE SPECTER

We fall and fall and hit the water so hard my whole body aches. We're sucked into the whirlpool at once, straight down the gurgler. The force of the current rips Violet and Hickory from my grasp. I bounce off a wall and flip end over end, dragged deeper and deeper into this black hell. The noise is deafening. The terror absolute. This was a mistake. I won't survive this. I can't. *You're gonna die down here*, I tell myself, *all alone*. But then my head smacks into something—a wall, a passing statue, who knows?—and everything changes.

I can still feel the pain, the terror, the swell sucking me down, but I can *see*. Dad's right there, hanging in the water nearby, just like in my dream. I reach out to him, kick my legs. I want to hold him one last time. Tell him I love him. Tell him I'm sorry I failed. I shape the words in my mind and cast them out into the water. Mom's there too, floating in the dark right beside him.

I tell her I wish she'd been there. I wish I'd found her. I wish, I wish, I wish.

Let go. Her voice comes to me again. Soft, whispered.

That eerie, underwater groaning echoes through the water. Tentacles of white light wrap around my ankles, my waist, and throw me against a wall.

The force of the impact drives the last gasp of air from my lungs.

Mom and Dad have vanished. The bubble-wash calms. The current fades.

The Specter rises before me, a beastly, blinding light. Shifting shapes and ghostlike. Ethereal. But I can just make out a pair of horns. And four legs. And the tentacles aren't quite tentacles at all, but long tendrils of light streaming from its sides, curling with the ebb and flow of the water. It's staring at me with its white-fire eyes. Staring *into* me, through me.

It's about to Grip me. Trap me in that place of nightmares. Fulfil its duty as a protector of the Manor, a Guardian of the Cradle of All Worlds.

The Cradle.

The key.

Lungs burning, I take the key from my pocket and hold it out. The Specter growls, so deep and loud it reverberates through the water, through my flesh, my bones, my very soul.

But it doesn't Grip me.

If you want to save the Manor, help us. I cast these words out into the water, willing the Specter to hear me. *Let me go. The creatures are coming. Buy us some time.*

The Specter floats a tendril of light over the key, around my hand. A spasm rattles my lungs, my throat. I shove the key back into my pocket and tell the Specter to make up its damn mind already. *Tick-tock. In case you haven't noticed, I'm drowning here, buddy.*

The Specter nods and retreats, disappears so quickly down the corridor it's as if it were never here at all.

The darkness returns. The bubble-wash roars. The current sweeps me away again and my whole body convulses, desperate for air. I think my spine's about to snap.

But then the pain begins to fade. The spasms ease. I stop fighting, overcome by an irresistible sense of calm. So this is what it's like to drown.

What was I so afraid of?

THE TIDE UNLEASHED

"Is she dead?"

"She's alive. Come on, Jane. That's it."

"They're coming. Get her up. We need to go."

Eyes open on the girl, leaning over me, wiping my forehead with her hand. Fuzzy at the edges again, fading in and out. The floor's trembling beneath me. My quake's still going strong.

"Violet?"

"Yes. It's me, Jane. Don't worry, you're safe."

"No, she isn't," Hickory shouts. "Help me clear this stuff."

Violet helps me up. "He's right. We need to go. Right now."

I lean against her. We're standing on a balcony. Behind us, a corridor of whitewash splashing at our heels. In front of us, a long candlelit hallway. Patches of strange, crusty white stuff on the trembling floor, sparkling slightly under the candlelight. Hickory's further down, trying to fight his way through a wall of egg-slop blocking our way forward.

"You found me?" I mutter to Violet.

"Hickory did. Fished you from the water just in time. What happened? We saw the light. Were you Gripped?"

I shake my head. "No, I—"

"Are you seriously swapping stories right now?" Hickory shouts. "Hurry up!"

We step up the pace. Violet parks me by the trembling mass of jelly-eggs and digs in with Hickory, elbows deep. He's half-buried in the stuff already, going nowhere. There's just too much of it. He yells at Violet. She yells back. I'm not exactly sure what they're saying because my mind's drifting again. I look around at the trembling Manor walls, and the rapids back down the hallway, and hope to hell the Specter's helping us out, flying around the hall of waterfalls from creature to creature, Gripping as many as it can. Even if it is, it probably won't be able to take them all out. There are too many.

We need to stop the creatures, but how?

Let go.

It was just a dream—a dream of a dream—but that doesn't change the fact that I saw something, felt something, heard something real. My parents in the water. My mom. I guess she's been with me all along, speaking to me, telling me what I have to do.

It's time.

I unwrap the bandage around my palm. "Violet, give me your knife."

"What? Jane, you can't stop these things with one knife."

"Yes—" I hold out my hand, "I can."

She realizes what I'm saying, takes a moment to believe it. Even Hickory stops digging through the muck and stares at me.

I stand as tall as I can manage.

Violet hands me the knife. She looks speechless, stunned, but grabs a strap of my Leatherhead get-up and pulls me close. "Go nuts," she says, and slaps me, hard.

I wasn't expecting it, but I can use it. The sting on my cheek. The shock. I bottle it up, turn, and stumble back toward the water. I breathe hard, feed the frenzy, fill the bottle even more with everything that scares me, every thought that makes me mad. The praying mantis and the weasel. Atlas, Peg, and Eric Junior. The Manor Lament. Winifred blowing up the tunnel. Booby traps, Tin-skins, and Leatherheads. Swinging chandeliers and carnivorous trees. The prison camp. The train. The crystals. The river. The creatures swimming our way right now.

And Roth. Imprisoning my parents. Holding a knife to Mom's stomach. Making Dad's feet dance. The sight of him. The deathly reek of him. His half-mask.

Those eyes.

Roth. Roth. Roth.

I let go. Uncork the bottle. Spill the furious tide of terror and rage. The stone around me trembles and cracks. The quake gets stronger, louder. I'm nearly at the balcony now and I can see the creatures coming to get me. Leaping through the water, climbing along the walls.

I grip the knife as tight as I can. Hold the blade to the wound and slice. The pain tears me apart, but only for a second. This time I rein it in, focus it, channel it through my hand.

I drop to my knees and skid. Slam my bloodied palm down on the stone.

And I can feel it. Everything. Every claw on the wall getting closer. Every vibration on the rock as the creatures swim through the water. But I'm not just feeling the stone, I *am* the stone. Every block. Every crack spreading out from my palm and coursing along the floor, over the balcony, up the walls and across the ceiling. Every enormous chunk breaking free and falling into the water. I am the cave-in. The collapse. The end of the line.

The power's incredible. All-consuming. I force my fury down the corridor and smother any creature I can, sealing the way. But the power's too strong. I can already feel it slipping away from me. Feel the cracks spreading above me, behind me, back toward Violet and Hickory, toward our only escape. Water sprays down from the ceiling.

The corridor above us must be flooded, and now it's coming through.

I cry out for help. Try to lift my hand from the stone, but I can't. Violet and Hickory are here in a flash. Grabbing me, lifting me, severing the connection. Helping me back toward the eggs. We're nearly there when the ceiling gives way right behind us.

The ceiling gushes like a burst dam. Boulders fall. We're swept off our feet toward the wall of eggs, through the eggs, all of it blasted clear. Then we hit something.

Another wall. A dead end. The force of the water pins us to the stone and fills the hallway in no time.

I'm drowning in darkness again.

I can hear Hickory and Violet crying out beside me. Feel their arms and legs hitting mine through the swirl of eggs and water. But just as I think we're finished, that nothing can save us now, I feel something else. A wall of honeycombed stone behind us. A gateway.

I slam my bleeding hand against it.

OTHERWORLD

We splash, tumble, skid, and roll. A tangle of limbs. The sunlight's so white, so blinding, I can't open my eyes. I'm pretty sure I elbow Hickory in the stomach. He knees me in the head. I think that's Violet grabbing my arm and squeezing. There's a stone-grinding sound behind us. The flow of water and egg-slop eases. I shield my eyes and look back just in time to see the stone door close. The jet of water becomes a slit of spray, a dribble, and then nothing.

The gateway has shut. Now it's just a mottled slab of stone in a small outcrop of rock. A tiny island rising from a desert floor. I see it, but I can't believe it.

Desert.

We're in a freakin' desert.

I turn over and cough up a lung. Feel the pain in my left hand. The slushy grit at my fingertips. It's real. We're sucking down the air of a brand-new world. Air that tastes old somehow. Bitter. I sit back and squint at the creature eggs scattered all around us, the chunks of blackish Manor stone. Beyond our mucky puddle, a flat sheet of white stretches all the way to the horizon, glaring so brightly it hurts. Suddenly, the patches of crusty white stuff inside that last Manor corridor make sense. Salt. There must've been an ocean out here, once.

"That," Violet says, "was too close."

She's kneeling beside me, catching her breath with her face turned up to the sky. For now, the heat's welcome. Soon it'll be unbearable. Hickory's already scurrying back to the gateway. He shoves his weight into it. Paws at it like a cat shut out in the cold, his eyes clenched tight. I bet he's afraid of all this space. The sunlight and the sky. He wants back inside the Manor already. This is what happens when you spend two thousand years indoors.

"Well done," Violet tells me. Her eyes are as squinty as mine. "Are you okay?"

"Not really." I try to clean my still-bleeding hand in the puddle. Unwrap a bit of leather from my leg and wrap it around the wound. It's all I can do for now.

Violet shields her eyes and looks out at the horizon. Her Leatherhead costume's as ratty and come-undone as mine. "I wonder where we are," she says. "Smells pretty bad." She screws up her face and sniffs her arm, shrugs. "Maybe it's the eggs."

This is all wrong. Sure, we escaped the river and the creatures, but we've lost our chance at finding the Cradle. Of beating Roth and returning home. This gateway's dead to us now. There's nothing on the other side but rock and water.

Worst of all, I've failed Dad.

"I've ruined everything. We're trapped out here."

Violet helps me up. "You did the right thing, Jane. We

would have drowned if it weren't for you. Or been eaten alive. Don't worry, we'll figure something out."

"If you tell me everything happens for a reason, Violet, I'll scream."

"You know it's true, though." She forces a smile but it doesn't last long. "I'm sorry Elsa wasn't there."

"Yeah," I say, "me too." I feel like an idiot, pinning all our hopes on a dream.

We must've missed something. Got out of the water at the wrong corridor. The trail's broken. The path to the second key. The path to my mom. Even if we somehow manage to find our way back inside the Manor, we'll never pick it up again, not without becoming breakfast.

I take the key from my pocket, hold it tight.

"Hey!" Hickory's still huddled against the gateway, pointing up at a strange little clamp-thing attached to the rock. A brick-sized scrap of metal with a bit of rope dangling from it. "What's that?"

"Calm down, Hickory," Violet says, but then I look up and grab her arm.

A trail of black smoke hanging in the air, fading by the second.

A flare, rigged to trigger when the gateway opened.

A signal.

Another voice echoes through my mind. Not Mom's. Dad's. *A desolate world. Ruined. Decayed. He'd been waiting a long time for the gateway to open again.*

Then I see them. Not one sun burning in the sky, but two.

"No, no, no." A cold shiver rattles my bones despite the searing heat. That bitter tang in the air tickles my throat again. A familiar scent, I realize, similar to the air we breathed on the train when *he* came onboard. I make binoculars with my hands and scan the salt flats, checking for a distant death camp, an approaching army. "We have to run. Now."

Of all the worlds connected to the Manor, why would it bring us here?

"Hey." Violet grabs my arm, stops me spinning. "What is it?"

"Two suns," I say. "And that smell. It isn't the eggs." I wave my hands at the desert. "We're in Roth's world. We came through a different gateway from my parents, but—"

"That's impossible," Violet says. "There's an infinite number of worlds connected to the Manor. The chances of us ending up in *Arakaan* are just—just—"

"There," Hickory shouts, pointing behind us. "Somebody's coming."

A smudge on the horizon. A dirty little cloud kicked up from the desert floor. A line of ant-sized figures in the heat-shimmer.

"Leatherheads," I say. "On horses. We have to run."

But we can't run. We can't hide. And we all know it.

"Don't panic," Violet says. "They won't kill us. Not if we show them the key. They'll have to take us back to Roth. Back inside the Manor. So they'll . . . they'll have to take us to the gateway by the dune sea, right? The

334

one John and Elsa used when they first came to Arakaan. Which means we'll have time to escape."

A volley of rifle fire rolls across the desert. Warning shots. Me and Violet kneel down and face the oncoming cloud together, our hands high in the air. Hickory shuffles over on his hands and knees, fingers sloshing through the salted ground, as if he's afraid he'll fall into the sky if he lets go.

I count nine Leatherheads thundering toward us, peeling off in formation, wheeling around and surrounding us before coming to a halt. Their glassy gas-mask eyes glint in the sunlight. The horses stamp their hooves and champ at the bits in their mouths, wild-eyed and ready to charge again.

We wait. And we watch. And we wait some more. Something isn't right. These jerks are too small to be Leatherheads. They have five fingers, not three. And they aren't *click*ing and *clack*ing, they're speaking. I can't understand them, but they're definitely voices.

"Humans," I mutter. "Bounty hunters?"

"Out here?" Hickory says. "Doubt it."

One of them dismounts. Sloshes through the puddle and debris right up to the gateway. Runs a hesitant hand over the stone and takes a quick step back. The others chatter among themselves and point at the gateway, at us, their rifles at the ready.

They're afraid.

Their leader approaches us, speaks to us, words trunky-muffled by his mask. Hickory and Violet glance at me, seeing as I'm in the center and all.

"Um. Hi, there. My name's Jane. Jane Doe."

Voices murmur. Two more men dismount and join the leader.

"'Hi, there'?" Violet mutters. "You start with '*hi, there*'?"

"What was I supposed to say? They clearly speak a different—"

The man yells at us, pulls off his mask. Bald head. A lazy eye. Trails of sweat shining down his face and neck. I ask who he is and that's when he notices the key in my hand. He shouts something to the others. Panic spreads. They all dismount and kneel on the ground.

A damned firing squad cocking their guns, getting ready to fire.

"No, no, no," I say, "it's okay. Please. We're not looking for trouble."

But we've found it. The men swarm and force us down onto our stomachs. Lazy Eye snatches the key and ties my hands behind my back while another guy takes care of my legs. Violet and Hickory are tied up too. Then Lazy Eye yanks me back up to my knees and grabs my hair. Forces me to look at someone else who's approaching us now. Someone shorter than him, skinnier than him. Someone who sways and staggers, seems a little unsteady on his feet.

No. *Her* feet. It's a woman, I'm sure of it.

Lazy Eye throws her the key. She fumbles it, drops it, snatches it from the salty puddle. Inspects the key carefully, gently, as if it were a precious jewel. Her breath quickens, amplified by her gas mask. Then she pulls off her mask and shakes out her wild, graying hair.

"Where did you find this?" she says, voice trembling.

The desert closes in all around me. I can hardly breathe.

"Mom?"

She recoils, as if the word itself were a hefty blow. She's much older than the woman I saw in my dreams, but it's her, I know it. She's just—well—wrinklier. We never lost her trail. The Manor led us right to her, after all. It must've brought her back here years ago. Back to the one place Roth would never think to look for the keys in a million years. Back to the very world he left for dead.

A bubble of laughter swells inside me and bursts before I can hold it back.

Hickory and Violet gape at us both.

"Mom," I say, "it's okay. It's me. Jane. I—I'm your daughter. We came to—"

She lunges forward, grabs my face, tilts my head back into the blinding light of the suns and forces my eyes open with her talon-like fingers. I can smell alcohol on her breath.

"*You*," she whispers. It's only now I realize her hands are shaking.

She backs away from me, shouts an order at the men and—*pfft! pfft! pfft!*—something sharp stings my neck. I collapse between Hickory and Violet. The desert spins and blurs. Voices echo. And the last thing I see? My dear, long-lost mom leaning over me, an old tarnished brass key dangling from a thin chain around her neck, identical to mine in every way.

Cradle symbol and all.

THE TRUTH ABOUT JANE

I come to in a pile of blankets. Head spinning, hand throbbing, vision blurred but clearing. I'm in some sort of hut. A small, mud-brick dome. Firelight dances over the rough walls from a flickering torch beside my bed. Even so, a crisp chill hangs in the air. Dad said nights were cold in Arakaan, but this is ridiculous. The salt outside might as well be snow.

Where am I exactly? How did I get here?

I remember the flank of a horse hot against my cheek. Violet, unconscious, slung over a chestnut mare trotting alongside me. Lazy Eye's shoulder digging into my guts as he lugged me toward a desert camp, the huts like a cluster of turtles tucked into their shells. I saw a well. Hickory being dragged away. A yard for the horses, and an odd goat-like creature that bleated as we passed. I'm pretty sure I waved a drunken hello to it before I blacked out again.

A tiny village, then. Could be worse, I guess.

I untangle myself from the blankets. Swing my bare feet onto the floor and shiver. Most of my Leatherhead disguise has come undone, and my tunic's sure seen better days. A fresh bandage has been wound around the gash in my left hand, tied off in a neat little bow.

Mom.

The strands of gray in her hair. The lines on her face. Those brown, blood-shot eyes glaring down at me. The reek of her breath. Her shaking hands.

What happened to her out here?

I run my fingers over the bump in my neck where I felt the sting.

"Blow dart," a voice says behind me.

Mom's right here in the hut, dressed in a pale brown robe now, slouched down against the wall and clasping an animal-hide waterskin that clearly isn't filled with water. The front of her robe's splotchy with dark, dribbled stains. She takes a swig, stifles a burp.

"Don't worry. They weren't poisoned. Just dipped in a mild sedative."

"Oh," I say. *Oh*, as if mild-sedative darts are perfectly acceptable.

"Your friends are fine, by the way. We woke 'em an hour ago." Mom adjusts a cushion behind her. "Had ourselves a nice chat. They told us everything. You've been through a lot."

"Yeah, I—I guess we have." I swallow hard. "Can I see them?"

Mom ignores me. "The key's also safe. Well done, keeping it away from Roth. Top marks, gold star, all that stuff." She gives me a thumbs-up. "Kudos."

But she doesn't seem happy or relieved. Not at all.

Something's wrong.

I shift on the bed, try to straighten my tunic. I'm not sure why. Mom can barely stand to look at me. Her watery eyes slide to the bed, the floor, the wall, the ceiling, the torch. She stares into the flames, lost in the fire. I clear my throat. "Mom—"

"Don't call me that," she says, a little too forcefully. "Please."

Okay. Baby steps. I guess we'll work our way up to that one.

"Elsa," I say. Where do I start? What do I say? Suddenly my ten questions seem so stupid. "Thank you. For saving us. If you hadn't come—"

"You would've wandered through the desert for days, like I had to." Mom grunts and gets up, staggers over to adjust the raggedy blanket draped over the doorway. Something on the back of her neck glints in the torchlight. The thin chain. Her necklace. The second Cradle key must be tucked under her robe. "Seems a lifetime ago now," she says, and shrugs. "I suppose it was."

Easy now, Jane. Gotta tread carefully.

"How long have you been out here, Elsa?"

"Forty-seven years," she says. "Nearly half a century of praying, watching, waiting for that gateway to open again." She chuckles to herself. "Now it's blocked on the other side—useless—all thanks to you."

Ouch.

I tell her I'm sorry. That I didn't have a choice. "And there's still Roth's gateway, right?" I add. "By the dune sea.

Please tell me you know the way from here."

"We know the way from here. We're leaving soon as we can. It'll be a long journey, but we'll manage." She stares down at her waterskin, gives it a swirl. "We always do."

Forty-seven years. I can't imagine it. The anger, the hurt, the frustration, the fear, the isolation. I can see her riding out to the gateway every day. Running her hand along the stone, pleading, wishing for it to open again, to let her back inside. Maybe she clawed at the gateway like Hickory, her way home so close, yet so impossibly far away. And all she could do was wait. Wait and grow old in this barren landscape. No wonder she started drinking.

"We'll pick up the true key on the way," Mom says now, catching me off-guard.

"I'm sorry, the—the what?"

"This," Mom yanks her necklace, snaps it, tosses me the key, "is a fake." I hold it up to the torchlight, confused. Even up close, the key looks exactly like mine. "It's a decoy, Jane," Mom says. "One of three hundred dummy keys forged decades ago. Scattered across the far reaches of Arakaan to conceal the location of the *true* key in case Roth ever returned."

"Three *hundred?*" What the hell? "Well, at least you were thorough."

"The true key's hidden in an ancient city to the west," Mom says. "A canyon hideout the people of this region fled to long ago. From there we head north."

"North," I say. "Okay. Good. I mean, it's not ideal, but it's a plan." I huff out a deep breath, feel the first glimmer of hope kindling deep inside. We're not alone anymore. After all this time scrambling in the dark we have a whole tribe behind us. "I've gotta say, Mom—"

She flinches at the word again. This time, it bugs me.

"Look, I know this is strange and weird and really, really difficult for you, but it is for me, too. Growing up without you was tough. I didn't know who you were, where you were, whether you were dead or alive. I didn't even know your name. It was just me and Dad and—"

Mom makes a strange sound. I can't tell if it's a sob or a laugh. Maybe it's a bit of both. She holds a hand to the wall for support. Shakes her head in disbelief.

"My gods, you really don't know . . ."

The pale, mud-brick walls of the hut seem to close in. "Know what?" I ask.

"I can't believe he didn't tell you," Mom says. She paces around the hut, running her hands through her hair, clenching her fists, like she's trying to wring out her brain. "He was supposed to tell you everything. First chance he got. He promised."

"Who, Dad?" I ask. Mom groans. I get up, take a step toward her. "He did tell me everything. We wouldn't have made it here without him, Mom."

"*I said, don't call me that*," she snaps.

We stand in silence. I don't know what to say, what to do. A tear rolls down Mom's cheek. Her lip trembles. She looks like a little girl now, a broken child.

"I can't do this," she says. "I thought I was strong enough, but . . . I'm sorry."

She clears her throat, shouts something in that foreign tongue. Moments later, somebody's pushed into the hut. My heart swells.

It's Violet. She's dressed in a brown robe of her own now. Looks rattled, even scared.

"Are you okay?" I ask her. "Did they hurt you?"

"I'm fine," she says, but any idiot could see she isn't.

Something's changed. She flinches just like Mom when I reach out to hold her hand. A subtle movement she tries to hide by tucking a strand of hair behind her ear.

Mom turns to her. "You tell her," she says. "Better she hear it from a friend."

"Don't do this," Violet says. "Please."

But Mom ignores her. Turns to me at last and looks at me. I mean really *looks* at me. "I didn't ask for any of this," she says, and ducks outside into the cold, cold night.

Just like that, she's gone.

"Violet, what's going on? Where's Hickory?"

"I don't know." She stares at the blanket draped over the doorway. "They took him."

"What? Where? What did they do to you? What did they say?"

Violet gestures to the bed. "You should sit down."

"I just got up."

"Please, Jane—"

"I'm fine where I am, Violet. What did they tell you?"

Violet steels herself. "They interrogated us. Me and Hickory. They beat him up. Right in front of me. Tortured him. Said they had to make sure we're *on the right side*. So I told them everything. Who we are, where we come from, what we're looking for. Everything that happened to us inside the Manor." She shakes her head. "Elsa was drunk. Rambling. Kept repeating, 'She doesn't know,' over and over. Said maybe John couldn't bring himself to tell you the truth because of everything you'd done for him. That maybe he didn't want to hurt you."

"Hurt me? How could he hurt me?"

Violet walks over to the torch, warms her hands by the flames. "You remember what he said. Everything he told us on the train about how he and Elsa were captured."

"Yeah."

"Then you remember there was a gap. He told us how they were imprisoned. How Roth went to see them when Elsa was in labor. How he wouldn't let John help her until he swore to find the Cradle. And he did. John told us he swore on their lives and Roth let him help her, but he never got to finish the story. Roth came onboard the train and everything went to hell. All we know is they escaped and found the Cradle and released two of the Specters, but John never told us about the birth."

Yes, Jane, you were born in the Manor, but—

"Something went wrong," I say, a new colony of wasps swirling round my gut.

Violet nods, turns to face me. "Roth let him go too late. John couldn't help Elsa. Their child . . . their little baby . . ." Her voice trembles. She wipes away a tear. "He died."

I shuffle on my feet, feel weak in the knees. What she's

saying doesn't make any sense. At all. Her brain's obviously been muddled by the not-quite-poisoned darts.

"Violet, I think you need to rest. Maybe lie down for a bit."

"I don't need to lie down, Jane," she says, forcefully now. "*Listen.* They had a baby boy, but he only survived a few minutes." More tears are streaming down her cheeks, shining in the firelight. "They did everything they could to revive him, but—"

"This is impossible. What you're saying is . . ." I can't stay still, can't think, can't breathe. This damn hut's too cramped, and it feels like it's getting smaller by the second. I need to walk, need to breathe, need to think. Why's it so hot in here all of a sudden? "You're telling me that—that I'm—that my dad isn't really my—"

No. It's unthinkable. Impossible.

"Roth kept them in their cell for months afterwards," Violet says. "The Leatherheads kept taking John out on patrols to find the Cradle—Elsa too, when she was strong enough to walk. And they were making progress. They discovered an engraving of the Cradle symbol in a chamber—a whole trail of them—but the trail always went cold. Roth was losing patience. John and Elsa knew they were running out of time, and that's when they managed to escape."

"Stop." The hut's spinning. I feel sick. I think I'm gonna pass out again. "Please."

"They fled deep into the Manor. Followed the trail again. But this time it kept going. They found the two keys in a chamber, on some kind of pedestal. They picked them up and the entrance to the Cradle revealed itself. They opened it. Stepped inside. They made it to the foundation stone and . . . and they found *you*, Jane. They took *you* from the Cradle."

Yes, Jane, you were born in the Manor . . .

". . . but you're not our child," I whisper to myself, dropping slowly to my knees.

Suddenly it seems so obvious, so real. Somehow, I can *feel* it. The cold, hard truth at last, sitting in my gut like a block of ice.

"It explains everything," Violet says. Gently. Softly. "The quakes. Your dreams. Your connection to the Manor. The reason Roth wants to capture you."

Hot tears sting my eyes as I claw at the bandage wrapped around my palm. Violet tries to stop me, but I shake her away. The wound's red and raw, starting to weep again. Not the blood of the man I've always called Dad or the woman I thought was my mom.

The blood of the Makers.

"It's me," I say. "I'm the third key."

THIS IS NOT
THE END

GRIM TIDINGS

He finds her in Outset Square, standing at the base of the Sacred Stairs, crimson cloak flapping gently in the breeze. She is staring up at the Manor, black against the starry night sky. She tells him he is late. Usually, he would protest, but not tonight. Even under the waxen light of the moon, he can see she is not well. There is a stoop to her shoulders.

"You look tired, old girl."

"Perhaps I am." Winifred sighs. "Lies can be such a weight, Eric, and I have told a great many of late. Withheld certain facts from you, Violet, Jane most of all." She turns to him. "But the time has come for me to tell you everything."

Atlas is surprised, wary. "Very well. Why did you send Doe away?"

"I have already told you. I sent Jane away to save our world. To save all the worlds."

"Save them from what?"

"A great evil I have faced before. An evil, I am ashamed to say, I failed to defeat."

Atlas has never heard Winifred talk this way. Has never heard of such failure.

"And you think a child stands a better chance than you?"

"Oh, she isn't just any child. She is a child of the Makers, and she needs our help." Winifred gazes up at the Manor once more. Turns on her heels and sets off across the square. "Come, Eric. We've no time to waste. War is upon us, and there is much to be done."

END OF
BOOK ONE

THE JANE DOE CHRONICLES
BOOK TWO

Stranded in a dying land, Jane has finally learned the truth about her past. Now, a whole world of danger lies between her and the Manor. With a little help from Violet and Hickory, she must find the courage to accept her destiny and face her darkest fears. Because the clock is ticking: John's life is in peril, Roth's grip is tightening on the Manor, and every soul in every world hangs in the balance. Will Jane get to the Cradle in time?

THERE ARE SANDSTORMS.
THERE ARE SCORPIONS.
THERE ARE NEW FRIENDS AND FOES.
THE ADVENTURE CONTINUES IN 2020.

ACKNOWLEDGMENTS

First off, a grand tip-of-the-hat to everyone at Hardie Grant Egmont for charging into the Manor with me. Your passion, dedication and encouragement blows my mind and fuels me every day. I've truly found my champions, and I couldn't be happier. Marisa Pintado and Luna Soo, you're absolute stars. Same goes for everyone at Carolrhoda Books who embraced *The Cradle of All Worlds* with such enthusiasm and gave Jane a home across the seas. Shaina Olmanson, Danielle Carnito, Amy Fitzgerald, Alix Reid, Erica Johnson, and anyone else I may have forgotten (please forgive me); you rock. Thank you ALL for making my dream come true.

Thanks also to agent extraordinaire Grace Heifetz at Curtis Brown Australia. I'm so very lucky to have such a fiercely intelligent, generous, and caring person in my corner.

They say you shouldn't judge a book by its cover, but we all do it anyway, and when your cover's this good, I say judge away! A huge thanks to HGE designer Pooja Desai and Italian artist Iacopo Bruno. You were the dream pick, Iaki, and I love this cover so much I nearly peed my pants when I first saw it.

A thousand hugs and high-fives to all my family and friends who have shown me so much love over the years. A special shout-out to Brooke Davis, number-one sounding board and light of my life (we're not in a relationship!); Claire Thompson, confidante and counsellor; Pip Smith, for opening one helluva big door; Charlie Mah, first teen reader; and Felicity Packard, who sparked the fire way-back-when. Thanks also to Sarah Hart, Mark Russell, Julia Loersch, George Poulakis, Simon Gauci, Steph Lax, Catherine Pye, Holly Ringland, Gabrielle Tozer, Amanda Bradford, Ollie and Rosie, Juully and Bill Lyons, team Oscar & Friends, Indiana Jones, Bailey the Golden Lab, and every cool dog I've ever met.

Mom, you really are a wonder. Thank you so much for your unwavering love and support. Sharing this wild ride with you has been such a thrill. Dad, I love you, I miss you. Tim and Nic, my dear siblings, thanks for putting up with me all these years. Karen, our life-long friendship means all the worlds to me. Brooke, yes, you get a second thank-you because you're pretty great. And to my future husband, I don't know who or where you are, but how dare you not be here for this. You owe me cake. Lots of cake.

Finally, a heartfelt thanks to all the storytellers out there, past and present, who have entertained, thrilled, consoled, inspired and educated me throughout my life, and to YOU, dear reader, for diving into Jane's world. I hope you had fun. I'll see you all again soon.

—Jeremy

TOPICS FOR DISCUSSION

1. Besides Violet, Jane has no friends in Bluehaven and she's forced to live in a basement. How does this isolation change her identity? How would she have been a different person had she been born in Bluehaven and grown up with the other kids? When can loneliness help us grow, and when does it hurt us?

2. Why are the people of Bluehaven convinced that Jane and John caused the Night of all Catastrophes? How have they convinced themselves of this? Do you think their small-town community made it easier or harder to start believing this as a group? When is a time in your life that you've had to deal with groupthink?

3. Jane says she had to stop hoping to be able to find her mother because she needed to focus on caring for John. Does shielding herself from more heartbreak like this help her or hinder her? When is it time to let go of the past? When is it time to let go of a person in your life? Have you ever had to do either of these things? If so, how did it affect you; if not, how do you think it has affected Jane?

4. When Winifred says Jane has a destiny, she hates this idea because it makes her feel like a puppet. When have you felt like a puppet in your life? Do you think people have destinies, free will, or a mix of the two? Would you prefer to have a destiny or free will? How are they different, and does thinking that you have a destiny or free will change anything for you?

5. Winifred has been following Jane her whole life, affecting her behind the scenes. How is this guardianship helpful to Jane, and when does it hold her back? Does Jane need Winifred? Does Jane want to need to Winifred? What is the right amount of supervision for young people, and when does it cross a line and become a burden to them?

6. Was Jane right to trust Hickory? Did she have a choice to team up with him or not? Do you think Hickory partly stays with Jane because he can connect with her, or is his interest in her entirely for the utility of the skeleton key? Why doesn't he just take the key and leave?

7. Jane realizes that she and Hickory have had very similar upbringings, but she knows Hickory has had it worse. What is the value in this comparison? Does Hickory's struggle invalidate Jane's struggle because his is harder? Why is it important for both stories to be accepted and acknowledged, and how does sharing them improve Jane and Hickory's relationship? Why does Hickory cry at the end of Jane's story?

8. Before Jane and Hickory enter the stomach of the plant, Jane has a gut feeling that it's a bad idea. Why does she know something's not quite right? What does it take to cultivate that sense? Should you always trust your gut, or can it lead you astray? What's the right balance between thinking and feeling?

9. John and Elsa completed extensive research on the Manor, but may have missed things. When John fills in Jane about how the gods created the Manor, do you think he has missed anything? What do you think is Jane's connection to the Manor? Why did the gods want to create the Manor? Does anyone deserve to control the Cradle? Why?

10. Do you think Roth kept John alive? Why or why not? Is John still useful to Roth or Jane, or neither? Do you think John likes being in the Manor?

11. How can Jane and Violet reconnect after being apart for six years? Has Jane lost that relationship forever, or can it be salvaged? How can it be salvaged, and do you think Jane and Violet want to put in the work necessary for that? Would you?

12. Jane doesn't have much control over what happens to her in the Manor; her abilities are powerful, but unknown. What do you think is Jane's greatest strength? Do you think she would rather keep these powers or have Violet's adventuring skillset? How much does Jane need her team of allies? Would you rather have an excellent team or be independent?

13. Violet pushes Jane to think more critically about all of the dangers they may encounter while trying to find the second key, but Jane is overwhelmed and just wants to go home with her family. Do you think Jane is making a mistake here? Should she plan things out more or deal with things as they come? Which strategy do you prefer to use, and why?

14. After Jane tells Violet and Hickory about the visions she's receiving from the Manor, Hickory says he believes her but Violet is skeptical. Why does Hickory believe her but Violet doesn't? Who is a better friend to Jane, and why?

15. Do you think Jane likes Violet? Do you think Violet likes Jane? Are Jane and Violet more committed to each other or to their mission? Do you think Hickory still wants to take advantage of their lack of experience with the Manor?

16. Of Jane, Violet, and Hickory, who do you think likes being in the Manor the most, and who hates it the most? Why?

17. Why do you think Elsa wants to go to the Cradle? Do you think she is on Jane's side or not? What about Hickory—is he still plotting against Jane? How will Jane unite these people to succeed?

ABOUT THE AUTHOR

Jeremy Lachlan was born and raised in Griffith, country New South Wales, and completed his honors degree in Creative Writing at the University of Canberra in 2004. Since then, he has won no writing prizes of any kind, but he did once take home $100 in a karaoke competition. He's super proud of this.

He now calls Sydney home, is slightly obsessed with dogs, and often wonders why we can't whistle and smile at the same time. *Jane Doe and the Cradle of All Worlds* is his debut novel.

Twitter: @jeremylachlan
Instagram: @jeremy.lachlan